D1607598

A Lethal Engagement

A LETHAL ENGAGEMENT

A MYSTERY

April J. Skelly

CROOKED
LANE

NEW YORK

Copyright © 2025 by April Jarien Skelly

Published in the United States by Crooked Lane Books, an imprint of The Quick Brown Fox & Company LLC.

Crooked Lane Books and its logo are trademarks of The Quick Brown Fox & Company LLC.

Library of Congress Catalog-in-Publication data available upon request.

ISBN (hardcover): 979-8-89242-105-8
ISBN (paperback): 979-8-89242-237-6
ISBN (ebook): 979-8-89242-106-5

Cover design by Marisa Ware

Printed in the United States.

www.crookedlanebooks.com

Crooked Lane Books
34 West 27th St., 10th Floor
New York, NY 10001

First Edition: April 2025

10 9 8 7 6 5 4 3 2 1

For my dear friend, Brittany Eden
Without you, Cora would never have
become an American
And that has made all the difference

CHAPTER 1

Cora

Engagements are lethal creatures.

But, of course, I didn't know that at the time. All I could do was stare stupidly at the ring on my finger, the enormous emerald flanked by two sapphires and a diamond on either side, and wonder what was to become of my life.

Because I had accepted this ring a mere twenty-four hours earlier, I was standing over a dead body now.

As it was, I gulped and yanked my gaze from my ring, only to stare at the puddle of blood seeping into the hardwood floor at the edges of the Turkish rug where it was too saturated to hold any more.

The woman lay unnaturally still, her skin leeched of color in stark contrast to her dark hair and the bright-yellow fabric of her dress that had been savaged from her body. Ripped and slashed, the corset was mangled beyond recognition, yanked back to expose her chest, abdomen, and lower.

My stomach turned, and I barely kept the bile that rose in my throat from making a messy exit. The poor woman had suffered the indignity of a murderer's message. Carved in a curve from her ribs to just above the flesh between her hips, the killer had slashed a calling card in gore.

I was terrified it was meant for me.

Twelve Hours Earlier
Airship Docks at New York City, New York
1890

The airship rumbled to life, the planks beneath my feet vibrating with the great whirring of machinery. Tipping my head back, I watched, awestruck, as the great blimp that would raise our enormous carriage into the air finished inflating. This was one of my father's ships, which was now *my* ship. The *Lady Air*.

A lump immediately formed in my throat. So much of me had gone dormant with the loss of my father. I wished he were still here and not buried on the family plot back on Hadaway Estate in Massachusetts. Perhaps I could regain some of my vigor for life on this journey across the Atlantic. Twenty was too young to wither away from sadness.

"Miss Beaumont, shall we retire to the observatory? I hear the wind is dreadful fierce when the ship leaves the ground," said Terrance, second son of Lord James Tristan, British duke of Exford and Debensley.

As of a few hours ago, Terrance Tristan had become my intended, officially.

Sunlight winked off the large emerald on the fourth finger of my left hand. His eyes were bright green, like the stone in my ring; they were kind, and his face was open, if a tad blank. His dark hair tousled not unattractively over his forehead. He was, by all accounts, an exceptionally handsome man. My gloved thumb traced over the golden band. I was the envy of all my fellow American heiresses—and their mothers—marrying into one of the oldest and most powerful aristocratic English families in Britain. Still, my belly trembled.

"Of course," I acquiesced quickly, even though the wild spirit inside me would rather have braved the harsh freedom of the winds. But as I preferred not to make a spectacle of myself on my first official outing with my fiancé, I thought it best to at least attempt the appearance of conforming to society's expectations.

A harsh breeze spun around the side of the great blimp.

Dratted skirts.

The frigid wind whipped underneath them and coiled my petticoats. They bunched uncomfortably about my hips, leaving my legs chilled and my bustle even larger than usual. I tried an unobtrusive hop, skip, and wiggle, but to no avail. They were firmly lodged. I hoped my fiancé liked big-bustled women. My cheeks heated at the thought.

"This is truly the most exciting thing that has ever happened to me," Lady Ophelia Hortense Davenport whispered at my side as she clutched my arm conspiratorially. "I have always wanted a bosom friend with which to share life's great delights—and possible scandals," she said, her voice low enough only I could hear. I bit back a smirk.

Lady Ophelia Hortense was possibly the pluckiest girl I'd ever encountered. I'd spent scarcely two hours in her company, and already she treated me like a dear old chum. Perhaps more impressively, Lady Ophelia had managed to earn more than one disparaging look from our shared chaperone, Mrs. Beesly, who had arrived from England on Lord Tristan's request for the sole pleasure of further instructing me in the customs of English society and to tame my wild American ways.

Better Ophelia Hortense than me. It was pleasant not to be the only one on the receiving end of Mrs. Beesly's most impressive stink eye.

"Tell me, as we are soon to be cousins, Miss Cora—and you *must* tell me the truth—do you suppose there will be any great scandal worth retelling while we're aboard the *Lady Air*?" Ophelia looked positively enraptured at the thought. I gathered she liked to gossip and wanted something salacious to report back to the friends she had left behind in England. As I understood it, she'd made the voyage with her cousins largely for the pleasure of the travel. Regardless of her reasons for coming and going, I was glad she was here with me now, as the *Lady Air* made ready to fly us swiftly toward my future.

"Even if there are no great scandals, surely taking the maiden voyage on the largest airship ever built is tale enough in and of itself?" I smiled as the pretty, dark-haired girl pursed her lips, quickly grabbing her hat to keep it from flying askew as the wind lashed about us with the halting rotations of the great turbines.

"Miss Beaumont is quite right," Terrance cut in. "Surely, traveling in such a grand manner will be story sufficient for all your gossipmongering friends once we land? Please do not go looking for mischief on this voyage, Phee." He said it with a rueful smile that told me Lady Ophelia would do as she pleased regardless of her cousin's pleas.

"Here we are. This way, ladies," he said as he opened the lead-paned rich-mahogany double doors that led to the first-class glass-walled observatory. His fingers ghosted over my elbow, and I gulped.

Taking in the room at a glance, I was delighted by how the images I'd seen on the blueprints had translated into grand opulence. As my eyes strayed from the costly velvet-covered lounges to the immaculate round tables set with white linens, fine bone china, and silver, I calculated seventeen members of the peerage, most of whom I had a passing acquaintance with. I might be the outsider American, but my parents hadn't left me completely devoid of culture. I'd been to England and traveled in high society, but it would be different this time, and not just because of the obvious ring that felt strange upon my finger. This time, I would be going to London as a properly engaged lady of the peerage— with all of British society watching me, waiting for me to make some mishap that was bound to put a black mark next to my name and give Ophelia Hortense a scandal she decidedly did not want connected to her family. I glanced at the members of the aristocracy as they languished around the lavish room. There, in the corner, a dark head turned, and green eyes focused on our small party.

Nicholas Tristan. Though I hadn't seen the duke's heir—and my soon-to-be brother-in-law—in nearly five years, his resemblance to Terrance was remarkable. Both stood tall and proud, with wide shoulders that tapered to a trim waist and a head of thick, dark hair. The aristocratic Roman nose was evident. Terrance's had a crook in the middle where Nicholas's did not, but their bearing alone was enough to assure even the most common passersby that they were descended from ancient bloodlines.

Bloodlines that were sure to cause that scandal Ophelia wished for once it reached the papers that I, the daughter of an American businessman, had solidified my engagement to the son of a duke. No American heiress had yet married so high into British society. I had money but none of the breeding that seemed customarily desirable in such arrangements. I cringed at the uproar that would likely cause. Never mind that Terrance was the spare and not the heir; dread still slithered in my unhappy gut, wrapping its ugly tentacles around the blueberry muffin I'd eaten before leaving Hadaway.

Society tongues would cluck at such blatant disregard for convention in marrying outside one's own class. Though from all accounts the Beaumont family had more wealth accrued than most of the British peerage, we did not descend from royalty. My father had merely had the good fortune to be born into a family of business-minded men. This had served both my father and my grandfather well, but I was a miss, not a lady, a fact that I was sure would be pointed out at some point on our journey to Southampton and London, where Terrance's grandmama waited at her imposing, ultrafashionable house at the edge of Hyde Park to inspect me like cattle and bestow her blessing—or not.

Suppressing a shudder, I pasted on a pleasant smile as Terrance led us to his brother's side. Waiting patiently for Terrance to make the proper reintroductions lest I make an exhibition of myself with an egregious social faux pas by speaking first—the horror—I clenched my fingers tightly in gloved fists around the ebony handle of my reticule.

"Nicholas!"

"Terry, glad you made it aboard," Nicholas answered, the deep timbre of his voice sending spiders skittering over my skin. There was something almost . . . magnetic about the elder Tristan son. Though they were so alike in appearance, Terrance was light and carefree, whereas Nicholas was dark and serious. The brothers smiled widely at each other, shaking hands firmly before Terrance turned and motioned to us with his arm. "May I formally present to you my fiancée, Miss Cora Beaumont, and the girls' chaperone, Mrs. Beesly."

Nerves raced through my extremities. There was no bitterness evident in Terrance's voice as my name slipped from his lips, though his eyes did not spark or crinkle at the edges. Was he happy with our betrothal? I hoped so. We had not yet had the chance to speak of it at length. Though ours was no love match, I did have hopes that we could form such an emotional attachment between us. We'd known each other as children, and titles aside, I could have done much worse than Terrance Tristan as my intended. He brought prestige and power to the Beaumont name, and I brought a hefty sum of Beaumont money to the Tristan coffers.

"Miss Beaumont, the years have been most kind. It is good to see you well," Nicholas said, politely taking my hand as I dipped a curtsy to him. His eyes were intense as they boldly met mine.

"It is good to see you as well, my lord," I replied, demurely enough that Mama would have been proud. My corset stays jabbed uncomfortably into my belly as I straightened and took my hand back. I secretly hoped I could go without the confining contraption a time or two while aboard ship. I'd packed some looser clothing for just such flagrant behavior. I had no doubt Lady Ophelia would join me if I suggested it.

"Phee, lovely as always." Warmth tinged his voice with sincerity, and the twinkle in his eyes indicated camaraderie with and care for his younger cousin. "Mrs. Beesly, how good to make your acquaintance," Nicholas said courteously.

Before Mrs. Beesly could simper out an answer, the ship lurched in lift-off and the knot of us pitched together ungracefully.

"Blazes," Ophelia muttered, decidedly unladylike.

Mrs. Beesly gasped like she'd swoon dead away. "Young lady," she admonished fiercely. "You will *not* use such base language." She practically growled the words.

I was a little shocked myself that Ophelia Hortense cursed so openly. A lady did not say such things aloud—not even brash

American women cursed aloud in polite company. Though I said *drat* plenty in my head and would likely cause Mrs. Beesly apoplexy if she heard me utter the word audibly. I quickly glanced to the two Tristan men. Nicholas remained impassive while Terrance rolled his eyes. Phee smiled meekly, chagrined, then rolled her own eyes when attention shifted to the older man making his way toward us.

Interesting.

Rooming with Lady Ophelia Hortense could prove an unexpected adventure.

"Ah, here is Captain Cordello. May I make introductions, sir?" Nicholas called to the captain as he tugged the bottom of his suit jacket and dusted invisible lint from his cuff. Nicholas's voice rolled deliciously along the vowels as his accent stretched sounds my American speech did not.

"My lords. Ladies." The captain sketched a quick bow. He looked smart in his white-and-blue CAB Airship livery.

"Miss Cora Beaumont," Terrance said, letting his gloved fingers brush my elbow familiarly. I resisted the urge to flinch away from his unexpected touch. We had known each other some as children, as our fathers were friends. But I'd spent the past few years in and out of American society and on archaeological digs with my father. Though my hand had been promised to Terrance Tristan once I entered my twentieth year, we had met properly as adults only two days ago. The arrangement had been agreed upon by our fathers and heartily supported by my mother. Though I was well pleased with my lot in the betrothal . . . it was still frighteningly new.

Captain Cordello's eyebrows rose as recognition lit his face at the mention of my last name. He'd been assigned to captain the *Lady Air*'s maiden voyage by the board after Father's passing, and I'd not had the chance to meet him beforehand. "Miss Beaumont, pleased to make your acquaintance. I am honored to be flying the *Lady Air* on her maiden voyage. Deeply honored. Your father was a man among men. I'm grateful to have been chosen for this undertaking."

Emotion swelled in my chest. "Thank you, Captain." I couldn't say more, as my throat closed suddenly, tears stabbing at the back of my eyes. My father should have been here to see this. To properly introduce me to the captain set to fly my inheritance across the skies.

"It shall be the crowning moment of my long career." Captain Cordello bobbed his head. Silver hairs peppered between the darker strands peeking from beneath his cap.

I swallowed in an effort to clear my throat. This man deserved a dignified response. It should have been Father—Clarence Abner Beaumont—standing here receiving this man's praise. Not me.

"Apologies, my good men, but now that we are airborne, we must retire to our quarters and refresh ourselves after the taxing journey to the ship," Mrs. Beesly broke in.

Relieved I needn't continue speaking about my father, I glanced at my chaperone. An hour in a hansom cab going from the hotel to the docks and mounting a ramp to board the airship was hardly taxing, though now that I was looking, she did seem a bit green. Swaying slightly, she waved the air in front of her face with her black lace fan.

"Mrs. Beesly, are you well?" I asked, genuinely concerned.

"Oh, I don't think she is. Lord Terrance"—Ophelia Hortense added the formality in the captain's presence—"have you the room keys?" she asked, her forehead wrinkled in worry as she took the older woman's arm.

"I do. I'll escort you there myself."

I dipped a quick curtsy to the captain and Nicholas, then turned and took Mrs. Beesly's other arm to help steer her toward our quarters. I could have sworn I felt eyes staring into the back of my head as I exited the observatory.

CHAPTER 2
Nicholas

I watched Terry escort Cora from the observatory. She had changed in the five years since I'd last seen her. Then, she'd been a girl. Now she'd blossomed into a young woman. She was lovely, with her auburn hair and womanly curves that were not present at our last meeting. But her eyes—those deep, blue-green orbs that could never quite settle on one color or the other—sent a shiver skimming over my shoulders. She'd met my gaze, and it was like she'd seen straight through me.

It was unsettling, and some strange combination of thrilling and terrifying, to feel so completely seen. She had always been straightforward as a child, and I wondered if age and society had tempered that. Part of me hoped they hadn't, as I had always found it a refreshing change from the rest of the world that seemed to pander to my position.

"My lord," Captain Cordello said.

I dragged my eyes away from the retreating form of my soon-to-be sister-in-law and gave my attention to the captain.

"There are things I must attend shortly. As I understand, the *Lady Air* has passed ownership with Mr. Beaumont's death. Would you care to accompany me to the bridge for a tour?"

"Indeed, I would enjoy that, Captain," I said, settling myself into the role of heir—talking business and representing our family name well. A familiar role, like an oft-used dinner jacket. "Thank you."

Captain Cordello bowed slightly and extended his arm so that I should precede him through the doors.

"Apologies about the wind; there's naught for it with the turbines going full strength. Watch your step, sir. Lift-off has commenced, but we're still ascending, so brace yourself." The captain's words were muffled in the wind as he mashed his hat down on his graying hair with one hand and maneuvered to the thick column of the tower where the bridge was located.

The world quieted as soon as the door shut behind us against the howling of the wind. Mechanical parts clicked and whistled softly as my ears picked up the strains of the ship. I smoothed my tousled hair self-consciously.

"Up this flight of steps into the main bridge. Should you need anything at all on the journey, please send word. My quarters are here." He indicated a door set into the pristine white wall, all but invisible save for the metal door latch. "I am at your disposal."

I nodded politely while sighing internally. As one of the highest-ranking peers in Britain, I expected this behavior, but I also found it exhausting. People always put on a mask of what they thought I should see. I doubted anyone knew what it was I truly wanted; sometimes I wasn't even sure of my own desires. As such, it was hard to find genuineness among those of my acquaintance. My position always seemed to get in the way. I was untouchable— and that made the best fodder for speculation and idle tongues, which were in manifold supply on both sides of the pond.

The tour *was* interesting—the mechanics of flying a great iron beast were fascinating. As the tour concluded, Captain

Cordello walked with me back down the other side of the tower that connected to the first-class lounge. Only a handful of people were present, having tea together at the far side of the distinctly posh enclosure.

"I shall leave you here, as I have duties to attend, but again, please do not hesitate to let me—or any of the waitstaff—know if you have any requirements while you are aboard ship."

"Thank you, Captain Cordello, and much obliged for the tour." I tipped my head. The captain reciprocated with a deeper bow and left to return to his post. Glancing around, I took in the size of the lounge. Though not nearly so bright and airy as the glassed-in observatory, the room was a picture of elegant leisure. There was even a row of bookshelves across one wall. It was a room built for relaxation. Maybe I'd find some on this trip. Maybe *Terry* would find some on this trip. He'd been sullen since we quit London two weeks prior before traveling to America—he to collect a fiancée and me to pursue a business opportunity that promised a good return to our stagnating coffers.

Something was afoot with my brother, but he had not confided in me. I sensed that it had to do with his impending marriage, though he'd always liked Cora well enough when we were younger. I realized my left hand had clenched into a fist at the frustrating thoughts. I willfully unbent my fingers, flexing them and releasing the tension.

So long as things carried on with the appearance of gracefulness, I'd do what I could to ensure things were as smooth as possible for my brother. Heaven help us all if the society matrons aboard got wind that there was discontent—they would be sharks scenting blood in the water. I had no intention of letting anyone connected to the Tristan name bleed for the sake of gossip. It would be bad enough once the news broke that

Terrance was marrying below his station and outside British class entirely.

I mused over these things as I let myself wander down the plush-carpeted corridor, simply enjoying the silence and company of my own thoughts after a hectic fortnight. A raised voice sounded around the next bend in the hallway. I glanced down in surprise at the red cordon attached to silver pillars at the top of a short stairwell and the sign cautioning me to stop. Ahead was second class.

As if lightning would strike should the classes mingle.

I rolled my eyes at the notion and glanced both ways to be sure gossipmongers weren't in the vicinity. Just because I thought a rule was silly didn't mean I was all for breaking it. The ramifications of gossip were like ripples on a pond. They spread, touching every shore. I breathed easier noting the coast was clear. Ignoring the cordon to satiate my own curiosity and rising concern as the voice—a woman's voice—grew impassioned and distraught, I stepped beyond the barrier and paced silently down the long hall to poke my head around the bend.

A woman with dark hair piled on her head, some falling around her shoulders, waved her arms at a man dressed from head to toe in CAB Airship livery.

"You dinna understand. I *will* be heard. You canna stop it. You *willna* stop it."

"Miss, I'm sorry, but you are not allowed up here. You do not hold a second-class ticket. You must remain in the third-class areas for the duration of the voyage. I assure you there are plenty of amenable accommodations—"

"No!" the woman shrieked. "You want t'stuff women away where we canna be heard, where we canna be *seen*. I got brains! I can think well as a man!"

"Miss." The man was beginning to sound harried. "It's not about what rights you do or do not have. It *is* a matter of being heard and seen. While you are aboard the *Lady Air*, you will stay in your designated area. Is that clear?"

The man firmly grasped her upper arm, turned her, and in so doing gave me the full image of her face. She was pretty—young, with wide eyes and a slightly upturned nose, her cheeks flushed with agitation. A wide yellow sash draped across her chest, a different shade than the yellow of her dress.

A suffragette sash.

"Unhand me, ye brute!" she shrieked.

"That's enough, miss. It's my job to see a tight ship is run among the staff and to see to the comfort of the passengers. While I'm sorry you're unhappy with the state of your affairs and the state of the country's vote, this is not the time nor the place. If you cannot contain yourself and comply with ship regulations, then I shall have no choice but to have you detained indefinitely until we reach our destination."

His voice faded as he marched her forcibly down the corridor and as she continued to thrash and protest loudly.

Unease gathered in my gut as I made my way back up the stairs and over the cordon into my own designated area. While I would not have been treated thusly if I'd been found outside my own class, there were lines in society that kept things in check. It made me uncomfortable to think about the suffragette movement. While some things did feel unfair, what the suffragettes wanted could also upset the entirety of the balance of Britain. One could not help but hear the murmurs in American society where women and the vote were concerned. The majority of women of my acquaintance were gentle beings—upset to the point of fainting by the wrong placement of the silverware at a dinner party. How could such delicate creatures hope to fare in the mortal coils of politics?

Then there was my cousin Ophelia. I nearly snorted. Not all women were so empty headed nor simpering, but even so, though Phee had a brilliant mind, she dashed headlong, willy-nilly, into everything she did. How was that any better when it came to forming the politics that governed the whole?

I sighed, resolved to cease thinking about it before my head began to ache, and made my way back toward the quarters I was to share with Terrance for the duration of the voyage.

CHAPTER 3
Cora

Poor Mrs. Beesly was positively puce by the time we reached our quarters. Terrance quickly thrust several keys into his cousin's hands.

"I'll, um, collect you for dinner?" He looked at me, and I was struck by how handsome my fiancé was, even if he seemed utterly terrified at the thought of Mrs. Beesly vomiting in his vicinity. Men could be so delicate at times.

"That would be lovely, thank you." I nodded to him. With a tight smile and fleeting glance at my chaperone, Terrance retreated down the corridor.

"In here, dear." As if she were the caregiving matron, Lady Ophelia Hortense led Mrs. Beesly through the door. Our quarters were on the port bow side, and they were every bit as lush as the first-class observatory.

We settled Mrs. Beesly comfortably abed in her adjoining room, then set ourselves to really look about our palatial accommodations.

"This is pure bliss," Lady Ophelia said as she turned in a circle in the middle of the room, her low-heeled silk slippers sinking into the multi-hued Turkish rug. A steaming silver tea service and plate of dainty sandwiches awaited us on an intricately carved sideboard.

"It's even grander than I imagined," I confessed as I peeked out the porthole windows that let in the fading sunlight before evening took hold. The ship rumbled, and I looked down, realizing we were already well on our way to finishing our ascent. "Lady Ophelia Hortense, look! The coast is already so tiny! Just a smudge on the horizon."

"Oh, pshaw. You mustn't call me *lady*. My name is an entire mouthful on its own. We are to be bosom friends. Proper chuckaboos. I am merely Ophelia. Phee, even, if you like." She gave me a cheeky grin as she sidled up to look onto the ground far beneath us. She whistled through her teeth, and I felt an instant kinship with this girl who loved scandal and balked at society's rules for young women.

Terrance had never been an overly stuffy child, and he didn't seem to mind his cousin's antics overmuch. Maybe he'd approve of them in his wife, so long as she behaved herself in public. It would be an agonizing marriage indeed if he did not.

I glanced out the window again, back the way we'd come. Dark clouds gathered on the far horizon, cutting a black swath across an otherwise pristine sky. Those clouds needed to stay where they were. While still a relatively new phenomenon, air travel was considered extremely safe, but not without some risk. A thunderstorm surrounding the ship would qualify as a significant risk, and floating over the mighty Atlantic waters for days didn't leave us many places to land. We had safety rafts, of course, but if a storm was great enough to bring down an airship, there was little hope of keeping a life raft afloat amidst such turbulent oceanic waters.

"I am so glad my father agreed to let me travel over with Nicholas and Terrance. I know they saw me as added baggage for part of the trip, but my father felt it was more advisable for me to travel with them than alone with only a chaperone aboard an ocean liner. Besides, this way I get to know you properly—and I can tell we're going to be the absolute best of friends—and now I have news to share among the peerage at home. Terrance was right. It is worthy of gossip to take the maiden voyage of such an incredible airship. Are you just thrilled to bits over it?" Ophelia smiled widely, no guile in her eyes.

"Thrilled to bits." My answering smile showed my teeth. "You'll have to teach me all your proper British sayings, so I don't embarrass anyone by speaking the wrong thing once we're in your country."

"You'll have plenty of time to learn everything you need." She whisked her hand dramatically through the air. "We'll only be in Southampton one night before we leave again for London, the social season, and Grandmama. Besides, it's not like you've never been to England, and not like you haven't mingled with the peerage. Your father has been in business with several of them over the years."

A lump rose in my throat. I swallowed it down. I hated using past tense when talking about my father. "You are correct."

"Oh heavens, I'm sorry. I'm such an insensitive clod sometimes. Forgive me if I've struck a nerve." The girl's face was wreathed in concern but not pity, and I found it eased some of the weight from my chest.

"It's fine. Truly."

Ophelia nodded hesitantly. "Has Mrs. Beesly been giving you all sorts of instruction? She has acted as my chaperone before. *I know.*" She winked, and I found myself grinning.

"She's tried. I fear I may still be a little rough around the edges."

Phee sighed. "It's all so romantic. An American heiress marrying into a duke's family. Someday this sort of story will populate romance novels across the continent." She smiled dreamily.

I chuckled. "You read a lot of romance novels, then?"

Phee rolled her eyes. "Brontë and Austen are about all I can manage to get my hands on. Someone who doesn't approve always finds the penny dreadfuls and confiscates them. You?"

"I have enjoyed Austen, Byron, Tennyson, Alcott, and such, but I haven't found much time to read in recent years beyond my educational and tutorial passages," I confessed. My reading time had been spent with poetry in snatched moments before and after long days spent helping my father on airship blueprints and other unladylike hobbies that would likely make the British aristocracy faint dead away if they knew all my comings and goings. Apprehension niggled at me.

"Still. You sound uncommonly well read." Phee glanced at the gilt clock hanging on the wall over the marble-topped sideboard. "But look at the time! What are you wearing for dinner and the opening ball?" she asked, wild excitement lighting her eyes.

I laughed, shoving my worry away. "What are *you* wearing?" We still had plenty of time to get ready.

"Let's see that everything has been properly unpacked. There is no point in sending all the luggage a day ahead if the servants don't hang things to let the wrinkles fall out." She opened one of the vast wardrobes. "Perfect. And just look at this gorgeous taffeta!" She glanced back to look at me, but her eyes slid past me to the door behind. "Oh, is that our own wash closet?"

I turned, walked over, and opened the door. Ophelia crossed the room and peered over my shoulder. "Dear me, it is. That's just some pumpkins."

I popped my head in, smiling at Ophelia's use of slang. It didn't sound quite natural, and I guessed she didn't have much excuse to try it out. A beautiful ceramic tub—large enough for a proper soak and with brass hot and cold water spigots—took up half of the white-tiled room. On the other side of the room stood a white porcelain washstand and a commode. The commodes had been a late addition to the ship. It would be nice not to have to use chamber pots, which most means of conveyance relied upon, for the duration of the trip. Indoor plumbing was quite newfangled and all the rage for those who could afford it. Not even our family estate in the Berkshires had plumbing up to this level. My eyes tracked to the passing landscape beneath us. The window here was utterly glorious for its humble appointment. It was full sized, not just a porthole, and let in the most stunning view of the sparkling ocean far below us.

"I rather feel this is wasted in the wash closet," Ophelia quipped, gazing out the window.

I snorted out loud. I knew the iron beams running the length of the ship and giving it support prevented a window like this in the adjoining room, but it did seem odd to have such a glorious view in the room in which one conducted one's private business. How awkward to have a curious bird peer in at you as you went on about lacing your stays or using the commode.

Ophelia smirked. "I knew we were destined to be the best of friends. Any high-society lady who can *snort* over a quip about the wash closet has earned her place in my heart."

"I must confess, I *am* glad you're not some uppity razzmatazz." I smiled at her. She had no idea how relieved I was. While my mother had done her best to drill into me the expectations of polite society, my father had indulged my every whim. I was the unexpected child of his second wife and of his old age, and he'd doted upon me—both my parents had. I'd grown rather headstrong with unconventional hobbies as a result, and not all the American peers looked favorably upon my eccentricities. But in the English peerage, money was still a language everyone spoke. And money the Beaumonts had. I'd spent the majority of the past two years since I'd properly entered society being alternately looked down upon because of my eccentric interests and entertaining offers of false friendship because money wasn't an issue for my father.

Ophelia grinned, a dimple appearing in her cheek. "Uppity razzmatazz? Tell me that's some delicious sort of scandalous American slang."

Maybe I wouldn't need to hide those eccentricities from Ophelia. We might even share an odd hobby or two.

I snorted again. "Um, an old stuffed shirt?" I attempted a British equivalent.

"Uppity razzmatazz. I simply *must* remember this phrase and use it at the earliest convenience." It was comical to hear the words in her properly cultured accent.

"So long as Mrs. Beesly doesn't catch you. She'd know you learned it from me," I added, not completely willing to break with all convention, if only for the sake of my father's memory and reputation, but I was amused at the twinkle that appeared in Ophelia's eyes.

"'Twill be our secret. Though, between the two of us, Mrs. Beesly can be an old uppity razzmatazz." She wiggled her eyebrows, and I bit back a laugh.

"I do hope Mrs. Beesly is well." My voice dropped to a whisper. "Though, truth be told, I was going to offer to walk the rest of the way to the airship if she gave me one more glare for my fidgeting fingers." Giving myself due credit, I'd been understandably nervous riding with Terrance and Ophelia. The whole idea of being engaged made me both giddy and anxious. As did being in the company of virtual strangers.

"Indeed," Ophelia said with an eye roll, looping her arm through mine and turning us back to the wardrobe, where I found a myriad of my dresses hung and organized.

"Oh, Cora, you *must* wear this." Ophelia ran her fingers delicately over the lavender silk. "Terrance will absolutely fall over his feet to fawn over you." She held up an evening gown with off-the-shoulder sleeves, a flat-fronted skirt, and a delicious fringe of lace and sequins at the bottom. My mother had given me an amethyst necklace and earrings to wear with it especially. I'd have to be sure to write to her that I'd worn it. She'd be most pleased.

"Ophelia . . . Phee . . . will you tell me more about your cousin? I haven't seen him regularly since we were children, and now that I'm of age and my fate is sealed with him, it would be nice to know more of Terrance as he is now. If . . ." I fiddled with the beaded edge of my reticule, which I still held. "If it's not too impertinent to ask, that is." I forced myself to put it down on top of a chest of drawers.

"I will tell you every possible detail. But you must promise to tell me every detail too. I have no romantic attachment of my own, though I do hope to have introductions to several of the peerage while on the *Lady Air* and potentially change that before my father can intervene. He might connect me to some aging viscount in some forgotten corner of the Continent, so until then, do let me live vicariously through you."

I chuckled. "I shall happily tell you any specifics that transpire, though I don't expect a great amount of swooning just yet. Bit early for that, isn't it?"

She sighed dramatically. "You are a practical sort. Never fear. Don't tell Mrs. Beesly—she wouldn't approve—but I've got a copy of *Emma* stowed away if we need romantic inspiration.

All the same, I'm sure Terry shall sweep you off your feet, and you'll be as besotted with him as he'll be with you."

I smiled, wishful that she be correct in her hopes.

"If I may be so bold as to ask, I overheard snippets of my parents' conversations that lead me to believe that your engagement is . . . unique. Perhaps more unique than the American-English connection." Ophelia's eyes shone as she gave me a sidelong glance. Part of me warmed to her enthusiasm while the other part of me cringed. It *was* unique.

"It is rare . . . on several counts." I shrugged as nerves flapped in my belly like seabirds with no place to land. I tried to ignore them. "I think we'd best have the tea."

"Tea would be grand. One can never have too much tea. We'll sip in between powdering our noses."

I poured us each a cup of the fragrant brew and ate, in two bites, a delicious mini sandwich of ham and asparagus with some sort of lemony sauce. Settling on the settee with my steaming white-bone-china cup imprinted with the blue CAB Airship logo, I refused to give in to the grief that swelled over seeing my father's initials—initials of ownership that I shared as Cora Alexandria Beaumont, as it was I who now possessed this ship. Instead, I waited as Ophelia gathered her skirts and sat opposite.

"And?" she prompted, curiosity lighting her eyes as she took a tentative sip of her own tea.

I swallowed a delicate sip and took a breath. "Well. My father befriended the duke when they were both in their early twenties, and then later he saved the duke—both his life in a boating accident, and then from a ruinous financial decision with a railroad company. In thanks, your uncle offered my father something unusually hard to come by in my society—advancement. We Americans have new money among our upper classes, but we have no titles. My father wished for his progeny to not only inherit the Beaumont businesses but to have the sought-after rank as well. Your uncle, though not particularly in need of funds, as I understand it, was willing enough to give this desired rank to my father in thanks for his help and friendship over the years. Hence my betrothal to Terrance."

Though part of me wanted to, I couldn't bring myself to explain the rest of the deal—how a social-climbing marriage would be my ticket to avoiding my half brother and his money-grubbing ways, and how he could jeopardize my chance at freedom should Terrance and I not be a good match. American though I was, it was still frowned upon for a woman to oversee her own finances, and it would be easy for my half brother to usurp my father's place without my engagement and the stringent stipulations of my dowry intact. Though not entirely sociably acceptable, a prenuptial agreement had been struck and signed shortly before Father's passing that would allow me to retain my own money—and CAB. But if my engagement was called off for any reason, it would be all the excuse my brother, who had no head for business, needed to take my dowry under the guise of caring for his younger sister.

"I was really hoping for something more lurid, though. It seems it was a good, honest bargain struck properly between fathers."

I nodded. "I hope Terrance is pleased with the arrangement. It was rather thrust upon us both by our parents." I was a willing party, given my other options, but it would be bad form all around to enter into a marriage already embittered.

"He's said nothing to me, though he wouldn't. But as a second son, he won't inherit the title or the dukedom. Rumor is that your dowry is a tantalizing accruement to even the most titled lord." Ophelia winked and took another drink of her tea.

A tiny smile played at the corner of my lips. My grandfather had invested heavily in the railroad and had been richly rewarded for his efforts. My father had invested heavily in airships and had quadrupled his already considerable wealth.

"You know, it's quite refreshing to find someone who doesn't mind speaking of things considered ill manners. Why must the most practical things be spoken of only in hushes behind fans and newspapers?" I took another sip of tea, realizing as I did that most young women of prominence wouldn't trouble themselves with talk of money. Most girls my age were in the process of marrying, so their financial status wouldn't concern them, merely their perception in society. A young woman's job was to elevate society's opinion of either her father or her husband. She needn't trouble herself with the mundane minutiae of accounting. I wondered if I'd spoken out of turn. Ophelia likely had no need to trouble herself with thoughts of her family's wealth.

"I suppose one must take scandal where one can get it. Isn't that what makes it so delicious, though? If it weren't so forbidden, it wouldn't be so enticing." Ophelia wiggled her dark brows conspiratorially. I smiled in return, glad she'd taken my frank words in stride.

"You have a marked point." I set my cup back onto my saucer.

"Now, we really *must* dress for dinner!" Ophelia said. "I'll ring for the ladies' maids. How shall we have her fix your hair? And who do you suppose will be available for dancing at the ball afterwards? I do hope I may set my cap at someone, or at the very least, make new introductions to some eligible suitors."

CHAPTER 4
Nicholas

"Terry, what troubles you? You've been quiet all afternoon," I commented as our shared manservant, Armand, finished tying my bow tie. The elderly man dusted the shoulders of my black dinner vest off before turning to Terry to assist him into his starched white shirt.

Terry was a little pale, and he *had* been quiet. More so than usual.

He glanced up and pasted on a smile that didn't quite reach his eyes. "Oh, I'm well. Just, just a little nervous about dinner tonight. With my . . . fiancée." He stumbled over the word.

Armand motioned for Terry to stand. The old man deftly buttoned up the shirt and flipped up the collar.

"Is something wrong in those regards?" I pressed lightly. "She appears well enough; you are pleased with her looks?" Terry put a lot of weight on the way a person looked.

"Oh, yes. She has turned out far prettier than I might have imagined. Perhaps I have a touch of airsickness too. Just nerves and the height."

I nodded, recognizing that Terry was politely shutting down the conversation. I'd have to trust that he'd tell me what was really bothering him when he was ready.

"Thank you, Armand," Terry said as Armand helped him slip into his black dinner jacket. Terry flipped the dark tails of his coat out, adjusting it to suit him. "Well then, I'm off to collect the girls. Join me?"

"Of course," I replied, accepting his olive branch. Armand helped me into my own suit coat. I locked our door and pocketed the key.

We walked the short distance between our chambers and the door of the girls'. Terry knocked politely.

"Ah, one more moment, boys," Phee said, opening the door and then dashing back into the room. "Cora, the boys are here!" she called far louder than was considered polite. I winced, hoping no one else along the hallway could hear Phee's unladylike bellowing. I loved my cousin—she was truly more like a younger sister to me than a cousin—but sometimes she had not the decorum of a bawdy house mistress.

"Right." Phee reappeared, her voice still too loud. She cleared her throat, shoulders going back, and it was like watching a caterpillar transform into a butterfly. Gone was the wild, unbridled joy that was Ophelia Hortense, and in her place stood a refined lady of society, her face arranged demurely, hands clasped gracefully in front of her.

Terry snorted.

"I'm so sorry to have kept you," Cora said softly in her American accent as she came up behind Phee. I swallowed. Cora smiled shyly at Terry, then her gaze flicked to me and she gave me a polite nod. I nodded in return by habit, taken aback by just how much she'd changed in the past five years. I'd had a good look at her earlier in the afternoon, but the way the lamplight from the room fell across the side of her face highlighted her cheekbones, the rounded bow of her lips, the elegant tilt to her chin, and the column of her neck that sloped down over her bared shoulders. The force of her beauty gave me a start.

As Phee looped her arm around mine, I blinked, then dumbly followed Cora and Terry down the hall toward the first-class dining hall.

"Your chaperone is not coming?" Terrance asked.

"She is not feeling well. She's opted to take a bowl of warm broth in her room," Cora answered.

"Nicholas, do promise me you'll introduce me to any of your eligible dashing friends who might be in attendance tonight at dinner. I so want to dance, and you know I must be properly introduced first. You wouldn't leave a poor cousin hanging about the side of the dance floor all night, would you?" Phee whispered, bringing me out of my stupor.

I chuckled. "I'll do my best, Phee, but promise me that you'll consider *all* your actions before charging ahead, hmm?"

Phee gazed at me icily from under her lashes. "I don't know to what you can possibly be referring," she quipped, not entirely successful at keeping her lips straight.

"There will be no sliding down the banister of the great stairway," I retorted.

Phee gasped. "Nicholas Tristan, I was three years old." She glared at me and pursed her lips.

I chuckled again to myself.

As it turned out, Ophelia did not disgrace the family name sliding down the banister, but her gaze sharpened like a hawk sighting prey when she caught a glimpse of her intended dinner partner. I stifled a sigh and dutifully pulled out my cousin's chair, then sat between her and Cora.

CHAPTER 5
Cora

Dinner was a lavish affair—a full seven courses—as I had expected it would be. Father and I had worked hard to take the best of traditions and expectations from both the British upper crust and the American elite, as The Mrs. Astor had privately started labeling them and mash them together in a display of glorious opulence that neither society could possibly disparage. I'd personally sat with Mrs. Astor in her grand brownstone sitting room and taken notes on her recommendations; Beaumont money wasn't properly "cooled off" to the third generation as Mrs. Astor insisted American high-society money should be. But neither could she pass up such an auspicious chance to leave her mark. It was the official pronouncement of my worth in American society. I only hoped the English would be so accommodating.

There were all sorts of entertainments planned for the duration of the journey. Nothing was spared for the first class. It was their gossiping that would help spread news of the *Lady Air* and how she cared for her passengers. If I intended to make my inheritance work for me and earn additional security, I needed to ensure everything was tip-top. I'd be watching tonight as well as putting myself on display for any who might be looking to the daughter of Clarence Abner Beaumont. With a small sip of frothy drink from my fluted glass, I swallowed down a bubble of anxiety at the thought of being on display—both for those who would approve and those who would not. If I was strutting about before God and kingdom, my engagement ring was sure to be noticed as well. The metaphorical cat didn't have much longer to wait before the bag surrounding it would be removed with the full force of the curious peerage behind it. My engagement hadn't been formally announced. I'd only just come out of mourning for Father, and Mother thought it would be in bad taste to have a lavish pronouncement. Better leave the festivities for the London season and the nuptials themselves. My engagement would be news soon enough.

I sighed. Pesky flock of vultures.

Gaslit chandeliers sparkled from the ceiling, their crystalline droplets rivaling the jewels of Queen Victoria's crown. Savory scents laced the air, and my mouth watered for the smelts and turbot I knew were coming after the soup course.

Nicholas was seated on my left, between Ophelia and me, while Terrance was seated on my right. Leaning ever so slightly forward and angling my head, I could just make out the animated sparkle on Ophelia's face as she conversed in surprisingly ladylike hushed tones with the nice-looking, mustachioed gentleman seated on her left. He was not someone I remembered meeting before; I knew his rank must be sufficiently high for him to be seated next to Phee but could call no name to memory. She tittered at her partner, and I hummed a smile to myself.

"Something amusing, Miss Beaumont?" Nicholas said, softly enough that only I heard him above the din of the room.

Straightening, I glanced at him, then inclined my head a fraction toward his cousin. "I believe Lady Ophelia Hortense may be working toward an attachment of her own," I whispered.

Nicholas raised an eyebrow, casting a furtive glace at his cousin as she playfully batted her lashes at the blond man.

"You may be correct," Nicholas muttered. "That is Lord Phillip Dawson Davies, son of the Marquess of Hamilton and Osborne."

A marquess? *Well done, Phee.*

Nicholas turned back to his glass of sparkling cordial.

"I say, is that the acting troupe that will be on board for the journey?" Terrance said before I had a chance to respond further to Nicholas. Terrance's face flushed, and his eyes took on a wild sort of excitement. He must care about the theater a great deal. I did not mind—an evening out at the theater with my husband on occasion would suit me well. New York had fine theater and opera, and I looked forward to more of its British counterpart. I glanced up, noting that the other side of the table was clear of occupants, so we'd have an unobstructed view of the stage.

"Oh, yes, did you see on the bill of service that they are performing multiple times while we're aboard?" the older woman on Terrance's right said louder than propriety called for, raising an eyeglass to her face and looking down her nose at Terrance to see him better. Lady Cadieux, if memory served. Bless the old biddy, she was hard of hearing. The scent of her old-fashioned eau de cologne cut through the savory dinner scents.

"I did, but I did not realize . . . that is . . . it is a merry-looking cast. Surely their amusements will be top rate." An animated glow, nearly like impassioned longing, seemed to emanate from Terrance's face.

"You are fond of the theater?" I asked my fiancé as a server refilled my water goblet.

Terrance turned to me. "Oh, yes. I thoroughly enjoy it, though it is a more recent passion of mine." He glanced back at the actors and actresses as they crossed to a section of the dining hall not yet occupied.

Lady Cadieux spoke, taking Terrance's attention from me once more. "What was the last show you attended, my lord? My daughter married a colony man. Quite properly, you know. Not like some that must flee our English shores due to unmention-able circumstances." She sniffed, and I noted that on the far side of Phee, Lord Dawson Davies inclined his head as if he were straining to hear Lady Cadieux—not that he had to strain much. The poor old bat was louder than a foghorn. I wondered if Lord Dawson Davies had someone of his acquaintance who had left England for India to spare themselves public ridicule. I'd heard it had happened on several occasions for children of the gentry who had found themselves afoul of society. The older woman sniffed. "But of India, she writes that the theater there is beyond description."

"And what do you think of all this mingling on the *Lady Air*?" Nicholas asked as Terrance chatted amiably with Lady Cadieux about the merits of the theater. Nicholas nodded at the troupe, thoughts clearly whirling behind his intense green eyes.

I took a sip of my water, pleased he had asked my opinion but unsure of his motives. "I think that actors and actresses are something of a rarity. Celebrities, even though many are from lower classes, are accepted into all levels of society, both American and English, because they are admired and put upon pedestals. It offers a bit of fun and respite on what might otherwise be a tedious journey." And the actors could do triple duty by providing amusements for each class, as they were among the few fluid members of our rigid societies. In this way, they saved the business money, which was part of the reason we had hired them for this maiden journey.

Nicholas nodded courteously. "An interesting observation, Miss Beaumont."

"And what is your opinion on the matter?" It was polite that I ask, though sheer curiosity prompted my question more than anything else.

A liveried server placed steaming bowls of terrapin soup onto our chargers. I inhaled the savory scents laced with a spritz of citrus and willed my stomach not to growl out loud.

"I think"—Nicholas picked up his spoon and seemed to tilt it in my direction—"that your father was a good businessman, and a good judge of society's wants and desires."

I lifted an eyebrow. It would likely do no good to mention that it had been my idea to have a troupe of actors on board rather than lesser amusements for each of the different classes.

"An interesting observation, Lord Tristan," I said softly. He met my gaze, a smile twitching his lips before he took a tentative bite of his soup.

We made it through the soup course, the fish course, and partway through the roast course before someone noticed the ring on my left finger.

"My gracious, is that . . . it is!" Lady Cadieux gasped rather loudly as she eyed my ring through her monocle. The gas lighting had hit it just right as I gingerly cut a bract of artichoke bathed in herbed butter, hoping it didn't drip onto my lap. But my lap and the possible dripping of sauce were forgotten as I froze, my fork poised to stab the unsuspecting vegetable.

Nicholas cleared his throat as Terrance heavily swallowed his bite of veal cutlet. Silence dropped over us like a burial shroud. Anxiety tumbled through me as Terrance remained mute.

"Yes, Lady Cadieux, Miss Cora Beaumont will be joining the Tristan house," Nicholas finally answered.

My mouth dried as I noticed fine lines of stress appear at the edges of Terrance's eyes, and my stomach dropped. Had he been so shocked into silence by her not-altogether-surprising question? The fine lines were subtle, but a negative change from the way he'd announced me earlier in the day. I wasn't sure what it meant, but it sent little tingles of foreboding slithering through my middle. My corset suddenly felt tighter.

The rest of dinner passed in hushed tones as furtive glances were thrown in our direction. We wouldn't have to wait for the news to hit the press pages aboard the *Lady Air*. We had our own gossip mill, and it was going full tilt, spiraling through the courses of dinner and carving my character—or lack of it, depending on which member of the peerage was consulted— along with the ham in apricot honey glaze.

When the chimes sounded at the doorway to signal that it was time to refresh ourselves for the ball, I was happy to escape the table and the vultures before they could pick away any more at my demoralized carcass.

"What a crowd of cads and old crows," Ophelia whispered, linking arms with me as we scooted as quickly as decorum would allow. I deeply appreciated that Ophelia had left Lord Dawson Davies's side to come with me rather than lingering near him. I needed the moral support. While I didn't care so much what society thought of me, I did still care very much what they thought of my mother and father and how they'd raised me. I hated to think that my actions in the face of irritating gossip might reflect poorly on the two people I'd loved most in my young life. Societal shunning was also decidedly not amusing. I might be accepted into New York's elite, but I was yet to be ensconced within the highest British social circles.

I needed the English aristocracy to want to fly in CAB airships. I didn't need people avoiding me like they'd catch the plague; that wasn't good for me or for business. To say nothing of how it would reflect upon Terrance and the Tristan name I'd be taking soon.

"Did dinner with the dashing marquess go well?" I whispered as we brushed into the ladies' powder room off the side of the dining hall.

Ophelia's eyes sparkled. "Maybe we'll be able to compare notes after all."

I smiled.

CHAPTER 6
Nicholas

I followed Terry down the short corridor to the smoking room, where he went directly to a mirror hung on the wall to study his reflection. My brow wrinkled as he meticulously adjusted his bow tie. Casting a furtive glance to make sure no one was close enough to hear us, I leaned in and whispered, "Terry, you must make sure to address the questions that are surfacing between you and Miss Beaumont. It wasn't my place to answer Lady Cadieux at dinner. For all she knows, she may think I'm the one currently engaged."

"I know, Nicholas," Terry snapped suddenly. My eyebrows lifted at his quiet outburst. He continued, irritated with me. "Don't you think I know what's expected of me? What I must do? I'm fully aware of my responsibilities; just give a chap a moment to accept them, for pity's sake." He brushed by me angrily and exited back into the hallway, leaving me perplexed and alone at the corner of the room.

With a sigh, I scrubbed a hand over my clean-shaven jaw, and turned to see one of my father's business associates coming toward me. I resolved to stay out of Terry's private life and let him work it out himself. After all, it wasn't as if I had any great experience to share with him. I had been engaged two years ago, to a girl

I'd scarcely known, but after visiting me, she'd gone home in the rain, contracted lung fever, and died within the week.

The arrival of Lord Nyland spared me from more morose thoughts, though I had a sneaking suspicion he'd like to put his daughter on display in front of me at some point during the evening.

"Lord Tristan, how do you fare on this historic voyage?" Lord Nyland shook my hand, his fluffy muttonchops bracketing his open, cheerful face.

"I am well, sir. How has business been this past season with the rain?"

"I was concerned at first, fearing it might hold up production, but the men have kept at it." He cleared his throat. "I wrote a letter to your father about a possible merger. Has he happened to reach any conclusions, or are there any caveats he'd like me to entertain?"

I kept my face carefully neutral. My father and I agreed that while Lord Nyland was a good associate with whom to do business, he was not someone we wanted on a permanent basis as a partner. But it was not my place to say so, even though I did hold the authority of the Tristan name.

"Or . . . any caveats *you'd* like to entertain?"

There it was. The daughter dangled like a carrot. I wondered if that was Lord Nyland's whole purpose in proposing the merger.

"My father and I are still in discussion regarding your proposition. We've received a few other lucrative opportunities and must best decide where to invest our resources, though you have been a valued associate for many years now." I hoped that was diplomatic enough.

"I appreciate those words, Lord Tristan. Nyland Industries will continue our support of the Tristan enterprises, despite the shortages of Indian manufactured goods. If you find you need things in greater quantity, don't hesitate to come to me. We are exploring other avenues for base goods now. Why, that's part of my reason for taking this journey. There are some top-rate American goods their new industries are producing. Their factories are impressive in their output." He smiled merrily.

"Are the Indian revolts causing much issue with your usual stock purchased from there?"

"Only a few things right now. We're monitoring the situation and keeping abreast of all productivity out of our Indian plant. I'll personally ensure the quantities and quality of all items produced by Nyland Industries."

"No doubt. You've always come through excellently in the past," I offered, placating the man, as I didn't wish to continue the conversation—either about his daughter or about the social class upheaval currently taking place in the far reaches of the British Empire. Both were likely to set my teeth on edge.

A flash of blond hair caught my eye across the room. Philip Dawson Davies, the toast of Ophelia's dinner, stood and casually leaned against the mantel. My eyes slitted slightly as I saw the same porter—the man who had escorted the suffragette from second class earlier—slip through an unobtrusive servants' door and surreptitiously slide a piece of paper into Lord Dawson Davies's hand. The porter made his exit the same way he'd entered, having scarcely been in the room more than three seconds altogether.

Dawson Davies hesitated a moment, scanning the room, then covertly unfolded the tiny paper and read its contents. He straightened and, with practiced ease, swept the paper into the fire, where it promptly sizzled into ash.

How peculiar.

Perhaps I'd better keep a closer eye on him after all.

CHAPTER 7
Cora

The ballroom housed in the belly of the *Lady Air* was by far the grandest and most lavish ballroom I'd ever been in aboard any sort of transportation. It was situated directly beneath the first-class dining room and took up the bulk of that level of the ship. The second and third classes were quartered below the ballroom, which had been designed to hold an entire class of people with room to spare, as well as laid out to accommodate the removable stage for the acting troupe to use during their performances. All in all, it made me a little giddy to look at it.

A small dais was situated in the far corner, where a quartet of musicians strummed lightly on classical instruments. The table of refreshments was set up along the wall opposite the musicians. If I strained, I could make out Terrance's wide shoulders as he stood in front of the white-draped table.

Ophelia gaped. "I have been in the ballrooms of many castles, estates, and chateaux. I must say, this is on par with all of them—grander than most. Is that gold laid into the mosaics on the walls? It's so bright and amazing, I fear I need to squint. And that shall ruin my face and set wrinkles in my nose," Phee whispered as she clasped my hand in hers, the silk of her elbow-length gloves sliding against the white silk of mine. "Also, don't look now, but Lord Dawson Davies is across the room. In a moment, casually glance over and see if he's observed me? Is my décolletage displayed appropriately?"

I choked back a snort of laughter. "Your décolletage has been so squeezed, stuffed, and plumped in your corset, and boosted with such layers of handkerchiefs, that you should take great care not to bend over lest it fall out and be on display for the gentry. And I warrant *that* is not the sort of scandal you wanted while aboard ship," I whispered back, grinning at her.

She smiled back happily, content to know that her assets were still where she'd put them. I rolled my shoulders self-consciously, making sure mine were still covered. I did not need to use layers of handkerchiefs to emphasize my chest, particularly in the lower-cut ballgown I wore.

The deep-turquoise velvet Phee had decided I should wear in lieu of the purple silk scooped below my collarbones and edged off my shoulders. The sleeves poofed deliciously, and I loved the drape of the dress around my naturally curvier frame.

"Ladies," Nicholas said as he stepped close enough behind us that we quickly stopped whispering. Phee shot me a look, urging me to glance across the floor.

I did, noting Lord Dawson Davies moving through the throng of people scattered between us. A puff of tobacco smoke whiffed as an older gentleman passed behind us.

"He's coming," I breathed to Phee. Her eyes danced and she sparked with excitement.

"Where is Terrance?" Nicholas asked quietly, a sharpness in his tone that sent the hairs on the back of my neck standing to attention.

"He was here a moment ago but went for a glass of punch," I said.

Nicholas visibly relaxed, and I filed that bit of information away to chew on later.

"Lord Tristan," a deep voice broke in, and I think Phee might have actually whimpered as she spread the folds of her fan faceup, as wide as they'd go, fluffing the air in front of her face ever so slightly. She might as well have written *available* on her forehead in kohl.

"Lord Dawson Davies," Nicholas responded. The men bowed slightly as Phee and I dipped quick curtsies. Phee sneakily moved her fan to the side so all her much-plumped décolletage could be inspected, should anyone happen to look. I bit the inside of my cheek to keep from snickering.

"Might I request the honor of this dance, Lady Davenport?" A smile hid beneath the kempt mustache on Lord Dawson Davies's face.

"I'd be delighted," Phee murmured as she glanced at the man from beneath her lashes.

The musicians began the opening refrains of a popular dance tune, and I glanced around again, irked that Terrance had deserted me. Nicholas sighed beside me.

"I fear I must apologize for Terry. Perhaps he was detained by someone near the refreshments." Nicholas shrugged apologetically. I nodded, acknowledging that people did often clog in lines to speak with those in the highest ranks of the peerage, though Nicholas was perfectly unencumbered presently. It was a pity Terrance was not so attentive as his elder brother. To be married into a duke's family at all was a rare and wondrous occasion, and I was grateful to have the less attentive brother. I could hardly fathom the uproar it would cause should a new-monied American marry an actual heir to a dukedom. The whole of Britain might collapse upon itself.

"Care to dance, Miss Beaumont?" Nicholas smiled, his eyes friendly and not pitying, so I agreed.

"Of course. Thank you."

He dipped his head and held out his hand. I let my palm rest against his as his other hand carefully touched my waist. With a swish of teal velvet and ruffled silk underskirts, we swept along the side of the ballroom.

Nicholas was an excellent dancer, and I found I didn't need to pay overmuch attention to ensure my slippered feet survived the intricate turns and twists. We clasped hands and he twirled me, my skirt swishing out far enough I felt my bustle lift slightly with the motion. I caught the barest hint of Terrance's shoulders at the punch table. A group of actors and a few actresses clumped around him.

Ah. His passion for the theater.

"Do you boast many trips to the theater?" I asked conversationally as we joined hands again and dipped and swirled in time to the steady music.

"A few times a season. Why do you ask?" The gaslit chandeliers cast a sheen on Nicholas's dark, wavy, carefully pomaded hair.

"Oh, I only saw the younger Lord Tristan speaking to some of the troupe as you turned me last. Forgive me if the question was impertinent."

"Not at all. I didn't realize he was there. You have keen eyes, Lady Beaumont."

"My father used to drill me on everything I observed as I studied ancient artifacts on his archaeological digs. He said observation was one of the greatest assets." I bit the inside of my cheek, hoping I hadn't said too much.

"You studied many artifacts?"

I couldn't respond immediately, as the dance called for us to separate and retreat behind the dancer to our left. Phee, three persons down, winked at me as she snagged my eye. Her cheeks were flushed, and I was delighted she was so enjoying herself. I was unable to study Lord Dawson Davies before Nicholas swept into my vision again.

"Artifacts?" he prompted politely.

"I did, yes. It's become a passion of mine."

"I see," he responded, though I couldn't tell from his tone exactly what he meant by the words.

The dance ended shortly thereafter. Nicholas bowed, and I curtsied to him.

"Shall we take refreshment?" He inclined his head toward my errant fiancé.

"Punch would be divine." And I'd like to *punch* my fiancé for ignoring me so studiously. I did not hold his love of theater against him, but it was quite rude of him to forget me for the inaugural dances. Especially tonight, as it was the opening ball of the voyage, and because he'd already failed to speak up at dinner, unintentionally though it may have been. Not to mention it was the first day of our official engagement. I'd have thought he'd want to make at least some sort of impression aside from his absence. Though maybe that was impression in and of itself?

Nicholas and I meandered through the throngs of the peerage that had clustered around the edges of the floor. I let my gaze wander and was surprised to see Lord Dawson Davies's profile as he glanced around the room, then made a hasty exit through one of the side doors meant for the servants.

That was odd.

I hoped Phee wasn't upset.

I nearly stamped my foot in impatience as we drew near Terrance. It was a full minute before he realized we stood next to him.

"Oh! Nicholas, M-Miss Beaumont," he stuttered. His face was flushed, and I wondered if he was bordering on drunk. I bit the inside of my lip.

"Forgive my tardiness." He inclined his head slightly. "I've been enraptured by the tales of such talented actors and actresses."

I lifted an eyebrow. I hoped that meant they were worth the money we had contracted to pay them for their entertainments.

"We mustn't keep you. We've got a dance number coming up, meant to entice all the first class to come back for every performance this week," a tall, lean man said. He twirled his right mustachio into a fine point and gave a quick bow before herding the rest of the group toward the far corner of the dance floor.

The lights dimmed, and the musicians began a new song. The peerage all clumped together toward the front of the room, clustering around the stage at the front of the ballroom. The music wheeled and dipped, comprising eerie notes and melancholy tones. The actors moved like wraiths in silken shrouds. Their gossamer skirts floated behind them like ghosts. The men, clad in black, lifted the ladies in their frothy skirts and spun them around as the music swelled and the gaslights flickered menacingly.

"Chillingly beautiful, don't you think?" Terrance whispered.

I nodded. He was correct. It was hauntingly, achingly beautiful. And slightly unnerving. The hairs along my arms prickled.

Chapter 8
Nicholas

I bit my lip and clenched my fists to my side to keep from throttling my errant brother. What was wrong with him? He was not typically so skittish, so remiss in his duties. I'd think, certainly, he'd have at least had the wherewithal to dance with his fiancée for the opening dance.

It was rude, and not only was it an affront to Cora, but it reflected badly upon the Tristan name. I glanced sidelong at him as the actors dashed about the dimly lit room in their glittering, whimsical costumes.

The darkened atmosphere gave me a moment to search its occupants. I found Lady Nyland, her gloved hand pressed to her heart, enraptured with the scene before her, her husband sipping a glass of punch next to her. He looked less amused. I sighed. I'd be less than amused if a duke's heir had politely brushed me off as well.

I put the thoughts from my mind. I would not speak for my father in business matters dealing with the Nylands. His daughter, Georgiana, stepped to her father's side. I mentally sighed. Nor would I encourage her attentions.

Though I wished to settle with a wife and someday have children, I did not wish to be cornered into a business marriage. I fully expected that my someday marriage would be of benefit to the family. But I hoped I'd at least be able to stomach my wife.

The music shifted, and I glanced at Cora where she stood beside Terrance. For one unguarded moment, I let myself study her. She was beautiful, but there was something else about her that raised the hair on the back of my neck. Her eyes spoke of a keen intelligence that bordered on frightful. She'd done nothing improper, but I couldn't help feel that there was something more to Cora Beaumont that lurked below the surface of her porcelain skin, flushed prettily from our earlier dancing. Irritation shot through me again as Terrance stood beside Cora, not touching her, not paying her any attention.

For the life of me, I couldn't understand why. He'd been agreeable to the engagement. Even excited about it when our father explained the situation. Then we'd gone to London in the weeks before the ocean liner took us from Southampton to New York, and Terrance hadn't been the same since.

Phee gasped beside me, drawing my notice and focusing my thoughts. Dawson Davies was nowhere to be found. He'd seemed uncommonly interested in my cousin's attention at dinner. I fully anticipated his asking my permission to see her again while aboard ship.

"Did you see how they lift the ladies? Do you suppose they have wires attached that make them seem like they're flying?" Phee whispered.

Truthfully, I hadn't been paying all that much attention to the stage. "Perhaps. Maybe you can ask them later," I whispered back.

Phee's eyes glittered. "Oh, what a delightful thought!"

I closed my eyes momentarily, resisting the urge to pinch the bridge of my nose while hoping Phee wasn't hatching another harebrained scheme. Though I wasn't sure what trouble she could get into just by conversing with a troupe of actors. Unless she tried to run off and join the circus upon docking in Southampton.

"You are absolutely forbidden from running off, forsaking your family, and becoming an actress," I said into her ear. Only half joking.

She covered her snort with her fan and glanced saucily at me from behind the sequined lace. I gave her a look to let her know I was serious.

Cora elbowed Phee surreptitiously on her other side. Phee leaned over to speak softly to her. I could only guess what she told her. Cora's eyes widened as her glance flicked to me, a smile tugging at the corners of her mouth.

I shrugged as Cora's eyes twinkled with laughter. I was glad to see that the years had not erased her sense of humor. A smile still flirting with her lips, she turned her attention back to the stage.

CHAPTER 9
Cora

Music floated over us as I took in the intricate ways the dancers moved—almost like a human knot. Skirts rustled behind me, the swish of silk across the parquet floor.

"Did you hear? The acting troupe is scheduled for a performance in the *steerage class* for a matinee on Wednesday. The audacity. I should think the classes would be better kept apart on a ship as luxurious as the *Lady Air*. To think of the same entertainment being provided to everyone! They might as well seat us down beside the peasants. It's just not done."

Heat flushed me from head to toe as the ugly whispered words carried softly over the ghoulish music the actors danced to.

I didn't dare turn around but strained my ears to pick up any replies.

"At least *we* are not expected to watch them from steerage." Both female voices—one British and one American—were deeply affronted. Marvelous. Both sides of the ocean were conspiring against my airship.

"It's a good thing too. Third-class quarters are simply beastly. Can you even imagine having to travel in such squalor? And aboard a ship reportedly so grand as this? There was a time when

Clarence Beaumont knew how to keep things at the level. But this? What a gross disappointment."

Blood boiled in my veins. How dare they sully my father's good name? A quick glance at Terrance saw him sipping from his punch, hardly aware of naught but the stage, watching the performance with rapt attention. I risked a look at Nicholas on Ophelia's other side. He appeared unaffected as well. Maybe the words hadn't been loud enough that other people heard them. Phee didn't seem to have heard them either, and of all my companions, I assumed she'd be the one to say something if she had.

One thing was certain. I would personally ensure that the third-class quarters were exactly as they were designed to be. They had looked sublime in the blueprints, but today was my first time aboard the finished *Lady Air*. Father's unexpected death had changed so many plans, but I was determined to *not* let rumors tarnish my father's name—or my future business. I'd simply have to sneak down into third class myself. Likely the women behind me were snobs of the first rate who found camaraderie in their complaining, but if there *was* an issue, I was in a position where I could fix things once the *Lady Air* docked.

Glancing at the ostentatious ring perched outside the thin silk glove on my finger, I smiled to myself. The engagement had done one thing: it had given me control of an otherwise uncertain future. The *Lady Air* was *my* inheritance, and it passed to me upon my engagement. I had the power to effect change within her walls.

With anger still simmering beneath my skin but resolve pumping through me, I forced myself not to turn around and confront the harridans behind me. I pasted a lovely smile on my face and clapped politely as the chandeliers were turned back up, light flooding the room again as actors bowed and curtsied.

"I hope you'll join us here for our performance Wednesday evening," the tallest actor boomed into the room. "It's the first of a three-part series of conjoined acts that will leave you breathless with anticipation, weak kneed with astonishment, and overjoyed with the ending!" The troupe all bowed and curtsied in tandem once more before exiting the stage and melting back into the crowd.

"Most excellent," Terrance said, his wide smile dimming slightly as it alighted on me. My skin crawled. Now that his attention was focused on me, I no longer wished for the spotlight.

"Indeed. Shall we be going to all three acts, then?" I tried to keep my voice toned politely.

"Most assuredly."

"Have you seen Lord Dawson Davies?" Phee whispered as she lightly tapped my elbow with hers.

"I saw him leave the room before the troupe took the floor," I answered.

Phee frowned. "We were getting on so well. I do hope nothing has offended him. He's such a dear. I confess I'm already quite besotted with him."

I snickered. "That didn't take long."

Phee pursed her lips primly. "We don't all have propitious fathers who make the best of matches for their daughters. Mine would wed me to old Lord Tavendysh given half a chance. The man practically has one foot in the grave." She shivered.

I patted her hand in sympathy. I'd met Lord Tavendysh. Nobody wanted to marry an aged man who stank of stale tobacco, had white whiskers to his waist, and was missing more than a few teeth.

"You see my urgency in securing another offer," she said. I nodded.

"Miss Beau . . . Cora." Terrance cleared his throat after the use of my first name. "They're starting the waltz. Shall we dance?" A light sheen of sweat covered his forehead, and some of my annoyance with him melted.

Poor man. Compassion softened me. Perhaps he was simply nervous or had a touch of airsickness.

"Of course," I replied, feeling my smile light my face. He returned the gesture, and we were off across the ballroom floor, glittering like a pair of sparkling gems.

CHAPTER 10
Cora

The waltz ended and Terrance smiled and bowed to me. "You are a wonderful dance partner, my lady."

"Thank you." *My lady* did sound lovely coming from my fiancé. Indeed, I'd be a proper lady and would be addressed as such as soon as Terrance and I married. I dipped a quick curtsy to him but was dismayed to find his eyes searching the room instead of on me as I rose. "Are you looking for something, my lord?"

"Oh." He startled as if I'd flashed my bloomers to the entirety of the peerage. "Oh. No, no, my dear woman. I find that I am overly excitable this evening. It is not every day one becomes an engaged man. Forgive me. I think I must take some air." He smiled tightly.

"Might I accompany you?" I offered. At least his nerves were now confirmed beyond question. Our engagement was far from normal, but it wasn't as if I were the first American heiress to marry into the gentry. Although I might be the first to wed into a duke's family.

Though the airship glided smoothly, my stomach dropped to my toes.

"I wouldn't trouble you. Go enjoy the ball. I'll be perfectly fine." He raised his hand awkwardly as if he were going to pat my shoulder, thought better of it, then dropped his hand and nodded to me before pivoting and disappearing through the double doors of the main entrance.

I was flummoxed. Terrance had never been so . . . unsure of himself in my memories of our shared childhood.

"Some men have a fear of matrimony," a singsongy voice whispered behind me. "It won't do to set your cap at that one. He's already running as far from you as possible."

I whirled around. Lady Tilly Remlaude stood, a mocking smile on her face.

"Some just have a fear of catching what the lower classes are carrying," her companion, Lady Georgiana Nyland, tittered behind her fan. She let her eyes slither over me, leaving me in no doubt as to just how far beneath her she considered me.

Irritation slid beneath my skin. I knew both these girls and had regrettably endured regular interactions with them at various society events over the past few years. Haughty, conceited, unkind, and the daughters of high-ranking nobles, they ruled the younger set of the British peerage.

How fortunate I was an American.

"Perhaps it's fear of catching some Egyptian plague. Wasn't that where you were off hunting your little relics this last time? Such an odious occupation. Not something for a lady of breeding. Not that'd you'd know. What it must do to your posture, never mind your skin—baking out in the hot sun, shuffling through sand like a barbarian. The whole thing is simply disgusting." Tilly scoffed and looked down her nose at me.

"Better sand in my shoes than sand for brains. Enjoy the ball, ladies." I turned and made it three steps before Phee linked her arm through mine. I caught a glimpse of Phee sticking her tongue out at Tilly behind her fan.

"Wretched class-mongers. Tilly and Georgiana may look like the jammiest bits of jam, but they eat vinegar with a fork!" Phee hissed while smiling pleasantly at those we passed as we meandered toward the other end of the ballroom.

I flipped my fan open so I could hide behind it. "It's a shame such pretty faces are wasted with such dreadful personalities."

Ophelia glanced around the room as we halted not far from the dais. "Oh, look." Phee fanned herself a little quicker as a flush rose in her cheeks.

"I see him, your dashing marquess," I said, following her line of sight.

"Of course, now we've parted ways with the two vipers, we're on the opposite side of the room from him. Should we shamble down that way again?"

"No. Let him come to us. It wouldn't do for you to chase after him too much," I advised. Men seemed to like to chase a woman a bit. Was that the reason for Terrance's absent nature—that he had not been given the chance to chase me? Did he want to?

Phee gasped as an unfortunate scene unfolded before us. Tilly sashayed brazenly across the parquet floor, her skirts swishing with the swaying of her hips, right up to Lord Dawson Davies. A flirtatious smile graced her lips, and the language of her fan could leave the young marquess in no doubt of her unmarried, unattached state. Anger seethed like a live coal beneath my skin. Tilly flipped a knowing glance in our direction.

"No! I've heard Tilly swear she'll settle for nothing less than a prince. She may absolutely not have him." Phee's deep-green eyes were huge in her face, her skin losing some of its rosy hue.

"She's likely only interested in him because he's been paying you mind," I whispered, jaw clenched tight in irritation. "You've been keeping company with the wild American." We rolled our eyes in tandem behind our fans before Phee riveted hers on Dawson Davies once more. To my surprise, and also to my relief, Tilly said a few words, then fixed her attention on Nicholas. Nicholas, who had been about to speak with Lord Dawson Davies, had politely waited to the side while Tilly fiddled with her fan. It appeared now that the duke's heir made a much more tantalizing target than a mere marquess.

"Oh, she's going after Nicholas. Tilly, that asp, has ensnared him." Phee harrumphed behind her fan.

Nicholas nodded politely at Tilly, then turned his full attention to Lord Dawson Davies, effectively ending his communication with Tilly Remlaude. A nasty glare flashed across her face for a single instant before smoothing itself back into a winning expression.

Phee gasped. "Nicholas *is* speaking to Lord Dawson Davies. Oh, so help me, if Nicholas messes this up for me, I'll strangle him in his sleep!"

I snorted, louder than I intended, and earned a raised eyebrow from a society matron some yards away. I smiled politely in return, and she turned her gaze back to the dancers. "I'd like to see you masquerading down the halls of an airship at night intent on strangulation."

"Oh, it wouldn't be all that difficult. The boys are bunked down the hall and through the one glass-paned door in the corridor."

"Phee, do be serious. My stays won't allow me the luxury of a proper laugh, and my cheeks are aching."

Ophelia's lips twitched. "Cora!" she whisper-squealed. "They're scanning the room. Tilly looks put out," she squeaked. Her face suddenly transformed into a mask of loveliness and decorum.

I only wished I could turn my charm on and off so quickly. Nicholas and Lord Dawson Davies bowed lightly to Tilly and Georgiana, who had joined their party, and then the men started toward us.

"Cora, I can't breathe. There are flapping things in my belly trying to escape!"

"I think that's called infatuation," I teased.

"Oh, you're so clever," Phee retorted, eyes flashing with excitement.

We waited in anticipatory silence as the men moved toward us.

"Ladies," Lord Dawson Davies said with a quick bow. Nicholas inclined his head, slight frown lines appearing between his brows. I trusted they weren't directed toward me. "Lady Davenport, I hoped I might entreat you to another dance," the marquess said.

"Of course." Phee batted her eyelashes, lowering her gaze and gasping. "Oh, my lord, have you injured yourself?"

"What? Oh heavens, no." His face lost some of its color. "S-some fool dashed his red wine and it splattered, though I didn't realize so much of it had landed on my cravat," he mused, glancing down and flicking at the dark-red stains dotting the snowy linen at his throat that draped down his chest. The splatter was thick and almost viscous in appearance.

As he flicked at the stain, I noticed a dark smudge across the knuckle of his white glove. "I fear I must beg your pardon for appearing so disheveled. I shall go and change at once." He dipped his blond head as the music struck up a tune for a dance that required the man's hands to land uncommonly close to the lady's waist as they turned. It was a favorite of the younger peerage, as it allowed the liberty of touching more than some of the other dances.

Phee's eyes sparkled. "Perhaps we could dance. It's not so very noticeable." The barest hint of a smile tipped her lips as Lord Dawson Davies smothered a grin.

"As you wish it," he acquiesced.

Nicholas rolled his eyes as the couple swept into the throng of the dance.

"You disapprove, Lord Tristan?" I asked.

"Disapprove is a strong word, Miss Beaumont."

I quirked an eyebrow but said nothing.

"My cousin is not known for her patience or her forethought." A grin tipped his mouth. "Though she could likely do worse than Dawson Davies," he said informally.

I let my eyes wander the dance floor until they landed on the dancers I sought. They seemed delighted with each other. Phee was radiant, and Dawson Davies was handsome, strong, and sure. As I continued skimming, my gaze snagged on Tilly. Her eyes slitted as she stared at me from across the room.

Because I wasn't English, or because I stood next to the quintessential titled Englishman?

CHAPTER 11
Nicholas

Lord Portsmyth, a mutual acquaintance of my family and the Beaumonts, had whisked Cora off to dance, and I made the mistake of lingering too long in one spot. That was all it took for Georgiana Nyland to pounce.

"Lord Tristan, you're looking dashing this evening," she purred, her words forward enough I had to fight to keep my brows leveled over my eyes.

I nodded, not particularly keen on her attention.

"I overheard my father saying he spoke with you earlier this evening. I do hope it was pleasant conversation." She made the comment casually, her hands clasped neatly in front of her as she held her fan open and faceup—indicating her single status.

That was fishing if I'd ever heard it. My insides heaved with a sigh. It would be considered a snub if we stood here and did not take a turn about the floor.

"Care to dance, Lady Nyland?"

"Of course. I thought you'd never ask," she replied, smiling brightly with a glint in her eyes.

The material of her dress was cool even under my gloved fingers, not warm and soft like Cora's dress had felt. I blinked, unsure why I had made such a comparison. We turned and swished our way through the dance. More than once, my eyes scanned the room. Terrance was missing again, and concern began to root in my chest.

This was unlike him—to shirk his duties, to disappear, to act in such an unreliable manner. Particularly with his fiancée, someone for whom he was responsible. Had he been suffering some ailment in silence?

"My lord?" Georgiana asked.

"Forgive me, please repeat the question?" Obviously, I needed to stop my woolgathering and focus more on the present.

"I asked if you'd heard those dreadful rumors about a suffragette strike. Can you even imagine such impertinence? I'm quite certain I could never make such important decisions myself without a husband to guide me. Don't you think that's the proper way of things?" She batted her eyelashes.

I grunted noncommittally. This was not a conversation I wanted to have with Georgiana Nyland.

"I've even seen some of those silly yellow ribbons pinned here and there since we've stepped aboard the ship," she continued. "The nerve of some women, and the nerve of the captain, letting them waltz in, brazen as Jezebel. It does make a girl feel unsafe, knowing there might be rebels about."

"Lady Nyland, I hardly think a few women wanting to exercise freedoms denied to them will take over the ship. I'm certain you have nothing to fear." Rebels indeed.

"My father says that's what started the rebellions in India. We have factories there, so he knows all about it. Not so much women wanting to vote, but people not accepting the position they were born into, and causing all sorts of unrest. Don't they know the British are only trying to improve their lives? The nerve," she repeated.

Easy words when one is on the top. I bit my tongue to keep from responding. Perhaps I should give more credence to the arguments surrounding the revolt—maybe even the suffragette movement itself? After all, I'd lived on top all my life. Perhaps I truly did not understand things as I ought. I pushed the thoughts away to unpack later when I had the time and mental capacity.

Georgiana scrunched her face. "The thought of all those politics makes my head ache. I don't want such a horrible thing to happen at home. Certainly not while we're all trapped aboard this huge flying machine."

"I'm certain the captain would adequately handle any insurrection that might arise." I could hardly blame the people of India for rising up. I'd heard rumors in every smoking lounge and newspaper of the cultural nationalism brewing in retaliation to the widespread western influence of Britain. It wasn't fresh news that the far reaches of the empire were having some impressive growing pangs.

"Certainly, the captain will be able to act accordingly when he has the best and brightest of the peerage to offer him council," she said, simpering and smiling prettily as the dance ended.

I dipped a bow and stepped back. "Thank you for the dance. Do excuse me, I feel the need for refreshment." It would have been more polite had I asked if she wanted any too, but I did not want to talk politics. Not tonight. I was too tired.

Instead, I scanned for Terrance. From the corner of my eye, I caught Cora curtsying to Lord Portsmyth and breaking away from him. Phee was still chatting animatedly with Dawson Davies where they'd ended their dance.

But where was my wayward brother?

CHAPTER 12

Cora

I wasn't sure the ball was ever going to end, despite the fact that it wasn't supposed to be an all-night affair as many balls were. The crew had to have time to come in and clean the ballroom in time for the troupe to set their stage for the play for the second class tomorrow. I'd obsessively memorized all the goings-on and happenings aboard my ship when I was too nervous about my upcoming engagement to do anything else. Waiting gracefully was not my forte.

Terrance reappeared to dance with me once more, but shortly after, the musicians played their last song, and I formulated how I was going to sneak around into third class to determine if the hateful words I'd heard earlier had any bearing or if the women I'd heard were simply full of themselves and their respective stations.

"Are you much recovered, my lord?" I asked Terrance discreetly as he escorted Phee and me through the exit. Nicholas trailed behind us, pensive, but his gaze was watchful all the same.

"Nothing a full night of rest shan't set to rights." He patted my hand where it was tucked in the crook of his elbow. I lifted an eyebrow. His face was flushed and held traces of both excitement and dread in a curious combination that I had no way of interpreting. He smelled strongly of spirits, too, which I assumed accounted for the red suffusing his cheeks. I sincerely hoped I wasn't marrying a drunkard. Surely it was just nerves.

"Cora, that was simply the most amazing ball I've ever attended," Phee gushed as I locked the door to our chambers.

"I'm delighted to hear it. And look at you, you who were afraid you'd not have any details worth rehashing. I dare say you had more of a romantic interlude than I did this evening."

Phee smiled sleepily. "Phillip is an absolute dream." She frowned. "I wonder if Terry is feeling some airsickness but is being too manly to give in to it?"

"That could be. He was a little flushed. Speaking of, I'll go check on Mrs. Beesly."

Phee rang for the lady's maids to come help us into our nightclothes while I checked on our chaperone. She was snoring softly, her smelling salts, an empty broth bowl, and a glass of water beside a large basin at her bedside. I eyed the basin, grateful there were currently no contents spewed into it.

Poor Mrs. Beesly hadn't left her bed but had at least taken the tray of warm broth. Who knew she'd get airsick? It was several days' journey to our destination, short in terms of travel but a long time to be miserable, bedridden, and mindful of one's charges as propriety might demand. Particularly when one of those charges was determined to make sure everything on her ship was running as her father had intended.

I saw no way around it. It must be done at an indecent hour, decidedly without a chaperone. I hoped my mother would never hear of the escapade on which I was about to embark.

Wind howled outside the porthole, and I shivered as I glanced out Mrs. Beesly's window. Night black as coal met my eyes. A flash of lightning far in the distance set my hair on end and my adrenaline spiking. I prayed the storm held at bay as we traveled overnight into the pitch darkness beyond with nothing but hungry waves far, far beneath us.

❖

Charith and Rose, the lady's maids, arrived only a few minutes after Phee had rung the bell, bearing a tray of tea. Charith stood just inside the door, positively quaking, hands trembling and clasped in front of her. Rose kept throwing her concerned glances as she went about turning down the beds and retrieving Phee's nightclothes.

"Charith, what is wrong?" I asked as I rose from toeing off my slippers.

She dipped a wobbly curtsy. "'Tis . . .'tis nothing, miss."

"You're shaking like a leaf. Come now. Tell us what has happened," Ophelia insisted. Though her tone was kind, it also invoked a layer of steel—much like others of the Tristan line.

Charith twisted her hands, her expression like a whipped pup fearful of its master.

"Rose, do pour Charith a cup of tea," I said, indicating that Charith should take a seat on the settee. Rose quickly crossed to the sideboard where the tea service still steamed.

It took some coaxing and gentle prodding, but we finally persuaded her to tell us what had occurred. "I was going to have a quick cup of tea before I came up here to attend you," she said. "But, as I entered the hallway, a man crashed into me from behind." She gasped, clutching her hands to her chest. "He had a knife and held it to my throat. He cut me just enough I bled." She stretched her neck as if subconsciously wiggling away from the bade, and she did indeed have a line sliced into her at the joint of her collarbone and neck.

I gritted my teeth, angry on her behalf.

"I was sayin' my prayers, my eyes clenched tight, as I thought it was my end, when all of a sudden, the man was lifted clear off me. Another man—I don't know who he was—had come to my rescue. There was a woman with him. A woman with long hair. I was so scared, I didn't dare stay. I'm not even sure which man attacked me. I didn't even see the men proper, just that both held knives. I was so, so scared. My ma would be ashamed of my manners. I just ran to the servants' lounge, where I found Master Porter and told him. He said he'd take care of it." Charith hung her head, still twisting her hands.

Rose urged the teacup nearer to Charith. The distraught woman took it up in trembling hands.

"You poor creature!" Ophelia cried, nearly moved to tears. Indeed, I was nearly struck dumb myself.

I needed to get to the bottom of this. This was *not* acceptable aboard my ship.

After repeated assurances from Charith that she was unharmed and did not need a physician, she helped me dress for bed quickly, as Rose did for Phee, then they left together under the protection of another male servant we had called to escort them.

Ophelia went straight to bed, and eventually, her breathing evened out and she did not stir. Tiptoeing into the wash closet, I didn't bother removing my nightclothes, relishing in the feel of the soft cotton flannel against my skin. I certainly didn't plan to run into anyone; therefore, I justified leaving off my corset. Scurrying into a dark woolen skirt and matching looser-fitting jacket, I did take pains to make sure the top button was done up under my chin. Just in case.

I took my master key—the one given to me by Father that no one else knew I had—and put it into my left pocket, then slid my knife into my right one. Father had taught me to always be prepared. A woman alone at night on an airship could meet with . . . unsavoriness. Thanks to poor Charith, I knew at least one such unsavory character roamed my ship. I clenched the hilt of my knife. I'd be traveling into less genteel areas where the clientele was largely comprise of the salt of the earth.

Not to mention I'd incur the wrath of several high-standing members of society if I were discovered. It was folly to go out on my own in the dark of night. But the conversation I'd overheard in the ballroom wouldn't leave my mind.

Terrance would receive a fat dowry upon our marriage, but all profits from the *Lady Air* belonged only to me, *not* my husband. They represented autonomy to me. Something I craved like oxygen in a society bent on putting me in my place. As a woman, and as an American. The society I'd come from was restrictive enough. The one I sought to enter was even more so.

Like a wraith, I crept from my chamber and through the shadows, taking twists and turns I'd memorized long ago on the blueprints Father and I had poured over. It was thrilling to see the plans on paper brought to shocking, vivid life within the walls of the *Lady Air*. The gas lamps, turned down now that night had fallen, ghosted spectral light along the corridors. Occasionally, voices would sound, and the soft strains of a violin wafted from the second-class commons room.

I smiled at the music as I rounded the bend that would take me to the staircase toward steerage. While not as posh as the one in second class and certainly not as grand as the one in first class, the stairway was still imposing, with its sleek carved wooden banister and tastefully carpeted stairs. There seemed to be nothing amiss. The area was nicer than most second-class train cars.

A door opened behind me, and footsteps shuffled toward me. Heart lurching up my throat, I descended the stairs as quietly and quickly as I could, leaning heavily on the banister to keep my tread as light as possible.

Making it to the bottom, I careened into the shadows, hoping I'd blend well enough not to be noticed. I fervently hoped the simple dark skirt and jacket would let me sink into the gloom. I wished I'd brought a cloak too. The storm, though yet leagues away, was bringing the already cool temperatures down even lower. I clamped my teeth down to prevent any chattering.

The footsteps disappeared without ever coming too near me, and I breathed a bit easier. Tentatively, I crept from my corner of darkness and assessed things.

Doors lined the corridor at regular intervals, gas torches interspersed at every other doorway—farther apart than in the other classes. While it was nice for the lighted doorways, it left the spaces between in near-total blackness. A chill that had nothing to do with dropping temperatures worked down my spine.

Perhaps I'd insist on better lighting in future airship models.

I inched along the hallway, fine hairs standing at attention on the nape of my neck. With a shriek of grinding metal, the ship suddenly pitched hard to the left. I lost my footing and careened headlong into a door.

With an ear-shattering crash, my forehead bashed against the door, jarring it open. As I looked up in horror from the crouched position where I'd fallen, the blood drained from my face one second, then surged to light me on fire the next.

"Oh! Oh, I-I-I'm so sorry; forgive me!" I stammered out.

A short man with intense dark eyes, a sleek mustache, and a hat pulled low over his brow glared at me. His arms were wrapped securely around a woman with beautiful brown, cascading hair. She was clad in a vivid-yellow dress, the full skirt swinging to cover the man's legs as he gripped her round the waist and across the bottom. Her arm was slung behind his neck, her body mashed against his. She hid her face from me, clearly mortified—as much as I was at having found the two caught in a lovers' embrace.

Shame, embarrassment, and the creeping feeling of humiliation clung to me as I clumsily stumbled out, fumbling the door shut. Hot prickles slid down my spine as I tried, and failed, to regain my composure.

Taking a deep breath to steady myself, I scuttled quickly, as quietly as I could, down the corridor. At the end, I turned the corner and immediately stopped. Wreathed in shadow, I paused and braced against the wall to allow my heart's pounding to slow. It still beat rapidly in my chest, and I cringed anew as images of the couple in their private moment flashed through my vision. Certainly not something meant for *my* eyes—given my innocent, unmarried station. Embarrassment nearly crippled me. No one else knew. The man and woman I'd barged in on knew nothing about me, who I was; I was simply an anonymous woman who had fallen through their doorway at a most inopportune moment. As members of the third class, they'd never have reason to suspect my identity. There was no reason our paths should ever cross again.

I blew out a breath and straightened my spine, determined to glance over the rest of the third class. A door opened and shut, and my pulse pounded again. Poking my head around the corner of the corridor and forcing the squirmy feeling in my gut to lie still, I glanced down the hallway.

My jaw nearly came unhinged. There, near the door of the amorous couple, the light of a gas lamp shining directly on his squared jaw, was one of the Tristan heirs.

CHAPTER 13
Cora

What black devilry was this? I blinked, disbelieving my own eyes. I was fairly certain it was Nicholas, but from this distance, it was hard to be certain. The man cocked his head as if hearing something, then gave me the profile of his ridiculously handsome face and removed any trace of doubt. The subtle bend in the bridge of the nose that Terrance had, and Nicholas did not, left no question that the man was my soon-to-be brother-in-law, and not my fiancé, staring at the offending door. I rubbed my scalp gingerly where a pulsing ache still resided.

Alas, I had bigger problems than the bruise forming at my hairline.

If Nicholas Tristan caught me alone in this hallway, he'd have my engagement to Terrance cut off in an instant, and I'd be left at the mercy of whatever my idle half brother could be bothered to do for me. My heart pounded at the thought. I could *not* be discovered here!

Moving as soundlessly and speedily as I could, I gripped my skirts and hiked them above my ankles most scandalously and hotfooted it down the corridor until I came to a door that led to either the waste removal or a supply closet. I was too frazzled to be sure. I prayed it was a supply closet. Footsteps thumped dully behind me.

Blast that man, he had turned into my corridor. I had approximately fifteen seconds to disappear before I was seen. Nearly yanking the pocket from my skirt, I took out my master key and inserted it into the lock. It turned, and the tumblers echoed like thunder down the hallway.

"Hello?" His deep voice, even whispered, sent a shock skittering down my spine and my heart lurching once again into my throat as I inched the door open and flung myself behind it. The scent of lavender and starch hit my nose, and my knees sagged in relief. It wasn't a waste-removal closet. It was a spare-linen closet.

I jerked a glove off and let my shaking finger run across the top of a sheet in the darkness. Smooth, not like silk, but a very nice cotton blend, my brain told me—reciting facts in an attempt to calm my choking anxiety. I inhaled the lavender scent and tried to hear above the pounding of my heart in my ears.

It might have been footsteps that moved outside the door, or it might have just been my hammering heartbeat. I dared not move. I stayed still as a statue until the ship pitched and a groaning of gears cranking dully was magnified in my small space. I caught myself on a pile of fluffy towels, knocking them over.

Resolving that I needed to get back to my room before I caused or happened upon some other catastrophe, I strained my ears. Hearing only the faint whine of machinery and the shriek of the wind as it zipped over and under the blimp above the ship, I cracked the door. Painstakingly inching my head out enough to peer into the blackness, I was rewarded with emptiness as far as I could see.

A chill worked up over my scalp all the same. I felt watched, though I could see no one. I wasted no more time. I'd have to complete my investigation of the third-class areas at a later date.

I came to a cross-section of hallway and squinted, trying to remember where each branch had led on the blueprints. Taking the right branch, I felt reasonably certain it led up a set of metal stairs not meant for the general public and out onto each of the decks. Rather than risking running into Nicholas or anyone else who happened to be awake at this hour—because surely nothing respectable went on at this hour—I decided to go up the metal steps to the first-class deck, cut across in the open air of the deck, then come back down the indoor, proper set of stairs that ended near my chambers.

Wind screeched along the hull of the blimp as I jogged across the outer deck. The air was biting and smelled of salt, even this far up. My skirts began whirling up my legs, bunching at my thighs. I sighed. Trousers would be infinitely more appropriate, though not even I was quite *that* brash.

Quickly stepping back inside the ship and out of the frigid wind, I descended the short staircase that would lead me to the first-class portside corridor and my room. I came to an abrupt halt as voices reached my ears.

Voices I recognized.

My heart pitched into my throat as Nicholas and Captain Cordello walked slowly but deliberately toward *my* door. Which I was currently not resting behind.

Drat.

Drat, drat, drat.

Was Nicholas my own personal haunt tonight? That brought me up short. What business could either of them have at this ungodly hour of the night that involved me *or* Ophelia?

I strained to hear as my heart pounded, threatening to drown out their hushed words.

"We cannot wait, Captain."

Captain Cordello tugged on his impressive mustachio. "I regret we must involve her at all."

"While I agree with you, the law is clear on this matter. We cannot proceed without Miss Beaumont." Nicholas swiped a hand under his eyes. His skin was ashen in the dim gaslight. I didn't have time to process possibilities, as all the air in my lungs whooshed out and a tight fist of anxiety lodged in my middle.

They were looking for me. And I was here, unchaperoned, unattended, most ostentatiously breaking all rules for my well-being and my fairer sex in general. If I was caught out here, the ramifications would be well beyond what my fragile social standing could take. Harsh enough to break my engagement and send my future up in a cloud of ill-timed smoke.

And if that happened . . . I shuddered as I beat a silent but hasty retreat up to the port deck. If my engagement was dissolved, I would have no recourse. I'd be at my brother's mercy, and the mercy of whoever might be willing to take a woman with a tainted reputation.

With panic threatening to clutch me in its grip, I inched to the side of the deck. My quarters were directly below where I stood.

Silently, I cursed a society that made things so ridiculously impossible. The mere idea that being caught alone outside my quarters could so upset my future made me chill with dread and boil with righteous anger.

I glanced down into the swirling mass of clouds. I'd abseiled down the side of a mountain. I could do this.

I looked down again and swallowed hard.

My mouth dried as clouds billowed up like black smoke, illuminated by the few cabin lights left winking against the darkness.

I'd used a rope to help my descent into a deep ditch to look at an archaeological site. Surely this couldn't be so much harder. *Could it?*

Without further thought, I caught hold of one of the grappling lines that attached from the blimp to the sides of the ship.

I was utterly certifiable. Bedlam was practically filling out my admission papers as I peered over the edge into a wide, yawning chasm of black death.

Mustering every ounce of courage, I gripped the line as if my life depended upon it—because it very much did—and swung my leg over the edge of the *Lady Air*.

CHAPTER 14
Nicholas

I dragged a hand down my face, stomach churning and shock setting into my limbs. I needed to take hold of myself. There were things at hand that I'd have to take charge of to protect those under my care.

I was loathe to drag Cora into this mess I'd been hauled into, but I had no other choice.

Blasted curiosity. I'd walked the halls, the corridors, the very route . . . if I'd changed course but a little, perhaps I could have stopped the atrocity committed tonight.

Cora had gone utterly rigid earlier at the ball when the women behind her had gossiped and then maligned the third-class quarters, which I was certain they had no firsthand knowledge of. But I also knew the happenings and goings-on of the *Lady Air* were important to Cora. Wanting to set her mind at ease if I could, I'd gone to investigate. I hadn't planned to do it this night. I was tired, but when Terrance stayed out overlate at his billiards game, I decided to see things myself.

And I'd run into madness.

Just before the staffer literally ran into me in his blind panic, I'd heard someone at the end of the corridor. What if I'd had the reprehensible one within my sights? The thought made me ill all over again.

"Are you certain this is how the terms work? You are certain you are not in charge of the airship? I've never in all my days heard of such hogwash. Surely you jest that . . . that the *woman* now owns this ship?" Captain Cordello gritted out between his teeth.

"We cannot wait," I replied, too numb with dread to address his ill-mannered words.

"I regret we must involve *her* in this at all," the captain grumbled.

"While I agree with you—a lady should never have to have such acquaintance with the macabre—the law *is* clear on this matter. We cannot proceed without Miss Beaumont."

Irritation flashed in the captain's eyes as his mustache twitched. I wondered if there was another reason for his ire. I ran a hand under my eyes, practically feeling the bags forming under them. Regardless, I was the son of a duke. The highest-ranking peer on this voyage. Which was why Captain Cordello assumed the *Lady Air* was in my possession. The captain would not cross me, though everything in his body language showed his disgust.

Captain Cordello knocked on the door.

No answer. Of course there was no answer. It was the middle of the night.

He knocked again, harder.

"Miss Beaumont? Phee?" I called softly through the door.

"My lady, please open the door. We've the most urgent matter we must discuss," Captain Cordello said, still quietly but with steel in his voice.

"Phee? Can you come to the door? Please?" I called.

There was muttering and a few oaths with a soft thump. If the circumstances had been less dire, I would have laughed at her grumping.

More soft thuds and then finally the door cracked.

"Nicholas Tristan, what in the name of all that's holy could possibly require my attention at this hour?"

"Lady Davenport, forgive the intrusion, but we must speak to Miss Beaumont. *Now.*" Captain Cordello was done waiting.

"Oh, Captain." She cleared her throat. "My apologies. Just a moment." She shut the door, and shuffling was heard on the other side. Phee cracked the door once again. "I, um, it seems that Miss Beaumont is . . . indisposed."

"We'll wait until she is adequately disposed." Captain Cordello harrumphed, and tension clenched the muscles in my shoulders tight.

Suddenly there was a loud crash, and the shriek of wind stood the hair on the back of my neck up on end.

Chapter 15
Cora

Invisible fingers tore at me, shredding my confidence and threatening to plunge me leagues below to my death, dashed against the unforgiving Atlantic. A whimper escaped my mouth, but I clamped my lips shut, determined that I would not give in to hysterics.

No matter how much I might want to as I dangled precariously from the side of the airship with nothing but my kid gloves and my iron grip on the ship's steel grappling line tethering me to life.

Squinting against the darkness that engulfed me, I secured my arm around the steel cable that attached to the side of the carriage so that the cable was between the crook of my elbow and my body and wrapped painfully tight against my left wrist.

Bracing my feet against the side of the ship, I belayed my way with painstaking slowness until I reached the blessedly large window of our washroom. I tightened my hold on the cable and steadied my feet as much as I was able in the tearing gusts and whipped a sturdy hairpin from my chignon. The wind thrashed my hair around my face, momentarily blinding me. Tossing my head like a wild horse, I shoved the edge of my sapphire-encrusted metal hairpin into the sill of the window and heaved on the bejeweled end.

Relief so potent I nearly loosened my grip on the cable burst through me when the sill gave ever so slightly. Wasting no time, I wedged the pin in farther, leveraging the window open more.

It was open enough I could thrust my fingers through the crack. I clenched my teeth around my hairpin like a pirate and jerked my hand upward, begging the window to open. Wind howled through the crack, whistling past my head as I shoved, pulled, and heaved with all my might to get the blasted window open far enough I could shimmy through, bustle intact.

Wretched fashion.

At last, the window opened enough I thought I could wiggle through. Though enough time had likely elapsed that they were all searching the ship for me . . . perhaps I could claim a violent bout of airsickness . . .

Oh, blazes.

I'd have to let go of the cable in order to get inside the room. I'd have to dangle like a leaf in the wind with no purchase for my feet.

Maybe I should have let my reputation shred into tatters.

No help for it now. I was committed. And likely *should* be committed . . .

I reached as far as I could into the washroom while still clinging to the cable like a second skin. I found the lip of the tub and gripped it so hard my knuckles popped.

"On three," I muttered around my hairpin, the wind carrying my words away. "One, two . . ." I loosened my grip marginally.

Just as I was poised to slap my other hand out to clamp around the edge of the tub, a massive updraft billowed up from below me, lifting my skirts and ballooning me to the sky. With a grunt any town drunk would have been proud of, I heaved, kicked, slithered, and then plopped with a crash into the porcelain tub.

I lay there panting, too tired to care for anything else. My feet were all akimbo, stuck up in the air, the bottoms of my white pantaloons peeking out, the lace edging brushing against my thighs in the wind coursing in from the outside. Hair and skirts tangled together over my face, puffing with each exhale.

"Cora! Dear, are you all right?" Ophelia's concerned voice was muffled through the door.

"Yes," I croaked. "Just . . . just a moment." My hairpin clanked against the tub as it fell out of my mouth with my words.

"Cora, are you ill? You sound awful. I'm coming in to help."

Before I could warn her off, she cracked the door, illuminating the space with light from the other room.

"Cora," she nearly shrieked. "What on earth?"

"The . . . the window came open," I offered lamely.

"I see that it has," she replied skeptically as she wrestled it shut. "You are going to tell me *everything* later," she whispered fiercely, assessing me for injury and helping me sit up in the tub. "But right now, my cousin and the captain are here. They said they must speak with you urgently. I've had to put them off, saying you were indisposed. I assumed you were sick in here like poor Mrs. Beesly." She lifted an eyebrow, sensing scandal like a bloodhound on a scent.

"Later. Help me." I gestured weakly to my hair, which must surely resemble the finest rat's nest after my tumble in the wind.

Ophelia *tsk*ed and quickly pulled my remaining pins out, twisting my tangles into a low knot at the base of my neck and securing it with the sapphire pin.

"Shall I call for tea? This seems the sort of story that requires tea."

I snorted. "We must have tea. The more bracing, the better," I muttered, wondering if I should attempt a drop of spirits in mine. I shook the thought from my head and took a deep breath. My legs shook like twigs in a stiff wind.

Ophelia patted my shoulder and helped me stumble out of the tub.

"Phee, is everything all right?" Nicholas asked through the door.

My cheeks heated.

"Fine. Cora, Miss Beaumont . . . just . . . she needed a moment. The crab bisque."

"The crab bisque was divine," I whispered, mortified at the insinuation of things exiting my nether regions in present company outside the door. I gathered my tattered courage and smoothed a hand down my jostled skirts. I cracked the door. "Excuse me, gentlemen, for having kept you." I put on my most cultured voice and tried to ignore the trembling remaining in my knees. "The window came open and gave me quite a shock."

"Miss Beaumont, are you well?" Nicholas asked, his green eyes assessing me with as much attention to detail as Ophelia had moments before. I willed the embarrassed flush crawling all over my body to stay away from my face.

"I am sufficiently recovered. What is so urgent that you needed to speak with me at this hour?" If either of the gentlemen noticed I was still fully dressed, though disheveled, while Ophelia clutched her dressing gown over her nightclothes, they did not comment.

The captain cleared his throat, looking perturbed. Lines creased the edges of Nicholas's eyes, his mouth tugging down. Unease slithered through my gut. "Miss, I think it best we discuss this . . . in private."

Ophelia balked. "You're taking the lady to parts unknown in the middle of the night with no chaperone? Naught to be concerned with there *at all*."

"Not now, Phee. This is serious." Nicholas's harsh tone sent my stomach dropping to my toes. He turned to me, and my knees quaked for an entirely different reason. "Miss Beaumont, as I am soon to be your brother-in-law, I shall take full responsibility for your person. Nothing untoward shall befall you. But we *must* speak with you. *Urgently*." His eyes crinkled around the edges, and my stomach quivered in dread.

"Of course." I nodded at Ophelia. Concern, trepidation, and a little sliver of excitement coursed through me as I moved to the door. What sort of happening could possibly have drawn the men from their beds and require my input? Unease tickled the back of my shoulder blades.

We passed through silent corridors, my heart still pounding painfully against my breastbone from my near-death escape, and from the coming confrontation—whatever it might contain.

Once we were ensconced in the captain's personal drawing room, a weight seemed to descend, pressing against my shoulders so that my knees wanted to buckle into the lavish carpet beneath me.

"Please tell me what's happened." The suspense was ratcheting up my anxiety, and it was already high.

The men looked at each other, the captain frowning and motioning to Nicholas.

Nicholas sighed and faced me. "Miss Beaumont, I am so sorry you must be involved in such vileness, but it cannot be helped. Once that ring slipped over your finger"—he nodded to the engagement ring mercifully still on my finger over the kid gloves I still wore, and I clenched my fists to my sides—"your dowry started to go into effect."

My eyebrows lifted. "My dowry? What of it? And what could it possibly have to do with clandestine meetings in the middle of the night?" Trepidation wormed in my belly.

A tired smirk lifted one corner of his mouth. "My dear Miss Beaumont, I am heir to the Duke of Exford and Debensley. I am intimately acquainted with all financial comings and goings of our house. Including the unusual stipulations of your prenuptial agreement."

I willed the blood not to rush to my cheeks. I don't think I was successful. I wasn't sure why Nicholas's knowledge of things made me so squirmy inside, though I was slightly surprised he knew *all* the particulars—or at least put on the front that he did.

"And this requires my attention at three in the morning?" I persisted to cover my unease.

Nicholas winced. "Something far worse, I'm afraid. But as it pertains to your engagement and your dowry, the moment you accepted the engagement to Terrance, the *Lady Air* transferred its title to you." *As you well know,* his eyes seemed to say. "And the law states that when . . . unpleasantness occurs, the ranking member of the staff must oversee said unpleasantness, or forfeit the right to the next ranking member, which would be Captain Cordello."

"Now, miss, if you'll just sign these papers transferring the right to oversee things to me, we'll let you get back to sleep, and having a pleasant rest of your journey." Captain Cordello bobbed his head and extended some papers and a fountain pen to me.

Unpleasantness?

I would not be removed from decision-making *that* easily. Not when it was within my power to make my own judgments.

I steeled myself. "I would know what this unpleasantness is."

"Miss Beaumont, truly, you do not wish to involve yourself in this. It is not something for a lady. Surely your sensibilities are far too delicate," Nicholas said, attempting to placate. His words had the opposite effect. I bristled.

"My sensibilities are perfectly adequate, thank you. Now. I'd know more details before I'm so put off."

Nicholas raised an eyebrow at my blunt words. Captain Cordello's face darkened. "Miss Beaumont, please just sign the papers," he urged.

I crossed my arms belligerently. "I will sign *nothing* until I am sufficiently informed."

With what certainly must have been my fancy and a trick of light, I clearly imagined the eldest Tristan's eyes lighting with something akin to respect. "There's been a murder."

A murder?

My blood chilled, and I felt my eyes growing rounder in their sockets. A murder on the maiden voyage of the *Lady Air*. *The poor victim!* My heart clenched, thinking about the family that must be informed their loved one had passed. Tears pricked my eyes as memories of my father's funeral bombarded my mind.

I blinked rapidly, shoving the unhelpful thoughts aside and focusing on the task at hand. A murder. A murderer was loose on *my* ship. Hurting *my* passengers. Risking my father's good name with wild, unscrupulous behavior. Risking my future.

I would not have it.

"Miss Beaumont, please sign and let us handle things," Captain Cordello encouraged again in a kinder tone.

My head came up and my gaze met his.

Resolve straightened my spine. "I will do no such thing."

Captain Cordello sighed, probably wondering if I was so daft as to not comprehend the gravity of the situation, or if I was so brashly American as not to back down. I was indeed the latter, for no one had as much to lose as I when it came to this airship's reputation.

"Miss Beaumont, I don't think you understand." The captain moved beyond placating to explain again that which I had indeed already comprehended. "A murder has happened aboard this vessel. It must be taken care of. In order for us to do that, you must sign over permission for me to take charge."

"As owner, you are the ranking member of the ship." Nicholas's eyebrows drew together in concern, his emerald eyes studying me, unsure.

"I understand perfectly, my lord. I will take an active role in this. I will not allow anything to tarnish my father's memory, or my future business. I appreciate your willingness to take control of things, Captain, but I'm afraid I must insist that I be intimately involved." I clenched my teeth, steeling myself for what I knew must come next. "Please take me to the body."

CHAPTER 16
Nicholas

I was impressed. Concerned but impressed. Cora straightened her spine, pulled her shoulders back, and with a look that said she'd spit in the eye of anyone who contradicted her authority, marched down the hallway alongside us.

I wondered if her bravado would last long enough to gaze upon the body.

Captain Cordello frowned, working his mustache frequently and stealing black looks at Cora every few steps. I didn't like the way he watched her, or his attitude. As unusual as this situation was, it didn't call for ungentlemanly behavior. Chances were good that Cora would faint away as soon as she saw the body. There were no women of my acquaintance who had the fortitude necessary to undertake such a heinous task. Maybe Phee, but I wasn't entirely convinced sometimes that she wasn't a changeling child and not human at all. For all Phee's facade of genteelness, she was as wild as they came on the inside. Even so, she might not deal well with a murder investigation. How could Cora?

Cora blew a quiet breath out, and I could practically see her resolve harden into a mask across her features.

Interesting.

Cora had always been a touch brazen as a child, but she seemed to have mellowed into the lady society would demand of her. I wasn't ready to forgo my thoughts that women shouldn't be involved with dead bodies, but as determination lit in the depths of her eyes, I wondered if Cora Beaumont might have a surprise or two in store.

We met no one on the way down to the third-class area. At the door, two liveried crewmen stood guard. Not another soul was in sight, for which I was thankful. The fewer people who knew a killing had taken place on board, the better—at least until we had the murderer in custody. The thought sent foreboding rippling down my spine. Whoever had killed must still be on the ship. There was no place he could have escaped.

A chill that had nothing to do with the wind lashing the outsides of the ship prickled over my scalp. If only I had started on my exploration sooner—I might have been able to stop this hideous thing from occurring. Regret tumbled into my gut, sitting uncomfortably next to the shock I was still processing. I swallowed. We stopped in front of the very door I'd paused at during my late-night excursion.

"Miss Beaumont." I forced the words out around the boulder of emotion clogging my windpipe. I cleared my throat. "Cora, this is the last chance for you to turn back," I encouraged, hoping the familiar use of her first name might endear her to my pleas for her to give up her involvement. "There is no need for you to view such a disturbance," I whispered, afraid somehow that even the corridors had grown ears.

She turned to face me fully, every bone in her body set straight and true. I knew then there'd be no convincing her otherwise until she'd seen the murder scene. Mentally, I prepared for what I was sure would be a spectacular reaction—one that would likely induce Captain Cordello's immediate assimilation of the case. Possibly smelling salts and a call for the physician. I blinked as she inhaled calmly.

"My lord, I appreciate your concern. But this is something I feel I must personally attend to."

The captain snorted, his mustache twitching furiously.

I nodded reluctantly.

CHAPTER 17
Cora

I appreciated Nicholas's concern. Truly, I did.

But there was a *murderer* aboard my airship.

And unless they'd tried grappling down the side of the ship and missed their washroom window, they were still aboard the *Lady Air*. There was nowhere for them to go.

"I must warn you, this is . . ." Nicholas shrugged.

I held up a hand to stop his protest. "I've been on many archaeological digs; I've seen desiccated mummies and things that would cause the better part of society to swoon."

"As you would, then." Nicholas glanced about to be sure we were alone in the hallway before cracking the door and letting the three of us inside, while the guards remained.

My bravado fled when I took in the very real puddle of blood oozing from beneath the young woman, her dress savagely torn open, a curved mark I didn't look at overlong cut gruesomely into the flesh of her abdomen, stretching from her lower ribs to below her navel—all the way to between her hips.

My stomach rebelled, and bile rose in the back of my throat. I covered my mouth with the back of my hand and felt Nicholas's solid chest at my back.

"Cora, surely you've seen enough now." His voice was kinder than I'd ever heard it, and his fingers ghosted over my elbow, silently encouraging me to turn away.

But I couldn't. This poor woman. Her dark hair streamed across the wooden floor, her lifeblood soaking the Turkish carpet beneath her torso. The hateful mark carved into her flesh. Anger rose within me that someone dared come against this girl—scarcely as old as I.

I looked closer.

Blazes.

Recognition slapped me hard across the face as I nearly swayed on my feet. I'd seen this girl before.

I locked my knees to keep them from buckling. I swallowed. Once. Twice. I shoved away the emotions that were rising in my throat and pulsing behind my eyes. They could not help me now.

The yellow dress. The abundant dark hair. This was the woman I'd seen in the man's embrace.

Letting the instincts my father had drilled into me rise to the surface while forcing down the horror, I took in the room clinically, as an archaeologist might. I pretended the woman at my feet was a mummy, the life within her long gone past the veil. Instead of focusing on her, I looked for details. For anything out of place or that would give me information.

I took a single step into the room, letting my eyes consume the contents while skirting the dead body for the moment.

"Her bed is made. She's still in her dress, not her night-clothes." I paused to swallow hard again. "The blood is drying at the edges where it's seeped onto the hardwood, but still wet everywhere else. She hasn't been"—I cleared my throat—"deceased . . . terribly long." I glanced around again. "There's a tea service." The teacup was half-empty. "She was alive long enough after dinner to request tea, but not to finish it. Nothing is out of order. There appears to have been no struggle."

"Meaning her murderer was someone she trusted enough to let inside her room," Nicholas finished for me.

The chill I'd been suppressing shuddered down my spine as a new nightmarish terror surfaced in my brain. This was the room where Nicholas had been poised outside the door. Had the woman known Nicholas? Had *he* known *her*? Why had he been outside her door? What of the other man I'd seen embracing her?

My gaze flitted to his. His expression was steady, concerned, and surprised, but held no guilt. Still, I had to be sure. The world contained some expert liars. I hoped my soon-to-be-brother-in-law was not among them.

"Now, my lady, surely you will sign the papers and let me take charge of this situation," Captain Cordello said brusquely.

My hackles lifted. Something about this man itched beneath my skin, and not in a pleasant manner. I turned to face the captain and felt Nicholas's gaze boring into the side of my face.

"My good captain, I have no intention of relinquishing anything. *I* will personally oversee this investigation. This is *my* ship. This atrocity has been done upon *my passenger*, on the maiden voyage of the *Lady Air*. I will let nothing tarnish nor sully my father's good reputation, nor his legacy. I thank you all the same." My knees quaked beneath my skirts—for once, I thanked high heaven for large bustles—as I strove for bravado I did not feel and forced the queasiness of what my brain attempted to process back into the recesses of my mind. I would *not* retch in front of these men. I tipped my chin and tried not to inhale the metallic tang of blood that permeated the air. "As the ranking official aboard this vessel, I shall take charge here. First, I am ordering that no one else be alerted to what has happened here. We will not incite a panic."

Captain Cordello's face was turning red—with anger or fluster, I wasn't sure.

"I . . . you . . . you just cannot . . . I will not take orders from a woman aboard my ship!" he spluttered.

My put-on confidence drained. I was not suited to this job. But I didn't trust anyone else to oversee it as thoroughly as I knew I would. This was my future at stake. Surely I could put my skills of observation to good use and find who had done this heinous thing to this poor girl. All while keeping my ship and society free and clear of the scandal.

Because this was a deep, steaming pile of scandal.

I took a steadying breath and set my jaw.

"As the legal owner and ranking official aboard the *Lady Air*, I think you'll find you *will* take orders from *this* woman," I declared softly. I was trampling all over the man's ego, and I didn't want him to have apoplexy there next to the victim. I attempted diplomacy, though my efforts were likely already shot to oblivion. "I have no wish to interfere with your duties or with the *Lady Air*. But this, Captain, is not something I will let go."

Anger lined the weathered sailor's face as a vein pulsed in his neck. With a black oath and some comment about *poxy Americans*, Captain Cordello turned on his heel and stormed from the room, leaving Nicholas and me alone with the body.

I shuddered.

"Shall I fetch the doctor?" one of the airship staff standing guard asked through a crack in the door.

"I'd best see to the guards," Nicholas murmured as he turned toward the door. He glanced at my face, head tilted in question, hesitating before stepping from the room.

I took a breath and fled the scene, letting Nicholas quietly shut the door behind us.

CHAPTER 18
Cora

I walked a few paces down the darkened corridor and turned, my insides a mass of writing snakes, both from the violence I'd witnessed and from the fading of the adrenaline that had surged with my own audacity. As I gripped my stomach, Nicholas bent low to speak softly to the remaining guard. The liveried airshipman stood taller and nodded seriously. Whatever Nicholas said to the man seemed to have inspired a great sense of duty.

A door opened farther down the hallway, and my pulse leapt into my throat, my hand going to my pocket. A dark-headed man in an undershirt popped his head out the door, sleepily rubbing his eyes.

"All right, miss?" he asked me, voice full of gravel.

"Oh, yes. All right. Thank you. Um, just . . . just an issue getting my porthole open," I lied on the spot.

Drat. I was a terrible liar.

"It's all fixed now. Thank you. You may return to your quarters." The fine hairs on the back of my neck stood up as Nicholas spoke softly but sternly. The man quickly shut his door. Even in the dead of night—bad timing for that expression—men didn't question Nicholas Tristan.

But I was about to.

Dread slithered along the back of my shoulders, and my stomach tied in knots.

"Come, it's appallingly late, and we're going to wake people," he whispered to me with a look that let me know how much I didn't want that.

I nodded. It *was* late. I knew my body was exhausted, but my mind flashed as fast as airship turbines.

"Wait. I would speak with you, Lord Tristan," I said, melting from the shadows into the dim light of the gas lamps hung along the hallway. The remaining guard still stood at rapt attention in front of the victim's door. I shuddered, thinking of what lay in the room beyond.

Nicholas stared at me, bewildered, and I ignored the strong urge to roll my eyes.

"Right now?" Nicholas blinked.

"Now," I confirmed without hesitation. I glanced at the guard, then swallowed down the blush that threatened to creep into my cheeks with my next hushed words. "But privately."

His eyebrows rose as his expression turned unreadable. He scrubbed a hand down his face. "Come. The third-class lounge is not far and should be deserted this time of night. The guard will stay sentinel at the door while the other fetches the doctor." It was curious that he already knew the general lay of the third class.

I nodded, my hand reaching into my pocket for the cool comforting grip of my knife.

Nicholas was right—the lounge was utterly devoid of life. It must be nearing four o'clock in the morning, and even the liveliest of passengers had gone to bed. A checkerboard and pieces lay scattered on a table next to a deck of cards in the silent room.

Nicholas shut the door quietly, and every one of my senses went on high alert. Thunder rumbled somewhere in the distance, and my anxiety spiked enough that my fingers twitched.

"Surely you've seen enough now and you will be reasonable and quit this nastiness. This cannot be pleasant for you. There is no need for *you* to do this—to suffer unnecessarily." His eyes were tired but focused. It was the sheer determination in that look that rippled gooseflesh like pinpricks over the back of my shoulders.

No, it was in no way pleasant, but I would not be deterred. My curiosity had been whetted, my concerns engaged, but I knew I must ascertain the truth of one thing more before I could move forward.

I saw no point in beating about the bush. I clenched my hand into my skirt and plunged full ahead. "I would know why you were seen near the victim's quarters shortly before you and the captain came to fetch me." I cleared my throat uncomfortably.

His face hardened as his brows drew low over his green eyes, piercing and intense as he took a step nearer me. I gripped the handle of my dagger within my pocket. I would not cower, but I would bite the inside of my cheek to keep the squeak inside my lips.

"Why such curiosity?" His voice was strong and unyielding. The voice he used when he spoke as heir to the dukedom. I didn't relish the tone turned on me.

"Please answer the question, Lord Tristan." I gulped a breath. "If it's a mere dalliance or a tryst, none of the peerage would think twice, but do just say so and let's be done with it. You were seen, and I would know your movements regarding the woman, or if you saw anything else that might prove useful."

His eyebrows hiked halfway up his forehead into the dark locks swept across it. "I beg your pardon?" Surprise was written plainly across his face.

Mortification slid through me. This was, after all, heir to one of the highest-ranked nobles in Britain, a man to whom I'd soon be related, and here I stood, accusing him of trysts and connection to murder. It was a mercy Terrance's ring still rested on my finger. I chewed the inside of my lower lip.

"I find it saves time to get straight to the point," I replied bluntly, figuring I'd already ensconced myself in enough trouble for the moment and more straightforwardness wouldn't hurt.

"She is not, and has never been, a mistress of mine. I do not keep a mistress. Your suspicions will have to land elsewhere, Miss Beaumont." I mentally cataloged the barest shake of his head, his expression of slight bewilderment mixed with disgust, and the steadiness of his voice, confirming his words.

I believed him.

But before I could consider relaxing, his eyes pinched at the corners. He took another step toward me, into a space society deemed inappropriately close. My hackles rose and fear coated the back of my throat. Nicholas Tristan was a well-built man. Even now in the scant lighting, I could see the material of his suit coat bulging over his biceps. He continued as I tried to hide my alarm. "But do tell me, what would the society matrons think of you, accosting me with such accusations in a dark lounge at this late hour, hmm? Or how you came by this supposed information in the first place?"

"They'd think more of you and your pitiful plight if you take one step more," I said with more bravado than I felt. I flicked my wrist, my dagger sliding silently out of my pocket and aimed at my soon-to-be brother-in-law.

Oh, what a blazing disaster.

"Is that so?" The words were low and in a tone that could be taken as a menacing edge or dark teasing. I didn't know him well enough to discern the difference but leaned toward caution, as his words sent the fine hairs on the back of my neck standing to attention. His left eyebrow lifted as he brought his leg forward to test my threat and stopped midstride as the tip of my unseen dagger pressed against a place that all men seemed to deem of the greatest import.

A strangled noise sounded at the back of his throat as his eyes went wide and he looked down in shock at the slender knife blade secured in my grip and angled against his manhood. Gingerly, he raised his hands in the air and took a large step back.

When he met my gaze again, his face had lost its menace, and I thought I saw the slightest flash of awe in the depths of his eyes. "Blazes, Miss Beaumont, you have been *ghastly* underestimated, lethal creature that you are. I shall never speak of you as one of the weaker sex again."

I bristled.

"Wherever did you learn to handle a knife? Most women of my acquaintance would swoon at the mere thought. Though I suppose I ought not be surprised. Even as a child, I remember you more courageous than most of the lads. I see a few years and society's influence have not diminished that." His arms slowly began to drop.

I lowered the knife, though I didn't put it away. A fact Nicholas took note of with yet another lift of his eyebrow.

"My father taught me," I said softly. Emotion rose in my throat, and I swallowed heavily.

"A good job it would seem, too." He slowly dropped his hands to his sides as his head canted. "Do you truly think me involved with the lady's demise?" All teasing was gone, his tone gentled.

I stared at him a full minute. The openness of his face, the concerned tilt of his eyebrows, the earnestness of his expression. When we were children, he'd always been the protective one, the one to call the rest of us to order when we grew unruly. I could not picture him a murderer. If his sensibilities had carried into adulthood the way mine had, he'd have done the proper thing, had the woman been a mistress and there had been . . . complications. Indeed, now that I looked at him, the idea of him doing such a thing seemed completely improbable. Nicholas was far too honorable to stoop so low as murder—much less such a gruesome killing as this was.

"No," I said at length, convinced. "No, I do not think you had anything to do with her demise."

Nicholas cleared his throat. "I'm glad that's settled, then . . . Shall I escort you back to your quarters?"

"I can manage, thank you," I said. Though I had no intention of going until I'd spoken with the doctor meant to examine the body. We also needed to wire Scotland Yard in Southampton. They'd need to collect the body as soon as we docked. And hopefully escort a murderer from my ship as well.

"Yes, I believe you can. Perhaps I should ask you to escort me to mine, lest anything more sinister than Miss Beaumont be lurking in the corridors," he muttered softly with a look that bordered on saucy. I tried to keep my lips straight as I turned, my skirts swishing around me as I turned to the bank of dark windows.

I allowed the tiniest smile of satisfaction to bend my lips.

"Miss Beaumont," Nicholas ventured after a moment.

I angled my head to see him.

"I am curious to know your witness."

My cheeks burned as my eyes found the floor. "Oh, I'd really rather not say," I mumbled.

Nicholas's reflection in the windows took on the look of a cat who has cornered a canary. "As a proper lady of society who is engaged to a son of one of the most influential men in the whole of England—a proper lady who would never jeopardize her standing in that society by wandering down darkened corridors alone at night—do tell me how you managed to speak with this witness from the confines of your cabin. Unless, of course, you've had someone spying on me?" His tone was definitely teasing this time, though there was an undercurrent that let me know he would have his query satisfied. I slowly turned and risked a glance up and was mortified all over again to see his smug expression as he crossed his arms over his solid-looking chest, waiting for my response.

I cleared my throat uncomfortably.

"Although, on those lines, I daresay I should ask your whereabouts this evening. As I am now intimately acquainted with your ability to wield a knife, I wonder if I ought to be in mortal fear for my life this present moment."

I wanted to stick my tongue out at him like a petulant child, though part of me was secretly flattered that he thought my skill with a blade was that impressive. I was ill the next moment, realizing that could make me a murder suspect.

I saw no hope but to tell him the truth.

With a heavy sigh, I told him. "I overheard some derogatory comments about the third-class accommodations during the ball this evening. It is the gossip of the classes that will ensure continued use of the *Lady Air* as well as other CAB airships. As you know, she and the business she brings are part of my dowry that stay within my control. I was afraid there was truth to the rumors I heard, and I set to see for myself, to ensure that things are as they ought."

"And *you* saw me rounding the corner, didn't you?"

"I did," I said tightly, curiosity burning like a torch in my brain.

A puzzled expression crossed his face. "I'll have you know, if nothing more than to ease your own mind, that I overhead the same comments. I was inquisitive. It seems that perhaps we are not so very different, then, in our desires for the *Lady Air*'s success. Though I came to your quarters at the captain's insistence. The body had been discovered by the man now at the door, and as the highest nobleman aboard vessel, Captain Cordello sought my opinion, thinking I must be the inheritor of the *Lady Air*." He paused, eyes narrowing again. "If you saw me in the corridor, then however did you manage to get back into your quarters without being detected? We came directly to your cabin. There is no way you could have gone to your cabin without the captain and me learning of your presence."

"I took the servants' staircase, cut across the upper deck, then gripped a cable for dear life and shimmied down the side of the ship into the wash closet window of my cabin."

Nicholas swore, his eyes round as saucers. I shrugged; it was naught but the truth.

"That would account for the crash, then, I trust?" I nodded before he continued. "I truly do not know what to make of you, Cora Beaumont. I hope Terry can keep up with you."

Indeed.

However, I was not done with shocking revelations for the night. There was one other thing Nicholas needed to know.

CHAPTER 19
Cora

"I think we should make a vow, right now, Miss Beaumont, to speak only the truth to each other from here on out," Nicholas said. "I shall be your shadow during the course of this investigation. If you cannot be persuaded to relinquish this horrid affair—and I cannot order you to relinquish it, as the law is on your side—you must know I will not allow the Tristan name to have scandal of this magnitude attached to it. I will ensure your safety, and you may rely upon my discretion, as I trust I may rely upon yours. But I want an agreement that honesty will prevail between the two of us."

Respect tingled at the base of my spine. Nicholas had all but offered me a place alongside him as an equal. Though he had not said the words and had voiced his opinion that he'd rather I stay out of the situation entirely, he acknowledged my right to be at the forefront of the investigation. Heat flashed through me as gratitude and something like gratification rose in my chest.

"Frank honesty would be most refreshing." I nodded, valuing the gift he was extending. "You have my word and my discretion. But there's something else you should know." I hated to burst his recently improved opinion of me so soon, but if honesty was to be the way of things between us, then I needed to make a full confession.

"I'm not sure I have the strength." He rolled his eyes—though not condescendingly. "Don't tell me you did your embroidery on the top of the blimp itself?"

I appreciated his attempt at humor, but exhaustion and the weight of the investigation to come pressed on me, so I didn't mince words. "I saw the woman. Before. I slipped from my quarters and came down here to search out if the rumors were accurate, as you know. I was down here the same time you were. Remember when the airship pitched sharply to the left? It would have been only moments before you came down the hallway."

Nicholas nodded. "I'd have fallen down the stairs had I not caught myself on the banister."

I grimaced. "I lost my footing. I slammed into a door." I swallowed. "The *victim's* door." I moved the hair from my fore-head, letting the bump on my head shine. Nicholas winced but didn't speak, and I continued. "I didn't recognize it as the same door when we first came to it—they all look the same. And"—my cheeks heated uncomfortably again—"I saw her . . . in an embrace with a short man. Hat, dark hair, small mustache, dark eyes—angry eyes—likely because I'd just walked in on a secret tryst. He held her in his arms in the middle of the room. That's all I saw. Obviously, I didn't let my gaze linger."

Nicholas dashed a hand down his face. "Do you think you could identify the man if you saw him again?"

"Perhaps? My lady's maid—her name is Charith—just this night was attacked by a man while another came to her rescue. She was unsure which attacked her and which helped her. She did not get a good look at either of them. I wonder if perhaps one was the murderer? One of them, she wasn't sure which, was with a woman." I bit my lower lip. "Could it be the same man? Charith's attacker was interrupted. What if . . ." What if. I frowned. "I don't know if it was her lover, or if it could have been her murderer, maybe both? Maybe he was interrupted and then sought another victim? What are the odds?"

"I am not schooled in such odds, but I do think we should speak with Charith," Nicholas said, a furrow appearing between his brows.

A light tap at the door had my heart lurching into my throat. My hand flew to my neck.

Nicholas crossed the lounge and cracked the door.

"Begging pardon, but the doctor's 'ere."

"Thank you," Nicholas said, and turned to me. "If you can't be dissuaded, I suppose we'd best go see if the doctor can tell us anything new. Truly, you do not have to do this, Cora. Certainly, after this evening, no one would think the less of you." His informal use of my name quickened my pulse, reaffirming his view of me as his equal.

But I was determined. "Yes I do, Nicholas."

CHAPTER 20
Cora

"Nasty, nasty business this. Just look at this mess!" The doctor, white hair mussed and clothes rumpled, shoved his spectacles farther up the short bridge of his nose. His linen suit jacket—completely wrong for this time of year with temperatures dropping—was hiked up awkwardly over his shockingly round seat.

"Can you tell anything pertinent, Doctor?" Nicholas asked tiredly as we stood at the far side of the room and let the doctor examine the body.

"Not as much as I could if she were alive. I'm a doctor for the living. Not the dead." The man's mustache twitched. "The fire's not lit, so at least she's not rotted and bloated in the heat."

"Sir, the blood is still fresh and barely tacky at the far edges. She's not been dead that long," I couldn't help interjecting.

"Eh, quite right, quite right." He touched the tip of his finger into the pool of blood. A slight, gummy smear came away on his finger.

I clenched my jaw to keep from heaving. My eyes stung. The doctor wiped his finger on a white handkerchief. The blood seemed to glow blackish red against the crisp white of the cloth.

"I need to clean this up to fully see what this piece of business is. So debasing, so ruthless, carving right into this poor girl's soft flesh." He shook his head, *tsk*ing.

"Any preliminary ideas?" Nicholas prompted. I was grateful. For all I wanted to take charge of things, I was nearing my emotional end.

"Not as yet, though it does look rather like a crude *C*, don't you think? It's hard to tell under the gore, but it looks like the blade may have slipped here, and there is a deep stab here where the blood has crusted. But it definitely looks like a *C* to me."

I willed myself not to jump to conclusions. But I couldn't help flashing back to the blue stamp on the white china that graced the ship. *CAB*. Clarence Abner Beaumont. Surely this murder couldn't be about my father.

I was being ridiculous. How could this have anything to do with me or my father? I'd never met the victim.

Nicholas glanced at me, his eyebrow lifting.

I sighed and shook my head slightly. I didn't have words; I needed to process. To think. To sleep, at some point. To organize myself and my plan of action.

"We'll see that a temporary place is set to house the body so that a full examination may be completed. We trust you'll treat this matter with the utmost discretion," Nicholas said to Dr. Bellson, his tone leaving no room for refusal.

I briefly wondered how often he'd had to use such a tone to become so good at it.

"Of course. Might I suggest somewhere near the coolers used for refrigeration? The scent of decomposition will turn even the most stalwart of stomachs. Will we be landing the ship to turn the body over to the local authorities?" The doctor squinted behind his round spectacles, reminding me of a mole.

"No. We cannot. The storm prevents us from turning back. There's nowhere to go but onward to Southampton," I said, suddenly feeling even more boxed in than I had moments ago. Ironic, seeing as we were surrounded by only endless air. All the same, it was safer to outrun the storm than to try flying through it back to New York, though America was yet closer than England. I hadn't even considered that I might need to obscure such a thing as a smell from my passengers. I groaned internally. "But we shall go directly and wire Southampton," I added, glancing at Nicholas.

He nodded. "Yes. We'll inform the authorities of the situation and make certain they are kept abreast of the investigation until we land, at which point they can take over." His gaze bored into mine. My head bobbed. I would be happy to let the police take over once the mess could be contained somewhere other than my ship, dangling above the crushing Atlantic.

"Bad form, that. This lady will be in bad form, too, if she has to journey all the way to English shores." At least the doctor didn't seem perturbed by my presence or my authority.

"There may be no help for it. I'll send the guards in to help you move her, and we can make arrangements for the ice." Nicholas glanced at me. I was emotionally numb but gratified that he sought my opinion. I nodded gratefully.

We discussed the details of how to transport the body without other passengers seeing, agreeing to disguise it under tablecloths in a food cart. There was a galley and a refrigeration bay on each level of the airship next to the dining halls for ease of meal preparation and delivery. We would deliver the body there. Regrettably, third class would just have to do without ice for the remainder of the journey.

"I can't decide if he's ridiculous or brilliant," Nicholas muttered as we traipsed toward the telegraph room as the body was conveyed to the bowels of the ship.

I cracked a weary smile. "For our sake, I hope it's the latter."

"Indeed. Miss Beaumont—Cora—if we're to be related soon enough and will be working closely enough with each other, shall we drop pretenses and use our Christian names?"

"It would save time. Nicholas is slightly less a mouthful than Lord Tristan."

He nodded. "Are you sure you're all right?" he asked, eyes concerned. It was a level of intimacy I hadn't expected but found I appreciated.

I shook my head. "No. I'm nowhere near all right. But I am determined to find out what has happened and get to the bottom of things. I will not stand for such monstrous crimes to be committed aboard my airship."

We paced on a moment more before he broke the silence.

"Tell me, how is it that a lady of your breeding and gentility has the stomach of a hardened investigator? Truly, you're most impressive."

"My father had three great loves late in his life: his daughter, his second wife, and archaeology. Andre, my brother, never shared interests with Father, and it was always a wedge between them. I helped uncover the tomb of Namasbasset. I broke the seal on his sarcophagus myself, though, of course, my involvement was kept far away from the papers." I smiled softly, remembering how proud I had been to help my father and Dr. Kautner find the shriveled, mummified remains of the ancient pharaoh.

"I had no idea you were so involved. I remember reading about your father's discovery, though. Terry and I were both proud to have known him. But you were . . . you couldn't have been older than ten then?"

"Eleven. My association with the macabre happened fairly early on," I confessed with some chagrin, and a burst of wind knocked the airship sideways.

Nicholas caught my elbow securely. "Perhaps those skills will indeed be put to good use now."

Pride burned through the fatigue and warmed me from the inside.

Even via telegram, we could tell Scotland Yard was surprised to hear from the *Lady Air* but took matters to heart and assigned us a Detective Morris as the detective in charge of the case on the mainland. On to disguising and moving the body.

We found the third-class galley to be locked. Not to be deterred, I fumbled my master key from my pocket, where it had mercifully survived my harrowing stunt working my way down the side of the ship.

"At some point, I shall stop being shocked and amazed at your ingenuity," Nicholas quipped as I attempted to insert the key. My hand was shaking—fatigue and fading adrenaline—so that it was hard to make the key fit into the hole.

Nicholas's large hand covered mine, steadying it. I sucked in a breath at the blatant contact but didn't shy away. I was unused to being touched by anyone of the opposite sex. Indeed, outside dancing or providing a proper escort, a man did not lightly touch a lady in either of our societal circles. Nicholas said nothing, merely steadied me as we inserted the key and turned the tumblers. Then the heat of his hand against mine disappeared.

I tried to shake off the jolt of electricity that seemed to scatter my senses and felt myself swaying on my feet. Exhaustion was setting in with a vengeance.

CHAPTER 21
Nicholas

I shouldn't have touched her. I'd shocked her, and she'd had enough of that to last a lifetime, though her hand had stilled under mine. Maybe my presence was helpful. At the very least, I determined to involve myself as much as she did, if for no other reason than to ensure Cora's safety and keep our joined families out of the tabloids and in society's good graces.

And—a small part of my brain confronted me—*for justice.* Rage burned inside my chest at the atrocity committed upon the girl. It was not right, and my overdeveloped sense of right and wrong warred against what I'd seen.

But as I glanced at the back of Cora's head, auburn strands escaping the low bun at her neck, I realized that my sense of duty wasn't nearly as irked with Cora's behavior as I'd have expected it to be. Maybe it was the circumstances. Maybe it was the lack of sleep.

Maybe it was Cora.

How she had taken my understanding of the fairer sex and shoved it right over the edge of the airship. Cora had displayed more backbone than most men of my acquaintance. I didn't think she was motivated by blind ambition but because she wanted what was right—admittedly, she had personal invest-ment, but I was convinced her motives were not purely selfish. At any rate, my eyes had been opened, and I was forced to con-front what I thought I knew about women. Maybe Phee wasn't the exception. My own mother was quiet, docile, and gentle in the extreme. Phee was a train rampaging down the tracks out-side the eyes of society. Until tonight, I'd thought Phee was the abnormality. Perhaps I should reassess what I thought about women in general.

Or at least about Cora Beaumont.

I couldn't afford to linger on that thought, so I shoved the unhelpful contemplation back down into the recesses of my mind and focused on the grisly problem at hand: how to move the body without attracting attention.

Cora finished lighting an oil lamp and set it on the large, polished wood countertop. She bit her lip as she glanced around the room. I followed suit, and my eyes landed on the ice cabinet.

"How outraged will the third class be without ice the rest of their voyage?" I asked, eyeing the large chest where blocks of ice were kept.

"Less so than first class," Cora quipped as she followed my gaze. She walked over and flipped the lid of the cork-insulated chest. "We can attempt to freeze her body and at least slow decay until we reach England," she said practically, though her fingers clenched into a fist as the words left her mouth. She sighed. "We'll say a water pipe burst; I'm certain it's ruined the space and put it quite out of operation. Third-class meals will have to be prepared sharing the second-class kitchens. It's not ideal, but certainly better than the alternative."

"Agreed—will there be enough food stores without using the food in here? If there is water damage, and that's the official word, will supplies suffer?"

"They shouldn't. There is food aboard ship in quantities sufficient to feed a herd of hungry elephants for a month. Some of the menus might need to be redrawn, and third class may get a sampling of some unexpected foods, but no one will go without."

Her bluntness both astounded and fascinated me. Even as spent as she must be, Cora was still thinking in terms of the larger picture. If I was being completely honest, I also found it rather delightful, subject matter notwithstanding. "Nicholas, look!" Cora pointed to a tiny space between the ice chest and the wall. Gingerly, Cora grasped the edge of a piece of cloth and drew it forward.

"Is that a gentleman's shirt?" I asked as she brought it all the way out and held it up. Blood crusted one sleeve and had spattered across the chest of the white material. I gulped as I realized it was, indeed, a gentleman's white shirt. Or a shirt that had been white at one time.

"Oh my heavens," Cora breathed. "Why is this here?" She laid the shirt out on a preparation table. "The fabric is not of a high quality." She frowned, a little crease appearing between her reddish brows. Keeping the garment some distance from her person, she grasped the material at the shoulders, then held it up to me. I flinched before I could stop myself.

She nodded. "It is a man's shirt, but too small to fit you. The man I saw with the woman, the . . . v-victim"—she stumbled over the word—"was a small man. I think this confirms it."

I took a step back and gave the offending shirt a critical eye. "You're right. This shirt would be far too short for me as well.

The man we're looking for is both small of stature and narrow of shoulder."

She peered at the stained sleeve again. "With the victim's room being down the corridor, I'd stake my inheritance that this is the murderer's shirt." She laid the bloody material back onto the preparation table. "Adds a whole new meaning to *agony in red*, don't you think?" she said, referencing a popular term for red evening wear.

"Indeed."

CHAPTER 22

Cora

In the end, we had to tie two carts together, as the poor woman's remains wouldn't bend. "Rigidity," the doctor mumbled as we wrapped and packed the woman's body in towels in hopes that more blood wouldn't seep out and drip down the corridors. We arranged cloches, trays, and a few cups along the table and atop her body, all double wrapped in tablecloths, lest anyone should happen to recognize a body in transit.

We walked ahead to ensure the path was clear while the two liveried airshipmen who had stood guard at her chambers wheeled the heavy cart down the long corridor.

At last, the deed was done and the body was in the third-class refrigeration chamber, where we'd also kept the bloody shirt, tucked away in an emptied cauliflower box we'd acquired for evidence. Relief sagged my shoulders as gravity pulled my eyelids downward even as I stood.

"If I may, I'll finish my examination of the body?" Dr. Bell-son asked us, unsure who to address, as he shoved his round glasses up the bridge of his short nose.

"Of course, Doctor. We'd be most grateful. Please let us know any findings you uncover," Nicholas answered after a brief glance in my direction. I was too tired to form coherent thoughts. I was drained like I'd never been before.

Dr. Bellson waved his hand in the air, letting us know he'd heard, but immediately went to clearing the long preparation table of its crocks and bowls and set out his doctor's case.

"You two, stay with him. Give him any aid he might require. He cannot move her on his own. I'll see to it that you're reimbursed for your time and your silence," Nicholas told the two airshipmen as he indicated we should take our leave. The two men stood straighter, their young faces serious, the weight of responsibility laid upon them by Lord Nicholas Tristan clearly having the desired effect. Though I'd found the offer of money often tended to have such an influence.

Nicholas escorted me back to my chamber just as the sky was graying into dawn light around the ship.

"I'll see you at brunch. Not a word," he whispered, his hand ghosting over my elbow.

"Agreed. Not a word. Thank you." The words slipped out as emotion welled inside my chest. "Thank you for supporting me in this, Nicholas."

He tipped his head to me, his green eyes as intense as I'd ever seen them, even with shadows cupping them.

A little shiver worked down my spine as I shut the door quietly behind me. Ophelia still snored from her bed, one stockinged foot hanging off the side and out of the covers, her right arm thrown casually over her face.

Barely stopping to kick off my shoes, I collapsed onto my own bed, jacket, overskirt, and all, and was asleep within seconds.

———•◦•———

"Cora, I've been as good as gold; I've done my best to let you sleep, but I am *dying* for details of what happened to you last night!" Ophelia whisper-shrieked somewhere near my head. I groaned, barely resisting the urge to swat her away like a pesky fly.

"Tea," I croaked as the fuzz slowly began clearing from my head.

"Already ordered. I've taken the liberty of pouring you a cup and put a bracing three cubes of sugar in yours."

I slitted an eye, taking in Phee's animated expression, her dark-green eyes wide and fringed with thick lashes that seemed to quiver in excitement. Sunlight lanced through the portholes, so I guessed it was sometime midmorning. I'd likely had as much sleep as I was going to get. It was not nearly enough.

"And guess what else?" she squeaked.

"You've tossed your corsets out the window and danced the turkey trot on the tabletop?"

Ophelia snorted. "Even better."

It had to be good if it were better than tossing corsets out the window.

"*Lord Phillip Dawson Davies* has invited me to luncheon!" She squealed his full name.

Lord Phillip Dawson Davies.

My brain fog cleared as my mind, still in traumatized cataloging mode, conjured up images of Lord Dawson Davies at last night's ball. With red wine spattered across his cravat upon his reentrance to the ballroom. His cravat and not his shirt. His shirt had been clean.

Red wine could look a lot like blood. Especially if one was not looking for blood and merely accepting the explanation given.

Whoever cut Charith's neck would have been close enough for spatter if the cut was deep enough. I'd seen the deep-red line. With adrenaline and her heart pumping at a far greater rate than normal, it was infinitely possible the attacker would wear evidence of his actions. Or if he'd cut a deeper mark across a different woman and changed his shirt after. There'd be evidence of that as well.

Evidence like the spatter across Lord Phillip Dawson Davies's cravat.

I bolted upright as a jolt of adrenaline worked through me and worry clawed at me. Images of the man Charith spoke of materialized behind my tired eyes—Dawson Davies hovering over her, knife extended. Cutting into her neck, her warm blood spurting across the snowy linen of his cravat. Images of Dawson Davies hovering instead over the mutilated body of the dead woman. Images of him changing his shirt, not realizing his cravat had sustained flecks of blood as well. My stomach turned, and I thought I might retch onto the rug beside my bed.

"Where are you to have luncheon?" I croaked in a tone that I hoped Phee interpreted as excitement, not panic. I tried to calm my racing heart. I was likely worked up over nothing. Lord Philip Dawson Davies was a respectable member of the peerage with an impeccable reputation, so far as I knew. He was not a devilish murderer who prowled dark corridors of airships at night, only to carve his knife into the soft flesh of unsuspecting women. Clearly, my imagination was up and going before all my mental faculties had thrown off the vestiges of sleep.

But my overtired, traumatized brain argued, *What lengths might a man go to, to protect that impeccable reputation?* Nicholas's words regarding the Tristan name floated to me. Scandal could sink even the most esteemed ship of the nobility. But what scandal could Dawson Davies have in connection to my chambermaid?

None, my brain argued. Unless he was a sadistic, murdering psychopath. In which case he'd need no connection. Just opportunity.

I gulped as Phee continued animatedly, her fingers twitching in her excitement.

"In the observatory. Publicly. Quite telling, don't you think?"

My heart rate began to slow a fraction. Public was good. "I—" I gulped. "That's delightful. Phee, do please make sure you're chaperoned at all times," I whispered. Fear for my friend coated the back of my throat and set my belly souring.

It was possible—likely, even—that I was worried over nothing, that perhaps Lord Dawson Davies was that clumsy and had spilled red wine on his cravat, or some other fellow had tripped and splashed him as he'd said.

Bile rose in my throat as I wrestled the images of the slashed woman from my waking eyes.

"Cora," Phee admonished with a gentle whack to my arm. "What's come over you?"

I rubbed the heels of my hands into my eyes. "It must be the late night." I winced. "But, um, there are some vicious gossips aboard, and you wouldn't want to fall foul of them. Tilly and Georgiana are not to be crossed if they can be avoided."

"This is true. Though I'd love to stick it to Tilly Remlaude."

I snorted. "Wouldn't we all?" Last night's events seemed to have stripped any decency from my tongue. My blunt words tumbled around us. Phee giggled in appreciation.

"Speaking of last eve . . . you must tell me what went on. For mercy's sake, what were you doing in the bathtub fully clothed with the window wide open?"

I winced again. "Where is the tea?" I croaked.

Taking a few sips of the well-sugared drink was a welcome reprieve. What could I tell her? *Look out, Phee. There's a murderer loose on the* Lady Air, *and since I've ruled out your cousin, the top of my suspect list now includes your dashing marquess and possibly an unknown man of short stature and angry eyes. They might even be accomplices— one man to clean up the other's mess, or one man to swoop in and take what the other man left.* That would go over swimmingly.

"I set off to see the third class for myself after the ball. After you were asleep."

Phee looked wounded. "Why didn't you take me with you? What debauchery were you up to?"

I shot her a look. "No debauchery." My cheeks heated. At least not on my part. There had been no wedding ring on the victim. I swallowed another sip of tea with the startling realization that I didn't know who the woman was. Add that to the top of the mental list. I pulled my mind back to Ophelia. "I'd overheard some women at the ball speaking ill of the lower accommodations. I'm overly concerned with it, as the *Lady Air* and her proceeds are, well . . ." I stammered, realizing I hadn't divulged that part of my dowry to Ophelia. "They will stay with me, even after I marry Terrance." I cleared my throat as Ophelia's jaw dropped. "The *Lady Air* is *my* inheritance. Not part of Terrance's dowry."

"You filthy-rich little heiress. What I wouldn't give to inherit money on my own and not have it go to the man I marry."

I smiled wanly.

"Well, do go on," Ophelia prompted, eyes large in her face. "But know I'm coming to you if whomever I'm saddled with is an old stick-in-the-mud." She winked conspiratorially and wiggled her fingers at me impatiently, urging me to continue.

I took a fortifying breath. "I wanted to ensure that things were as they ought, not as they'd been insinuated by malicious gossips. So, I poked around alone. In the dark. At a less-than-respectable-hour of the night," I haltingly admitted. Saying the words aloud made me sound like a criminal—a criminal whose crime was overstepping the bounds of polite society. Which could offer a sentence every bit as ruinous as committing an actual crime. Heaven help me if Mrs. Beesly overheard my confession.

Ophelia's eyes were shining with awe. "You're the brickiest girl I ever knew!"

"Yes, well, you'll appreciate that I also went out sans my corset," I whispered. Ophelia giggled in delight. I cleared my throat. "At any rate, I caught sight of Nicholas and the captain coming down the hallway on my way back. I didn't think they'd find me *bricky* out and about alone—batty and rebellious more like—so I did the only thing I could think of at the time. I swung down through the washroom window. It was the only way to get back into the room I could conceive of without them seeing me." I gestured to the only door leading to our cabin.

Phee was utterly speechless.

A feat I'd never thought I'd live to see.

"You mean to tell me that in order to spare your reputation, you . . . you swung out over *oblivion* like a wild ape and in through the washroom window? Well, I never . . ." She trailed off, hand over her heart, and just stared at me like a dazed cow.

"Yes?" I didn't mean for it to come out as a question, but it did, my voice sounding all high pitched and funny.

Ophelia fanned herself. "I'm not the swooning type, but I'd faint dead away if I had to leap off the side of an airship. *Blazes,*" she murmured. "And it's not even properly scandalous," she said at length. "Now if you'd been caught . . ." She waggled her eyebrows. I couldn't help the smile that spread across my lips.

A knock sounded at the door. "My ladies, we're here to help you dress." Rose said softly, her words muffled through the wood of the door.

Phee leapt up to let in the pair of maids, who were dressed in the white and blue of the *Lady Air* staff. In tandem, they curtsied deeply, and I hid a yawn behind the back of my hand.

"Are you well this morning, Charith? Any other . . . incidents?" I asked, sleep fleeing with the remnants of my yawn. Rose set about opening the chifforobe while Charith opened my drawer for a fresh chemise.

"I am well, thank you, miss. How can I be of service?" Her eyes were trained carefully to the ground and her hands clasped politely in front of her, the drawer and fresh chemise forgotten at my direct address. Charith looked paler today. I hoped this girl was stout enough to lace a corset. She looked as if a stiff breeze could blow her over.

"You're sure you're unharmed?" Phee asked again.

Charith nodded. "I apologize for troubling you yesterday. It was not my place."

Rose snorted softly, seemingly offended on Charith's behalf.

My heart ached. I hoped she hadn't gotten into trouble on our account. "You are mistaken," I said gently. "You are important. If something else occurs, you are to come to me immediately, and I will see that it's taken care of."

Charith glanced at me from beneath her pale lashes, cheeks coloring slightly. She dipped another curtsy. "Truly, miss, thank you. But I am here to help *you*. Yesterday is behind me."

I wasn't completely convinced, and I wanted to press her for more information about her attackers but needed to wait until

Phee was no longer present, lest I alert her to the murderer running amok on the *Lady Air*. The maids' entrance had distracted
Phee from asking anything more about my late-night excursion
with her cousin and the captain, and I doubted my luck would
hold long enough to evade such tenacious curiosity again.

"If you're sure, I'm ready to change for luncheon," Phee said
to Rose, pointing to the open door of the wardrobe, an array of
dresses peeking out.

"Yes, my lady. Which shall I lay out for you?" Rose waited
with anticipation, her eyes gleaming over the shining dresses.

"Oh, dear. Cora, what do you think?" Phee pursed her lips.

I scrubbed a hand down my face and wished the biggest
thing facing my day were the color and style of my dress.

The sun was clouding over by the time we reached the first-class
observatory. I paused outside the door, glancing back. Worry
knotted in my gut. Even if we hadn't been flying over the mighty
ocean, we would not have been able to land sooner and let the
authorities take over things. If we were to detour, the only place
we could land before Southampton was the Irish coast, and they
had no operating airship docks. Landing an airship in an undesig-
nated spot held all kinds of heavy ramifications. We'd just as likely
be blown to kingdom come as to land safely. In addition to the
difficulties inherent in landing a behemoth of an airship, dark
smudges of clouds, bruised and angry, still swarmed the horizon
behind us. The storm hadn't fizzled out—if anything, it looked to
have gained in magnitude. Which, in a sense, left us trapped in
the sky. We'd be fine, so long as the storm remained behind us.

"Cora, are you coming?" Phee said, popping her head back
out the glass-paned doors. She was set to meet Lord Dawson

Davies, resplendent in a deep-green gown that made her dark hair and light skin tones radiant. Her green eyes, a trademark of all the Tristan line, I'd decided, fairly glowed like newfangled green lightbulbs.

"Of course. Merely watching the sky." I suppressed a shudder. Just like last night, I felt as if I were being watched. An itchy-skin feeling crawled up my neck and burrowed into my scalp. But how absurd. The only people about were a scant few airshipmen and maids. One young married couple, members of first class, took in the bracing air. I entered the conservatory, and the door whooshed shut behind me. Phee was chatting happily with two other girls—Gertrude and another whose name I couldn't remember, though I should have been able to recall it. I was too distracted still by thoughts of murder and mayhem. The three of them looked adequately engaged, however, so I took the opportunity to move to the far corner where I could observe the room.

I collapsed in as ladylike a fashion as I could muster into a white chair. A member of the waitstaff immediately came to the table bearing a steaming tea service, complete with a tray of toast, butter, and jam as well as tiny quiches that were nearly too adorable to eat.

The man bowed, pouring tea into my cup. "Will there be anything else, my lady?"

"No, thank you."

The man bowed again and moved back to the counter along the far end of the room. I put a cube of sugar into my tea and watched it slowly dissolve, wondering if the murdered woman had felt her life disappearing like the sugar in my cup.

I swallowed thickly and shoved the unpleasant thought from my mind. The need to find out who she was pulsed behind my eyes. Only a few of the gentry were up at this hour—it was still considered early after a late ball. Or later investigation. After scanning the room and noting nothing worthy of more import than the tea in my cup, I took a sip.

As I lifted the cup emblazoned with my father's initials, I saw the edge of the *Lady Air News* poking out from under the plate of toast. Excellent. I tugged the sheet of paper from its anchor and flicked it out so I could browse the headlines. Having a telegraph on board, the airship got daily headlines from Britain and America and printed up sheets of newsprint in the print room before distributing them to the passengers—the same technology that had let us wire Scotland Yard a few hours prior.

Price of Hogs Escalates as the Queen Requests Bacon for Breakfast

I rolled my eyes. Surely there were more important things happening in the world than the queen's choice of breakfast meats. Personally, I liked a good sausage link.

The tea was warm and comforting as it slid down my throat.

Wool Set to Be the New Silk

I wondered what the Ladies' Mile shopping district north of Union Square would say about that. I skimmed the article. Wool was practical, though silk was infinitely more comfortable. Wool itched in unmentionable places.

New Expedition Set to Uncover the Ruins of Amarna—Deaths Expected!

A new dig at Amarna? I devoured every word.

The Egyptian Antiquities Service has cleared the king's tomb at Amarna. Such discoveries have prompted the English to send Flinders Petrie and his assistant, Howard Carter, to do a

*thorough excavation. Their discoveries could change the history
of the pharaohs as we know it.*

Oh, I ached to be a part of such a thrilling expedition! The
rest of the article outlined some of the finds they'd already made.
With a sigh and a light crunch of toast and jam, I moved to the
next article.

Indian Caste Upheaval Displaces British Nationals

Political upheaval? Now that *was* newsworthy. I was not
ignorant of the attempted reforms taking place in India, but the
fact that people were being displaced from their homes was news
to me. I followed the headline to the brief article below.

*As revolts tear across the country and the caste system is thrown
into chaos, British colonials are uncertain of their future in the
country. Indian women are asking for freedoms historically denied
them. There are rumblings from women in both Britain and
America. Is the world to be overrun with feminine affectations?*

I scowled at the paper. I hoped the Indian women won their
freedoms.

"Anything interesting this morning?" The deeply rumbled
words echoed in the small space of the corner and sent the hairs
on my arms prickling to attention. Glancing up quickly, I covered my surprise. I'd been absorbed in the paper and my
thoughts. Nicholas sat down opposite me and nodded to the
pamphlet.

"Nothing quite so exciting as other recent events," I quipped.
A half smile tugged at the corner of his lips.

"I got word that the doctor finished with *things*"—he cleared
his throat—"and we may observe his findings."

My eyebrows shot up. "We must go at once."

"May I have a square of toast first? I'm famished. Terrance should be joining us shortly. It would be good form if we can keep appearances as . . . normal . . . as possible. My brother knows nothing," Nicholas finished softly.

"Neither does Phee." I sighed. He was right, but I chafed to get as much information as I could. The pressure to find who had hurt one of my passengers pressed upon me. For that matter, so did *whom* exactly had been hurt.

A slight breeze circled the observatory then as Lord Dawson Davies's blond head appeared through the door. He immediately found Phee and crossed to her. He bowed as she curtsied, and the two other girls with her hid their smiles.

The toast in my belly turned to ash. Nicholas straightened in his seat as he observed them.

I leaned forward and whispered. "We must discuss Lord Dawson Davies."

Nicholas's brow puckered before a thought seemed to lodge, giving him a jolt. "What do you perceive?" He whipped around in his chair, scrutinizing his cousin and the man escorting her to a table before facing me again.

"What if the red wine on his cravat last eve wasn't red wine?"

A strangled sound stuck in the back of Nicholas's throat as his face paled. "Surely not. What possible motive could he have had?"

"Not to speak ill of the dead, but what if the man I saw with the woman wasn't her only lover? Dawson Davies was also gone a respectable amount of time from the ballroom. Plenty of time to do damage. And Charith said one of the men who might have attacked her was with a woman. The way Charith was cut—the attacker very well could have sustained some spatter.

And what if the victim was the woman with the man?" I whispered so softly I wasn't sure Nicholas could even hear all my words. The graveness of the situation was not lost on me. I'd not known Ophelia long, but already she was one of my dearest friends. The thought of losing her to a murderer—or even a mere lecher—was nearly more than I could bear. "Should we warn her?"

A muscle jumped in Nicholas's cheek as he paused, his eyes discerning the pair. He turned back to me. "I think not yet. We have no real evidence, only suspicion. And it's weak suspicion at that. Merely wine and happenstance. If something of this magnitude got out and was linked to a member of the peerage, it would condemn them and critically hurt any future business dealings for them. But so help me, if it wasn't red wine . . ." He drifted off, the knuckles on his clenched fist turning white.

"Ah, you rise early," Terrance said as he pulled out a chair and sat next to me. My fiancé had dark smudges under his eyes, and I wondered if he was coming down with something.

"Terrance, good to see you up and about," Nicholas said as he helped himself to a square of my toast. I resisted the urge to bat his hand away. Nicholas met my gaze and had the audacity to wink at me as he took a bite.

"My lords." The waiter appeared as if from thin air and deposited a second tray with additional cups, boiled eggs, toast sticks for dipping into the yolks, and more toast and jam.

"Nick, you were gone uncommonly late last night. Was there a secret billiards game I wasn't privy to?" Terrance cracked the top of his egg with his egg spoon, sending a spider web of fissures across the surface of the delicate shell.

"No. Nothing so exciting as that. How did your own billiards go?"

Terrance raised an eyebrow much the same way Nicholas might. "Won more than I lost," my fiancé answered with a rueful smile. When Nicholas said nothing further, Terrance turned to me. "And how are you this morning, Miss Beaumont? Did you sleep well?"

"Well enough. And you, my lord? Are you sufficiently recovered after last night?"

Nicholas's head came up as if to question Terrance's whereabouts as my fiancé's cheeks pinked.

Oh dear.

Terrance cleared his throat. "'Twas nothing. Just too much excitement and . . ." He trailed off as Nicholas looked on, unimpressed.

I took a sip of tea. Because that is what one does when one is uncomfortable in the presence of one's fiancé and soon-to-be brother-in-law.

Scanning the room, my gaze fell on Phee and her dashing marquess. Her face was wreathed in smiles. His back was to me, and I resisted the urge to scowl, as I couldn't see his face. But just then he picked up his teacup, and across the backs of his knuckles, a bruise or scrape splatted like a little dollop of plum preserves. I recalled the smudge on his white gloves last night at the ball. Somehow, he'd injured his hand. Perhaps in attacking my maid? Or in hiding a bloody shirt, misjudging the distance, and ramming his knuckle against the heavy frame of the icebox?

Another strike against him. I'd help Nicholas disembowel the dirty swine if he laid one finger on my friend.

Nicholas cleared his throat. "Miss Beaumont?"

My attention snapped back to the two men at my table. "Yes? I'm sorry. I seem to be woolgathering this morning."

"Shall we take a walk along the promenade once we've finished breakfast?" Terrance asked. I did not want to promenade with Terrance after breakfast; I wanted to go squeeze every scrap of information from the doctor that I could. I hesitated. Nicholas's foot tapped against mine under the table.

My eyes narrowed as I resisted the urge to hiss at Nicholas. "Of course," I answered Terrance with a gracious smile.

CHAPTER 23
Nicholas

I gritted my teeth as Terrance escorted Cora from the observatory. Cora spared one more glance toward Phee, and my eyes followed, landing firmly on my cousin and Phillip Dawson Davies. I scrutinized the man as best I could without being outright rude, lest I draw unwanted attention from the gaggle of eligible girls who were flocked in the opposite corner, just waiting for the right moment to ruffle their feathers and swoop in to roost as close to my dukedom as possible.

Scanning the headlines of the paper Cora had left by her plate, I glanced over the top of it and watched Dawson Davies. He was far enough away I could not hear the quiet rumble of the dialogue he carried on with Phee, but if Phee's expression was anything to judge by, he was doing an ample job of holding up his end of the conversing. Her cheeks flushed and her eyes sparkled. Her fingers wiggled animatedly as she enthused in her response to him. If anyone had been in doubt, it was clear now to the peerage for whom she'd set her cap.

My gut clenched. I muscled down another bite of egg and toast and chased it with a swig of tea. I'd have groused about her lack of propriety were I not so worried for her safety. Surely we were jumping to conclusions. But on the off chance Dawson

Davies was a less respectable man than he appeared . . . I clenched my fist, wrinkling the newssheet. When Phee giggled, my pulse pounded behind my ears, and I could stand it no longer.

Leaving the rumpled paper on the table beside the remains of my breakfast, I tried not to stalk across the floor and plastered on a mask of politeness.

"Ah, good morning, Lord Tristan," Dawson Davies said with an open smile as I hovered near the edge of their table.

"Good morning, Lord Dawson Davies. I trust I'll see you this afternoon at the card game in the men's smoking lounge?" I asked the first thing that popped into my head. I was not rested enough to have this conversation. My blood simmered beneath my skin.

"Of course. Save a seat for me, will you?" His blond mustache twitched. I wanted to glare at the fashionable lip covering. "Also, while you're here . . ." His voice dropped to a conspiratorial tone. "I wondered if I might request your permission to escort Lady Ophelia Hortense to this evening's entertainment—the first of the plays."

I resisted the urge to growl. I had no proof that Dawson Davies was anything other than an upstanding man of the peerage, but I cared for my cousin, and an uncomfortable sensation was growing in the pit of my stomach the longer I looked at Dawson Davies and Phee's hopeful face.

I cleared my throat. I had no real grounds to deny his request. It was uncommon that I felt my choices were so limited. I did not care for it. "Of course," I said tightly. "Though it would be a pleasure for us all to attend together, would it not?"

Phee covertly rolled her eyes as her lips thinned.

"A pleasure indeed. We shall all attend the play together then, if that suits, Lady Davenport?"

Phee's annoyed expression melted as Dawson Davies turned his face to her. "I would be delighted," she said in the perfect imitation of a lady.

I sighed internally, hoping this was one less hurdle I'd have to navigate today. Despite my earlier words to Cora, I was anxious to hear what the doctor had discovered about the victim. I wanted the whole affair to be done and over, the murderer caught, and the Tristan name miles from any hint of scandal.

Just as the silence was drawing toward awkward, Tilly Remlaude sauntered up, flirting with the lines of protocol as she sashayed close enough between Dawson Davies and me that the feathers rimming her dress threatened the black wool of my suit coat.

"Such a pleasure to see you all this morning," she crooned.

"Lady Remlaude," Dawson Davies said politely.

I dipped my head, forgoing any words lest I growl them at her. Phee's smile turned brittle.

"Hello, Tilly," Phee said, bordering on rudeness in her address.

"Ophelia Hortense," Tilly replied, a coy smile gracing her porcelain features, even as her eyes narrowed a fraction. "I was so hoping you would join Lord Dawson Davies and me for a stroll through the hothouse. I have not yet observed their famed delights, and Lord Philip did promise to take me. Would you care to join us?"

The marquess cleared his throat uncomfortably. Whether or not he'd promised to take Tilly to the hothouse was beside the point. It would be a breach of etiquette to say so in front of an audience. Neither Phee nor I missed her casual use of his first name either.

"Oh." Phee bit her lip. She glanced at Dawson Davies. "I was just to have luncheon with Lord Dawson Davies," Phee began. She glanced at him, her face shuttering. I would not wish to be on the receiving end of Phee's displeasure, if she had a chance to voice it.

"Oh, splendid," Tilly responded enthusiastically. "Let's all have luncheon together, then go as one. You too, Lord Tristan." She batted her eyelashes at me, and I resisted the urge to roll my eyes.

"Regrettably, I have a prior engagement. Perhaps another time." I nodded in her direction.

Tilly pouted. "But you'll come, then, won't you?" She turned her winning smile on Dawson Davies and Phee. There was no polite way out of her invitation for Dawson Davies unless he planned to make a public statement about his interest in Ophelia. Since he had not come to me prior to, his hands were tied. Tilly really was a conniving little vixen. Phee's face was a frozen mask of politeness. I wondered if steam would start fizzling out her ears.

Dawson Davies cleared his throat again and glanced apologetically at Phee. "Of course, Lady Remlaude. But we'll meet you there once we're done with luncheon."

I lifted an eyebrow. Phee beamed.

Relief and consternation warred in the muscles of my shoulders. Relief that Phee would not have the opportunity to be alone with Dawson Davies—because she was just daft enough she might spurn the rules if she could—and consternation that I couldn't formulate a better excuse for her not to see him at all until his name was cleared of any suspicion.

What a fine mess.

I clenched my jaw, excused myself politely, and made my way into the sharp wind on the deck. It was time for answers.

CHAPTER 24

Cora

With a final nod toward Phee and Dawson Davies and a shared glance with Nicholas, I exited the glassed-in observatory with Terrance, and we made our way down the chilly promenade.

"I do love the briskness of the air in the morning," I said, the wind whipping my words as my hair tried to tug free of the pins Charith had bored into my chignon earlier.

"It's so different up here. It's . . . almost like breathing damp." Terrance frowned as if he couldn't quite figure out the weather at this altitude.

"I suppose it is, as we are literally going through the clouds, but isn't it glorious?" I asked, forgetting the seriousness of things for a moment and enjoying the cool. A dark peal of thunder rumbled and my skin prickled. "That does not bode well."

"Surely a little thunder won't hurt a great ship like this, no?" Terrance tried to placate me with a pat to the hand that was looped through the crook of his elbow.

"Thunder, no. It's the lightning that precedes the thunder that could prove troublesome. The *Lady Air* is largely made of metal."

"Oh." Terrance's brows drew together. "I see the problem."

Was he really only now considering the ramifications of being caught in a storm in an airship? I gave myself a mental shake. I should have more grace; not everyone was as familiar with the ins and outs of airship construction as I.

"It should be fine—so long as we continue to stay ahead of the storm, no harm shall befall us. I'm sure Captain Cordello has everything under control," I tried to reassure Terrance, who had suddenly gone pale.

We continued to walk around the outer rim of the promenade deck, nodding graciously at a few of the other members of the upper crust when we crossed paths.

"Do you have plans for the day?" Terrance asked once we neared the observatory doors once more.

"Oh, I . . ." I stammered, unsure how to respond. I couldn't very well tell him I was burning with curiosity over the dead body currently chilling in the third-class icebox a few levels below us.

"Do not trouble yourself," Terrance said quickly, seeing my dismay. "I was going to beg your forgiveness, as there are several members from one of the London clubs in attendance on this historic voyage. I have been invited to coffee and cards with them. Would be good if I can make myself known among them." He winked, and I was startled how much he looked like Nicholas as he did.

"Ah, the Crackford Club?" I concluded.

Terrance blinked. "How did you surmise that?"

Heat bloomed in my cheeks, sending an uncomfortable flush over my chest, covered by my layers of jacket and shawl. "A fortunate guess?"

"Really, how did you know? There are dozens of high-society clubs in London."

"Yes, but only four that the son of a duke would willingly be seen at, and of those, only two serve coffee as their beverage of choice. I also saw Lord Jamison at the ball last night. He is known to frequent the Crackford."

Terrance stared at me with a look of confused awe. I cleared my throat.

"Enjoy your cards and coffee?" I ventured.

"Right. Of course. If you're sure you don't mind." He gazed at me quizzically.

I squirmed internally but forced a pleasant smile to my face. "Not at all. Thank you for the walk along the promenade."

The door opened behind us, and Nicholas exited. "Nice morning for a stroll," he commented. His jaw was clenched.

"Indeed. Nick, would you mind terribly to escort Miss Beaumont to her next engagement? I've got one of my own and don't want to be late." Terrance consulted his pocket watch and flashed us a smile. A dimple appeared in his left cheek.

"Have a lovely time," I said. Nicholas stood silent beside me as Terrance trotted through the wooden door that would lead him down the stairs to the upper-class corridor.

"Where is he off to?" Nicholas canted his head, a fleeting expression of displeasure marring his handsome looks.

"He said he'd been invited to coffee and cards with some men from the Crackford."

"Conceited lot, if you ask me." He raised an unimpressed brow.

"Didn't you warrant an invitation as well?" We started walking toward the far entrance that would lead us inside nearer to the servants' staircase.

Nicholas snorted. "Of course I did. If they invited Terrance, they certainly also invited the Tristan heir." He sighed. "Truthfully, though I have no desire to view a dead body, the excuse not to attend a Crackford meeting is welcome."

I pulled my shawl tighter. "Do you think it's safe to leave Phee with *him*?" I whispered.

"Today, Lady Remlaude's antics suit our purpose. Whatever her game, she's determined to remain close to Phee and Dawson Davies. I doubt they could shake her attentions if—when—they try."

I seethed at the mention of her name. "Tilly Remlaude is a cat," I gritted between my teeth before my eyes went huge at the realization I'd said the words aloud and in front of Nicholas. "Oh, I . . . do forgive me. That was quite rude," I stammered.

Nicholas chuckled darkly. "Please. Save your apologies. Don't tell the society matrons, but I find your brash honestly refreshing. Coyness is tiresome, and all the rules of politeness do wear on a person."

I smiled tentatively at him, and he nodded.

"Shall we attend to other frigid matters?" I asked.

"Posthaste. I hope the doctor has something useful to tell us."

<hr />

I was surprised to find the doctor still in the refrigeration room as we entered the chilly confines. Part of me had expected a written report or a note rather than the man himself. I braced myself, set my jaw, and suppressed a shudder as my gaze landed on the sheet-draped body laid out atop a bed of pink-stained ice.

"Yes, yes, come in, come in," the doctor said as he shoved his spectacles up the short bridge of his nose. "There isn't a lot to tell, especially as this isn't my specialty, but as a few of my esteemed colleagues who teach the mortuary sciences say, the dead always give up at least a few secrets, and so she has."

Nicholas and I stopped beside the vat of ice. The doctor gently uncovered the woman's face. He'd cleaned the body. Four buckets of soapy, bloody water stood sentinel against the back wall, evidencing his ministrations. Even so, the ice below her wasn't clear but pinkish. The woman's face was now devoid of blood spatter, her hair brushed back respectfully from her face.

"Oh, blast," Nicholas murmured. I glanced at him. His face was as ashen as the corpse before us.

"Nicholas?" I only just stopped myself from putting my hand on his arm. He truly looked distraught.

"You aren't the only one with an unexpected connection to this woman. I didn't realize last night—her hair, and so . . . so much blood." He swallowed heavily. "I saw her in the hallway. She is . . . was, a suffragette. A vocal one, from the sounds of my unintentional eavesdropping." He met my gaze.

"You think politics could be involved?"

He shrugged. "I think it's too early to tell. Lots of people have extremely strong feelings about the suffragette movement. She was making no secret about it—quite the opposite. She and the head porter were having angry words when I observed them. She had her suffragette sash on. She was making the porter's job rather difficult, though he handled himself well enough before he became exasperated." He paused, a thoughtful expression coming over his face.

"Well, she got into a tussle with someone. Likely her assailant. You'll note these bruises here." The doctor uncovered the side of her upper arm and showed us long, dark, horizontal bruises that wrapped around her grayish skin. "Someone grabbed her arm hard enough to leave these behind. But you'll also note that she has deep bruising around her neck. It's hard to tell, but her assailant may have strangled her into unconsciousness before carving into her."

Nicholas shuddered. "The porter had a grip on her arm," he said softly. "Just where the bruises are. She thrashed and struggled against him."

"Do you think he could be in any way connected to her death?" I asked.

"I think the possibility bears enough weight that we should speak with him, at the least." Nicholas glanced up at the doctor, then meaningfully back at me. I lifted an eyebrow, understanding that there was more to be said, but not in front of the doctor. Electricity buzzed beneath my skin. I sent up a lightning-quick prayer that the sensation had naught to do with the storm coming nearer.

The doctor seemed oblivious to everything but the body before him. "It appears that full postmortem rigidity has commenced." He peered at us. "That is, all her muscles have stiffened. Now, if the lectures I've attended on mortuary sciences are correct and my memory serves, that means she's been dead roughly ten to fourteen hours, as there seems to be some blood pooling in the back, parts of the thighs, and buttocks as well. Frankly, given the size of that puddle we found her in, I'm surprised she had any blood left to pool."

Ten to fourteen hours. I whirled calculations. My head had bashed in the door of the poor woman's quarters nearly exactly ten hours ago.

But fourteen hours ago was time enough for a certain member of the peerage to deal in darkness and return to the ball with blood spattered upon his cravat.

Bile threatened to rise even as I frowned. Dawson Davies *could* be innocent. At least of this woman's murder. But with blood on his glove and the slice on Charith's neck, could he yet be a brigand? Could she have been the woman with the men who attacked

Charith? If she was, could Charith identify this woman? And was the man I saw her with her murderer? I strained my brain for any details I could remember. I hadn't looked at the floor of her room. My eyes had arrested on the couple in a lovers' embrace, then shot to the ground in front of me—missing what might have been a bloodstained carpet entirely. I had seen no blood on the woman, but as I cataloged my mental image, I realized it was possible she'd already been dead.

There were signs of strangulation on her body. The man had held the woman pressed to his chest. I'd not have seen if all the blood was still to the front of her—if none had dripped down the sides of her dress. The man's suit jacket covered part of the woman's middle, which would have disguised any additional bleeding. It would appear I'd seen her at least before the killer had carved her flesh, though perhaps she hadn't been living when I saw them.

If she had . . . if there was something I could have done . . . I bit my lip, banishing those torturous thoughts.

"One moment, please." I excused myself to the door, where two airshipmen still stood sentinel. "Would one of you please fetch the lady's maid Charith Mount and bring her here?"

"Right away, miss." The shorter of the two men bobbed his head and dashed down the hallway to do my bidding.

Closing the door behind me, I gritted my teeth in frustration. I had no more solid answers now than I did before coming to the refrigeration chamber. I took a breath through my mouth, determined not to gag, and focused once more on the doctor.

In a clinical manner, he covered her arm, covered her face, then lifted the sheet from the bottom. My stomach dropped as the woman's body—feet, ankles, legs, thighs—then her grievous wounds were exposed. Nicholas cleared his throat, glancing away, obviously as uncomfortable with this as I was. My father was likely to turn in his grave if he knew I was standing here, unmarried, with two gentlemen—at least one of them also unmarried—staring at the utter exposure of this woman. I forced my hands to stay at my sides, though the urge to hide myself with them was strong.

The doctor quickly placed a towel over the worst of her nakedness, though the deep lacerations went nearly to the complete end of her trunk.

"Now that the gore has been cleaned, you can see here that this was likely the killing wound, though there are still the neck bruises to contend with. She has some hemorrhaging in her eyes from at least partial strangulation, but I think it most likely that she was alive, but unconscious, when she was stabbed here." He pointed to the deepest slash, bruising around the outside. "The knife used to kill her had a hilt. You can see the outline of it outside the wound tract here. Then there are some minor hesitation marks surrounding the wound here." He pointed to some tiny slices surrounding the deep gash. "The killer seems to have thrust a slender blade in deep, puncturing the lungs and the very bottom of the heart, I'd warrant, though I'm not about to cut this poor thing open further to find out. Here, the knife has been dragged downward to make this slash into the flesh. It could have happened if the woman struggled and the knife tore through the flesh, though it appears a clean cut. I think it more likely that it was intentionally cut this way.

"But this." The doctor frowned and shook his head as he pointed to the ugly curved slash. "This is an atrocity beyond the murder. Even washed cleanly, it does look like a C has been carved into the soft tissues of the belly, her skin peeled back to expose a wider slice of muscle under the skin. The killer likely has some experience with butchery—you'll note the internal organs are all still present and only the top few layers of flesh have been removed. This took some power to accomplish, too. This is a wide mark. It starts just beneath her breasts and descends to the top of the pubis, with the separate killing stab, and a slash to the upper right side." The doctor frowned. "This seems to be an odd mix of experienced butchery, but someone inexperienced with killing. The slash and the hesitation marks are not as clean as if done by someone who knew what they were about. But the carving, this shows deviousness beyond a simple murder."

"So we're looking for someone completely unhinged, smart, strong, and possibly with a political grudge?" I said, mostly to myself.

"That would seem to sum things up," Nicholas agreed as the doctor nodded.

"Well. That's all I can say on the matter for the moment. There is one last thing here. This bruising is most curious." He gently covered the woman's body again, then once more uncovered her face. Dr. Bellson pointed to the side of her head. Right on her temple, there was an angry bruise forming, but it wasn't just a blob of blues and purples. There were distinct lines. Bile rose in the back of my throat while buzzing sounded in my ears. Dr. Bellson's voice was far away. "Now. If you'll excuse me, I've not slept since being dragged from my bed to see to this poor wretch. I'll take my leave now. If you have need of me again, don't hesitate to send for me."

The doctor rinsed his hands in a basin of red-tinged water, dried them, and left us alone in the refrigeration chamber with the dead girl.

CHAPTER 25
Nicholas

I was still reeling at the unholy sight before me, brain churning, stomach too, and willing myself to think things through critically.

"Nicholas." Cora's voice quaked. Before I could answer her, she shakily drew a key from her pocket. "Look at the end of this key, then examine the bruise on the side of her head."

With a dead weight in the pit of my stomach, I took the key and examined its bow. The rounded head wasn't hollow but had the raised logo and typeface of CAB Airships. A tiny hole at the top allowed for a silken tassel to attach to it.

"It's the master key. But look at her bruise." Cora's trembling voice echoed in the stillness of the chilly room.

I bent at the waist, loathe to look upon this woman in her current state, but forced my eyes to fix upon the abused flesh near her hairline. My pulse pounded up the side of my neck as I made out the bruised indentations. They were larger than the bow of Cora's key, but the pattern was eerily similar.

Someone had struck this woman with an object bearing Clarence Beaumont's airship emblem. Slowly, I raised my head and met Cora's tortured gaze.

She blinked and turned to the body, gently covering the woman with the sheet, and I found having her nakedness obscured helped. What had been done to this woman was undeniably wrong, and though I was trying to find out what had happened to her—who had murdered her—staring at her wounds and her unclothed state made me feel as if I was adding to her degradation. "How could this have happened?" Cora asked softly.

"I don't know," I answered honestly.

"We must find out her name—who she was," Cora whispered, staring at the filled ice chest.

I nodded. "Yes. That must be one of the first orders of business. We also need to make a list of . . . suspects." I paused, thinking of Phee. I swallowed and willed the unease rising in my throat to go away. "We also need a list of persons of interest who may be able to shed any light on things. Your maid and the porter, for one."

Cora was silent, staring at the table. My eyes followed.

This was a heavy burden to bear. Despite my own misgivings, I was glad neither Cora nor I had to bear it alone.

"Cora?" I said softly.

She cleared her throat and ripped her eyes from the sheet-shrouded body and met my gaze. "I think I may have been the last person to see her aside from the murderer. If she did die ten or so hours ago, ten hours ago was nearly the moment I stumbled upon the woman and her lover."

She blinked. "It's just . . ." She groaned.

"Cora, what are you saying?" Alarm tingled down my spine as her blue-green eyes grew wide in her face and her mouth parted.

"Oh, to say it aloud . . . Nicholas?" The words left her mouth hushed as nausea crawled up the back of my throat. "What . . ."

She swallowed heavily. "What if I wasn't intruding on a lovers' tryst at all? She was draped across the man's chest. He had an arm around her back and one hand"—she blushed furiously— "one hand cupping her . . . bustled area. I thought at the time she must surely be hiding her face from me in mortification, but what . . . what if she was already dead and the killer was moving her, or propping her up before he cut her? What if he'd already strangled her into submission but hadn't cut her yet?" She paused. "Or what if he was cleaning up after someone else? I was too shocked, it was too frantic, that I never saw the floor, or any blood that might have been there. And now I see this C carved into her and find my father's airship symbol pressed into her skin."

Cora struggled to draw a breath as I processed the words she spewed.

"What if I looked her killer straight in the eyes?" A violent shiver worked over her, propelling me to action. Though it would be frowned upon if anyone chanced to see us, I rubbed my hands over the tops of her arms anyway. I wanted her to know she wasn't alone, and the blood was draining from her face. We couldn't afford to have the indomitable Cora Beaumont falling into shock.

"Cora?" I called softly, concerned.

Tentatively, she met my gaze. "What if it wasn't Lord Dawson Davies but *that* man—the one I looked straight in the eyes— who killed her? And I all but witnessed the actual act?"

I blew out a breath, thankful that she hadn't happened upon the scene any earlier or later than she had. "Either way, we must find the mystery man and question him. Obviously, he will know something." Her eyes cleared, resolve steeling her features. I stepped back.

She cleared her throat and changed subjects. "What was it that you wanted to say earlier when the doctor was still present?"

My mind flew back to the moment I'd connected the girl to the porter and the porter to Dawson Davies last night.

"Last night, in the smoking room before the ball, I saw the porter, the head porter who had escorted the girl"—I nodded to the table—"discreetly slip a note to Dawson Davies. He read it and then tossed it into the fire. He was acting very secretive."

"This doesn't bode well for Lord Dawson Davies. Or Phee," Cora said, worrying her lower lip between her teeth. "Possibly also the porter."

"Better we find out what the trouble is before Phee gets in too deep." Trepidation for my cousin still scratched inside my chest.

"Do you think questioning the porter should be the first order of business? Charith should be here any moment. I wish to see if this is the woman with the men in the hallway last night. Should we check in with Captain Cordello? Not that he'd be eager to see me." Cora bit her lip.

I smirked at Cora's self-deprecating tone. "I think you intimidate him."

"I intimidate him? Whyever for?" She blinked. "I'm certain I anger him and have caused him great annoyance at my insistence to be involved in this. But surely he cannot be *intimidated* by me."

I smiled. "Clearly you underestimate the effect a woman can have on a man," I responded dryly, ignoring the way my pulse wanted to quicken. "In this case, you own this ship. Until last evening, the captain was under the impression that the *Lady Air* belonged to me. Not to Terrance, and certainly not to you. To find that his ship is owned by a young American woman was shock enough for him, but to then find that you've got more than fluff between your ears and that you refused to be cowed, well, I think it's put him in fear for his position and in great concern that a woman could replace him. You've quite turned his world inside out and upside down."

Cora studied me for a moment.

"Do I intimidate you?" she asked, her voice concerned and questioning—her tone asking if I approved of her.

I felt myself softening toward her as one side of my mouth turned up. "Cora Beaumont, you terrify me." *In the best way possible.* "You've surprised me, certainly, but I also think I know your person well enough to know you don't take this lightly, and that you do have the best interest of everyone involved in this at heart. Would I prefer you not to be center stage in this gruesome affair? Of course. I want no scandal attached to the Tristan name, nor do I want you to put yourself in danger." She bit her lip again. "But I can also understand why you would take this upon yourself."

Her shoulders slumped in relief as she exhaled. I did understand; many of the things I did were to uphold the appearance of the Tristan name. I did so out of love and respect for my father, the same as Cora sought to do.

"I'd like to look at her quarters again. Look over things for any details—perhaps something connected to her suffragette ties, find out her name—and then speak to the head porter." She glanced up at me, pursing her lips. "On second thought. I might have a better, though slightly scandalous idea."

I felt my eyebrows hike up my forehead. "Scandalous, you say?" I asked dryly.

"I have a master key to the ship." She held it up where I'd placed it back in her hands moments ago. "It won't unlock the individual cabins, but it will unlock the cabinet where the chamber keys are kept. Moreover, I know where the chamber keys are held. What if we were, perhaps, to abscond with Dawson Davies's chamber key as well as our victim's and do a search of his rooms while he is out with Phee? It might lay our suspicious to rest and allow us to relax in regard to Ophelia's involvement with the man."

If she were a man, I'd say she had a steel pair.

"I cannot believe I'm agreeing to this." The desire to eliminate my cousin's potential suitor from the list of suspects was strong. We were already in over our heads; we might as well swim around while we were underwater. I nodded. "Agreed. Let us get the keys to his rooms under the guise that we are retrieving the key to the women's cabin. We'll search Dawson Davies's, hope we find something that exonerates him, then browse the ship's records for a name, peruse the woman's room, then send for the porter."

And start a manhunt for the woman's lover.

CHAPTER 26
Cora

A quiet knock sounded at the door.

"I trust that's Charith." I cracked the portal open to find my maid waiting for me. "Come in," I said, and quickly ensconced us in the chamber, leaving the guards at their post.

"Oh, oh my merciful heavens," Charith blabbered as her eyes grew huge and her hands covered her mouth as she beheld what could only be a body beneath the stained sheet.

"Charith, look at me."

Her frightened eyes swung to my face, her lips trembling and skin paling. Nicholas shifted so that he obscured Charith's line of sight to the dead woman.

"Charith, I'm sorry to ask you this, but I must swear you to secrecy, and I must ask you to tell me if this woman was with the brigands who set upon you last night."

Charith's mouth moved, though no words exited. Finally, she took a breath and squared her shoulders.

We moved to the table. With a glance and a nod from Nicholas, I carefully drew back the covering only enough so that the woman's face could be seen.

Charith exhaled heavily. "I don't know, miss, but I don't think so. I caught a flash of long blonde hair on the woman, but that's it. I don't think I'm mistaken."

Disappointment clawed at me, but there was nothing more for it. With quiet thanks and an oath to keep her silence, Charith returned to her duties and Nicholas and I set off to retrieve cabin keys.

Nicholas's acceptance of my involvement in this mess meant more to me than I'd realized. Not to mention he'd just agreed to breaking and entering a fellow peer's quarters. He must be worried for Ophelia indeed. I was quite certain Nicholas Tristan would *never* stoop to such criminal activity were he given an alternative course of action.

Part of me thrilled at the thought of such intrigue, while the other part of me flinched at such ghastly behavior and any excitement connected to it. Even so, as we left the refrigeration chamber and made our way to the captain's quarters, there was a lightness to my step that his words had brought. Even though thoughts of Captain Cordello threatened to quash it.

"Do you suppose he'll put up a fight, parting with the ship's passenger list or access to the keys?" I asked as we exited the servants' staircase and into the hallways of first class.

Nicholas snorted softly. "I doubt you'll give him much choice. It's not as if the passenger list is any kind of secret. We all got our copies of the list so we could see who the celebrities among us are." He shot a sideways grin at me, which, despite the gruesome circumstances, filled me with sparkling confidence. My lips twitched. It was a common enough practice. All the big ocean liners and airships provided passengers with a booklet of travelers booked on their transport. It was a way of marking one's social standing, making connections, being seen by the right sort and so forth. But the captain's copy would note the cabins assigned to all persons aboard ship. As owner of the *Lady Air*, I had a right to that list, but it might not come easily.

"I'm willing to bet that the captain thinks those passengers' cabin accommodations are of the utmost secrecy." I gave a mental sigh, expecting the captain would do what he could to interfere with *my* investigation.

I was right.

"You want my personal banking papers as well?" Captain Cordello bellowed, bushy brows drawing together as he flung the neatly written passenger list in its record book toward me, glaring, and pointed to the domineering cabinet that held all the chamber keys. He fisted the cabinet key into Nicholas's hand.

Nicholas cleared his throat testily. The captain wilted under the glare of one of the highest-ranking men in all of Britain.

"Not unless your banking papers have something of relevance to our current line of inquiry," I retorted. Captain Cordello's face purpled.

I spread the pages of the book toward the window to catch the best light. The captain's quarters where the register was kept was blessed with a large window that let in a ray of early-afternoon sunshine. Neat script in crisp black ink graced the pages. I ran my finger down the page, looking for the cabins I needed.

"One more page over," Nicholas said softly, his breath teasing tendrils of hair beside my ear as he read over my shoulder. My pulse jumped. I hadn't realized he was so close. As I flipped the page, the air caught in my lungs.

Third Class, Cabin 173, Mary Albright, Resident of Hastings, England. Traveling alone.

"Mary Albright," I whispered. Tears sprang to the back of my eyes as my emotions refused to behave.

"We have a name now," Nicholas said, his breath brushing the fine hairs behind my ear again. Shivers tingled over my shoulders.

I flipped a few more pages, ascertained the quarters of Lord Phillip Dawson Davies, and closed the records book, blinking rapidly. "We have a name, but still no identity of her *friend*." I nodded subtly to the key cabinet. He raised a brow, almost as if in challenge, to see which of us was going to get the keys. I felt my own eyebrow lift in answer. A smile hid in the corner of his mouth as he deftly stood with his back to the room, effectively cutting off the view of anyone who might happen to be watching. He casually unlocked the cabinet, and I wasted no time in snatching both keys.

Heat rushed to my cheeks, but it wasn't as if we were doing something naughty—we just didn't want anyone to know we were investigating a member of the peerage in the event that he really was innocent. Reputations could go up in flames in moments and take years to repair. I didn't need that added weight on my conscience.

"In time. We'll find her friend. Make no mistake. Let's go search her quarters." Nicholas turned to the captain, whose face had mottled to a reddish tone from its earlier purple, bruised-ego hue. "Thank you, sir. I trust if you find any other useful information, you will bring it to us posthaste."

Captain Cordello cleared his throat. "Of course, Your Lordship."

Wretched ratbag of a man.

Phee's slang must have rubbed off.

I bit my lip, wondering how Phee and Lord Dawson Davies were getting on. "Do you think we should check on Lady Ophelia? Before we check on *other things*?" I whispered as we moved decidedly away from Mary Albright's quarters and third class. It was too good an excuse to pass up to search out Lord Dawson Davies's chambers while Phee unwittingly had him occupied. We headed for the carpeted first-class stairwell.

Nicholas sighed. "I'd like to confine her to quarters, but I doubt it would go over well. They should be visiting the hothouse. Which I think is on the opposite side of the ship from where we'll be . . . *directing our inquiries*." He glanced at me for confirmation.

I nodded, appreciating his unspoken question. The hothouse was one of the unique features I hadn't yet been able to explore, but I did know where it was located. It was nowhere near the third-class passenger cabins or the side of the ship where Dawson Davies's chambers lay.

Nicholas continued, "I truly don't think Lady Remlaude will leave them either. She seemed quite attached."

"You mean like a leech?" I mumbled uncharitably under my breath.

A faint look of amusement flitted over his face, and his lips twitched. "Even so, it would be highly inappropriate for him to take her off somewhere alone." He paused, and I could practically see his wheels turning. Likely he was wondering if Ophelia was brash enough to take Dawson Davies somewhere, which would give him an unsavory opportunity in the event he was Charith's attacker or the killer of Mary Albright and looking for another victim. Nicholas shook his head. "No. I don't think they'd go off alone at this stage."

"In the meantime, let us make good use of his absence."

"Agreed," Nicholas said, ushering me into the hallway that led past our own set of quarters and down the corridor toward Dawson Davies's.

The servants had not yet been in his room to clean things, and the man obviously wasn't traveling with a personal valet. Papers lay strewn across the coffee table, and a book lay facedown, pages parted in half, at the foot of the bed. His coverlet was wrinkled, and his black tails were tossed over the back of his chair.

He'd worn his tails last night.

"Nicholas, I think these are the clothes he wore at the ball." I pointed to the chair and the rumpled clothing. Nicholas's eyes widened as we crossed the room together to riffle through the discarded clothes.

"No cravat," Nicholas muttered as he held up the black suit coat and a limp white shirt, the starch having worn out. I noted it was similar in size, though seemingly longer in the waist, to the one we'd found stuffed and bloodied behind the refrigeration box.

I shied away from a clearly worn charcoal-gray sock and shivered. "It's cold in here. Typically, one of the staff would ensure the coal burner is kept going lest the room cool too much. And it's overly chill in here. They'd also tidy up the space. Why would he forgo these things?" I mused aloud.

Because he had something to hide.

"Cora." Nicholas's tone had me whipping around fast enough my bustle rose a few inches with the action.

I watched in fascinated horror as Nicholas gingerly pulled a tattered piece of white fabric from the coal burner. Barely a scrap, but there was a little spatter of red along the unburned edge. Clearly, it had been burned last night, as the coal was now cold.

Ice formed in my spine, leaching the heat from my midsection and spreading little tendrils of frost across my shoulder blades.

We stared at each other. It still didn't prove anything definitively, but it certainly didn't help the case for Lord Dawson Davies's innocence.

CHAPTER 27

Nicholas

Room 173 was hushed—almost as if Mary Albright's ghost were lingering, daring anyone to enter and disturb the memory of her last moments.

Breathing through my mouth as I'd advised Cora to do, I let my eyes wander the gore-streaked room. The suffragette sash was draped lovingly across the back of a chair in front of a mirror on the far wall. The closet door was open, but the few clothes were hung. Nothing seemed askew. I glanced through the contents of the closet. On the floor, tucked behind a hatbox, was a reticule. Swallowing down the unease that rose in my stomach—a man should never touch a woman's purse—I opened it anyway.

"This is unexpected," I blurted as I took in the carefully folded banknotes.

"What is it?" Cora asked, coming to stand next to me to peer into the reticule. Her skirt brushed against my thigh where I crouched, and I swallowed as awareness burned through me. Straightening, I pulled out what I'd found and showed her.

"That's a wad of cash for someone in her position to be carrying!" Cora exclaimed.

I turned the wad sideways, taking a cursory count of the folded bills. Even if they were all small notes, it would be a questionable sum for a woman in third class to have on her person. And the first three were fifty-dollar bills. Likely more than six months' worth of wages. "It is, indeed. Just the same, I don't think robbery was the motive. It wouldn't have taken much searching to find this."

"Mm," Cora grunted as she turned back to the rest of the room, one hand on her hip, one finger tapping her lips.

I wasn't sure what else I was looking for, and I found my gaze straying to Cora as she examined the room.

Her eyebrows were pinched together, her lips pursed. It was as if she'd shut down the part of her that was soft and feminine and replaced it with a calculating detective. Much to my own surprise, I found myself drawn to both halves of this puzzling woman. I was certain she observed things the rest of the world missed.

"What do you see?" I finally broke the stillness.

She turned to me, her deep blue-green eyes wide. "Nothing in this room is disturbed. There is one bite taken from a biscuit on the tea tray. The killer doesn't seem to have taken anything, unless it was so small it was only of an intimate nature or something from . . . from Mary herself." She blinked twice, then moved in front of me to the nightstand. A whiff of rose and lemon cut the bitter tang of the blood as her dress swished over the tops of my boots as she moved close to me to avoid stepping on the blood-stained carpet. I blinked as my hand rose to touch her of its own volition. Fisting the offending fingers, I quickly forced my hand into my pocket lest I do something completely inappropriate.

Cora slowly pulled out the drawer in the nightstand. A rosary and Mary's passenger book were neatly arranged.

"Well, if he did take anything, I don't think we have any way of knowing it now." Her lips pulled down at the edges. "Look, Nicholas. She's put a marker here."

I glanced down and picked up her passenger booklet, thumbing to the place where an unmarked piece of paper was stuck between the pages. As I skimmed the pages, the blood drained from my face.

Cora gasped beside me as her gaze tore down the page and arrested on one name. It was underlined.

Miss Cora Beaumont, daughter of Clarence A. Beaumont, of Hadaway.

She shivered as we stared at each other.

"Nicholas, what if that hateful mark carved into Mary *was* a *C*? The bruise on her temple. What if this is somehow tied to my father? Tied to me?" Her blue-green eyes were wide and determined. But a hint of fear cowered in their depths.

I held up the book as I swallowed.

My name, Terrance's, Phee's, and Dawson Davies's names were all on the double-spread pages too. But none of us had a famous father whose name started with *C*, and none of our names were underlined.

Suddenly, the neck of my shirt was too tight. I put the book down and strained at the button. Whatever was going on, we were no closer to finding the truth of the matter. But the threat seemed eminently nearer.

CHAPTER 28
Cora

My blood ran cold, my body numbing with the shock of our discovery.

"I have no ties to Mary Albright. I've never seen her before last night, and to my knowledge, my father had no ties to her either. What do we make of this, Nicholas?" My voice quavered on the last words. I swallowed down my fear, refusing to let it conquer me, though I'd rather take myself down the side of the blimp a dozen times than face the curdling terror spreading in my midsection.

Nicholas took a measured breath. "We stay calm. We have a servant posted at the hallway entrance to your quarters to act as guard. You go nowhere alone."

An invisible noose tightened around my neck with the restriction of my freedom. I knew Nicholas only suggested it for my safety, but it felt smothering all the same. Still, I nodded my head.

"We tell no one." His pained words dragged my gaze to his face. "The fewer people that know you may be a target, the better. The more insulated you are within society's folds, the safer you should be. Your position will still gather people to you. If they know you're in danger, they'll keep themselves away, and I don't like the thought of you isolated."

"All right," I acquiesced. The irony pricked that the society I frequently spurned was to be the insulation between me and a madman.

Nicholas glanced around the room. "Is there anything else you want to look through here?" He pulled out his pocket watch from his vest pocket and glanced at it. "Luncheon is long past. It seems I've also missed afternoon billiards in the men's smoking lounge. I had mentioned it to Dawson Davies at brunch." He sighed. "So much for that."

The play! I needed time to dress and have my hair done properly for it. Blast.

We sneaked back through the winding servants' corridors, earning a strange glance from a maid we met along the way. I cringed but carried on. Nicholas personally deposited me at the door to my chambers.

"I'll go and speak to the captain about posting someone as we discussed. Do not leave your room until I come for you. And it goes without saying, but do not admit anyone not of your acquaintance."

I nodded as a wash of skitters flitted over my skin at the intensity of his gaze. He offered me a strained half smile.

"No strange men in your quarters."

I gasped at his blatant insinuation. He winked, and heat flushed my cheeks as my stomach tightened.

"Nicholas Tristan," I started.

"There's the fire." He smiled kindly. "Don't worry overmuch if you can help it. I swear I will do everything in my power to get to the bottom of this, keep you safe, and keep your arrangement with my brother intact." His expression sobered. "Terry and I will collect you girls in time for the play." He sighed. "If Dawson Davies comes for Phee, stall him so we may all go as one group."

"Wait here, to be sure Ophelia is back, lest you need to search for her too," I whispered as I unlocked the door to my cabin.

"Cora! There you are. Wherever have you been?" Phee gushed as I poked my head into the room. I breathed a sigh of relief as my shoulders immediately lost some of their tension. The scrap of burned material from Dawson Davies's quarters fairly ignited a hole in my reticule where I'd stored it for further inspection. Nicholas whooshed out a breath behind me at his cousin's voice. I turned my head and nodded to him once, seeing the same relief cascading down his features. He nodded back and gently closed the door behind me.

"Was that Nicholas?" Phee asked, coming up short as she caught a glimpse of her cousin behind the wood paneling of the door.

I cleared my throat. "Yes. Captain Cordello needed my input on some documentation." I shrugged noncommittally, opting for a half-truth and cringing internally as the words left my mouth. "Owner of the ship and all," I said ruefully. I put my reticule onto the sideboard, wincing as the purloined keys clanked together. I needed to return them to the captain's quarters.

"You are so fortunate," Phee said, clasping her hands. Her eyes sparkled. "But. Ask me how my luncheon was."

This was one topic I wanted every detail from, though the reasoning was nothing that Ophelia Hortense would ever entertain.

"Tell me every word," I said, my voice sounding breathless even to my own ears.

Phee squealed. "Oh, Cora, Lord Philip Dawson Davies is the most elegant gentleman I think I've ever met. I just want to stroke his blond mustachios!"

I snorted despite myself. "Phee," I admonished, shocked, but not surprised at the girl's brashness. "Mrs. Beesly may be sick, but she's not deaf," I reminded my friend.

Phee smiled cheekily. "He was so attentive. Even when that viper Tilly slunk in, ready to pounce, he all but ignored her except what would be considered the barest minimum of politeness. Even when she insisted she accompany us to the hothouse—which is utterly marvelous, by the way—the hothouse, not the nincompoop—he was polite to her but nothing more. He even offered me his arm. And he most decidedly did *not* make the same offer to Tilly Remlaude, even if she took his other arm anyway." Phee's eyes narrowed at the memory.

"At least he has better taste than that," I quipped. Murder suspect aside, I envied Phee her gentleman's attention. I wished Terrance acted as dedicated to me when we were together. I shook my head. I was certain things between Terrance and I would improve once we were back on his native English soil and we had time to really sit with one another. Things were too frantic aboard the *Lady Air* right now. I cleared my throat. "How is he as a conversationalist?"

"I think him to be a man of varied information. He spoke of world events, and even about going to the queen's court early this season." An intense look of longing scrolled across her face, and I desperately hoped her dreams wouldn't be crushed if Lord Dawson Davies did harbor something sinister.

If he did, I would find it.

A knock at the door sounded, and my heart jerked into my throat.

"I'll get it!" I said with a little too much force as panic careened inside my chest. I slipped my hand into my pocket, gripping the comforting handle of my knife. Willing my breath to settle and my heart to leave my throat, I cracked the door.

Relief surged through me again as Charith's pale face emerged, Rose close behind her.

"Afternoon, miss. We're here to see to your hair and help you dress for dinner," Rose said softly.

"Of course, do come in."

The girls entered, Rose balancing a tea tray, Charith with a thin sheen of sweat on her upper lip. I wondered if the viewing of the body this morning had been too much. Or if something else had happened.

I stared hard at her.

"I'm fine, miss. Promise."

I nodded, still not completely convinced she would even know if something was amiss toward her. She was such a meek little thing. Rose put the tea tray down and stood to the side, awaiting instruction, while Phee dramatically threw open the armoire doors.

"Cora, what shall I wear? I must dress to impress again this evening." Phee's eyes grew frantic before narrowing in calculation. "I was thinking of the green damask, but I'm wondering if I should go for something lighter in color."

I snorted, focusing on the task of dressing up and shoving the dread away. "How many kerchiefs will that take?"

Phee giggled and threw a satin pillow at me.

Mrs. Beesly would faint dead away if she could see our antics.

CHAPTER 29
Cora

A few minutes before I expected them, Terrance and Nicholas knocked at the door. I had on a deep-orange silk with a cream-colored lace flounce. My laces were too tight and my bustle too large for my liking, but I had to admit to myself, I did look a fashion plate.

Phee poked her head out. "Is Lord Dawson Davies not with you?" she asked with a slight frown.

"I'm sure he'll meet us at the doors to the ballroom," Nicholas offered.

"What's this?" Terrance asked, glancing between his cousin and his brother.

Phee waggled her eyebrows at him. Terrance smiled ruefully.

"Let me grab my reticule," Phee said.

As Ophelia ducked back into the room to collect her things, I stepped out of the room, briefly meeting Nicholas's gaze. He gave the slightest nod. I let my gaze fall to Terrance and gave him what I hoped was a sweet, winning smile.

"Good evening," I said.

"You look lovely," Terrance said as he offered his arm. I lightly laid my gloved fingers in the crook of his elbow.

"Thank you," I said softly as my reticule thumped softly against my thigh. The one downfall of this dress was its lack of pockets. I made up for that with a reticule that was slightly larger than was appropriate, in which I happily stowed my knife, my skeleton key, our room key, and a spare handkerchief.

It is always advisable to have a spare handkerchief.

"Was coffee all that you hoped it would be?" I asked Terrance as Phee dropped something loudly inside the room.

Terrance beamed. "It was top rate. Should be visiting the Crackford once we're back on home shores."

I smiled at him as Phee bustled out the door. "So sorry," she said. "Getting any clumsiness out before we attend the play." She locked the door behind us, and we were on our way, padding down the carpeted hallway as our dresses swished along the blue fibers beneath us.

"Phee, how was your luncheon?" Nicholas asked conversationally as he escorted his cousin behind us.

"It was divine. Thank you for allowing me to lunch with him." I could hear the happy smile in Phee's voice. "Could we enter via the grand staircase?" she asked innocently. I bit back a smile. I knew she wanted to be on full display if Lord Dawson Davies happened to be in the vicinity. Resplendent in her light-pink gown with a sequined fringe, puffed sleeves, and just a hint of décolletage, plumped with a modest four handkerchiefs, she was sure to attract all the right sort of attention. I just hoped that attention wouldn't be used against her. Anxiety thumped my heart against my breastbone as we rounded the bend to the massive staircase. All the great ocean liners and airships alike had a promenade for the first class, complete with a grand staircase on which one could display wealth, prestige, and status.

Because those were the grandest pastimes of the rich and famous. The bulk of our collective American and English upper crust was nothing more than strutting peacocks.

But even strutting peacocks were inclined to spend their money where their strutting could best be put on display. Knowing this, Father had spared no expense on the carved mahogany stairwell, the posts intricately wrought in knots and ending in columns with busts of the Anemoi, the Grecian goddesses of air. It was carpeted in rich, lush fibers of variegated blues, with the CAB Air logo woven into interlocking circles.

Bile burned the back of my throat, and I took a cleansing breath. Training my eyes on the rippling wooden curls of the Anemoi at the end of the staircase, I refused to look at the carpeted logo that so closely resembled the hideous mark bruised into Mary's flesh.

"Are you well, Miss Beaumont?" Terrance whispered. He must have felt my body go rigid.

"Perfectly well; thank you for asking. Though you know you may call me Cora." I smiled gently at him from beneath my lashes while I told my muscles to release their rigidity, which only made me think of poor Mary's body, still and unyielding in its decaying state.

I took another breath and forced the grisly thoughts from my mind, determined to keep a sharp eye out for any details I might uncover.

Terrance gave a soft, nervous chuckle. "Of course . . . Cora." He said my name like it was a foreign food, rolling it around on his tongue, trying to decide if he liked the flavor or not. I mentally chastised myself. It wasn't as though he hadn't used my Christian name when we knew each other as children. We just needed to get to know each other once more so we felt at ease together again.

We managed to make it to the bottom of the staircase with no more mishap, though partway down the stairs, I did see Phillip Dawson Davies emerge fully from the shadows overhanging the staircase. His eyes were riveted on Ophelia as she and Nicholas descended. Glancing quickly over my shoulder, I saw her catch his eye, her whole countenance lifting. When I glanced back at him, Dawson Davies was positively entranced as well.

I wondered how good an actor he was.

Or if his enrapture was the eyeing of a prize he sought.

"Lady Davenport, you are a picture of radiance," I overheard him say. Turning slightly, I saw the pained expression that passed quickly over Nicholas's face as he passed Ophelia over to Dawson Davies's arm. Phee murmured her thanks delicately behind her fan, and I let myself be led a few steps nearer the entry to the ballroom.

"Wasn't orange last season's shade?" Tilly Remlaude whispered viciously as she passed me in her froth of honeydew-colored satin on the arm of Antony Blakeney, Lord Tallcot. I bit the inside of my cheek. Orange was perfectly in vogue this season, as she well knew.

We were seated in the same configuration as the night before, as the order of the aristocracy hadn't changed. 'Twas a slight shame it was so immovable.

As red fish chowder and then fish cakes fried in brown butter were served, conversation flowed around me. Terrance chatted amiably with Lady Cadieux—who flashed her enormously large ivory cameo bracelet, which could only have come from India—and me, and the strain I saw earlier had diminished. It was a relief after such a horrendous night and day searching for a murderer. At least I wasn't worried about my fiancé presently. Lady Cadieux was hardly competition.

However, on my other side, Nicholas sat stiffly, Phee and Lord Dawson Davies on his other side. The murmurs of the room were loud enough, combined with the steady thrum of the ship, that I could make out very little of what they said. I made a mental note to ask Nicholas for details later.

The servers placed white china plates and lifted silver cloches off roasted capon stuffed with herbs, spices, and truffles, nestled next to a bed of sea greens and a miniature venison pasty in red currant gravy over a tiny pile of mashed potatoes. The gaslights dimmed, and the musicians played their opening notes— hauntingly morose—as the actors and actresses took the stage.

Beside me, Terrance sighed audibly as he slowly chewed a bite of capon. I hoped it was because the bird was that satisfactory. His attention turned to the play unfolding, as did mine, though I paid only half attention to the performance. While it was marvelous and the music and costumes were phenomenal, I was more interested in the patrons.

No one was above my scrutiny. Both to my delight and my disgruntlement, nearly every eye in the ballroom I could make out was trained to the stage. There were a few whispers and the soft clinking of cutlery, but nothing that particularly stood out. I wasn't expecting anything grand—the man I'd seen with Mary was no one I recognized. I knew every member of the peerage currently on board the *Lady Air* on sight. I'd gone over my own list of passengers and confirmed all the names. I'd have to find a way to access the second and third classes for additional suspects without calling attention to myself.

As I sat poking at the savory sea greens, I muddled over the facts in my mind. I was convinced of several things. One, the man I'd seen with Mary was either the last person to see her alive or had something to do with her death. Two, Lord Phillip Dawson Davies had been missing from the ballroom long enough to cause Mary's demise—and he'd come back to the ballroom with a substance that, upon closer inspection of the scrap found in his coal heater, was decidedly blood spattered on his cravat. He also had a bruised knuckle, which could have happened in a struggle. This put him more in mind for Charith's attacker. But if he'd been intent to kill and had been interrupted, he could have sought out Mary Albright after the ball and done her in, if violence was his goal. Three, there was a *C* carved in Mary Albright's midsection, the CAB emblem bruised into her temple, and my name was underlined in her passenger book. Cora, Clarence . . . CAB Airlines . . . I shook the thought away.

There was one more avenue of thought surrounding her murder. Four, Mary Albright's murder could have been politically motivated. The fact that she was an outspoken suffragette didn't bode well. Among the upper echelons of male society, the word *suffragette* was anathema.

Which unhelpfully brought me circling back to the peerage and men of the American upper crust.

I was annoyed that I didn't have a better vantage for Dawson Davies.

Five. The thought floated to me as I swished a morsel of mashed potatoes in tart red currant gravy around my mouth. Mary Albright could have been a mistress. Possibly to more than one man. I was fairly confident I'd found her in a lovers' embrace with the short, dark-haired man. If she were the lover of one man—and I even hated to think this—what prevented her from being the lover of more than one? We had found all that money in her reticule. It had to have come from somewhere. The potato soured in my stomach. Was she a lady of the night? She had been a pretty woman. If she was desperate enough, might she have turned to prostitution?

Forcing such ugly thoughts from my head for the moment, I tried to turn my attention to the players. I scrutinized every one of them as well, hoping I might spark some memory or one of them might seem familiar.

I had no such luck.

At last, the gas lamps were turned back up and light flooded the grand ballroom, reflecting off the gold and mirrors along the walls of the room. Applause echoed in the cavernous chamber as the actors bowed and the actresses curtsied.

"Thank you for being a wonderful audience this evening. I hope you'll come back tomorrow for the second installment of our little tale. But in the meantime, please feel free to come forward to meet our troupe and introduce yourselves," the principal actor announced to the crowd.

"What fun," Terrance said as he put his napkin beside his empty dessert plate and rose. Taking my cue from him, I rose as well.

"Shall we?" I asked, indicating we should go together as society would expect.

"Oh, of course. How inconsiderate of me. Do you wish to go?" he asked.

"I'd be delighted. Particularly since I know you're fond of the theater. I hope it is a passion we might share."

"Lovely," he said with a smile, though the fine lines around his eyes did not crinkle. I did not have time to dwell on it, however, as Nicholas bumped me lightly as he rose.

"I'm so sorry, do forgive my clumsiness," he muttered, clearly appalled.

"Of course," I replied. He smiled gratefully, and I couldn't help comparing the lines that *did* crinkle around his green eyes, so like his brother's.

As the ranking peers, our little knot was given a clear path to the actors. Tilly and Georgiana, devoid of their dinner partners, quickly flanked us. I was fairly certain Phee stuck her tongue out at Tilly behind her fan. Her features quickly changed as Lord Dawson Davies sidled between Tilly and Phee.

"Lady Davenport, might I escort you to the stage?" he asked politely.

"I'd be delighted," Phee murmured appropriately.

Tilly then slipped in next to Nicholas, wedging herself between us, her bustle all but knocking into me. Red haze burned behind my eyes.

"Can I help you, my lady?" Nicholas asked, letting his arm be ensconced in Tilly's forward grasp.

"Did you not adore the play this evening, my lord?" She batted her eyes. Rumbumptious cow.

"It was a fine performance." He nodded toward the line of actors and actresses in heavy makeup.

I shut out Tilly's prattle and focused on keeping my *orange* silk out from under her vicious, slippered toes.

"It was such a pleasure," Terrance said graciously as we sidled up to the first few actors and actresses. There were some among them who were clearly enamored with the idea of meeting and rubbing shoulders with the aristocracy. Stars shone in a few eyes, and it wasn't long before the majority of the actors were ensconced within the numbers of high society. I laughed softly to myself, smirking as I realized the ladies who had so vehemently cried out against the ship's entertainment the night before were now chatting animatedly with the troupe—all of whom were far from the upper echelons of either American or English society.

For the first time since last night at dinner, my shoulders truly relaxed. For the moment, things were well. There was still a murderer loose on my airship, but there was no immediate threat right here in this place.

At least, I thought so.

My hackles rose right back up once my gaze landed on Dawson Davies as he smiled widely at a lovely actress in a blonde wig. Her eyes were broad and her smile gentle. He said something that made her laugh. Phee was still standing next to him, and I hoped he had a care for her heart.

If he didn't, whether or not he had anything to do with Mary's demise, he'd find himself on the receiving end of my prettily—and fashionably—orange-clad wrath.

CHAPTER 30
Nicholas

The evening wore on, and Lady Remlaude wore on me. Her incessant chatter, her nattering, her ploys for attention were exhausting. Repeatedly, I found myself looking for a way to rid myself of the pest.

Respect for my father was the only thing that kept me from rolling my eyes as Lady Georgiana Nyland joined us.

"My lady, you're looking resplendent this evening," I said with as much kindness in my tone as I could muster. It was a stretch of the truth. She looked as if she'd imbibed a bit too much at dinner. Red dots stood out on her cheeks, the rest of her skin pale.

"Thank you, Lord Tristan. Have you seen my father?"

"I beg your pardon, I've not. May I assist you in finding him?" Anything to get away from this cat.

She blushed. "Oh, don't trouble yourself. I only thought he may have spoken to you."

I lifted an eyebrow, not wanting to tread in those waters. Business deals should not be discussed with the daughters of the business associate. Though it didn't stop my mind from wandering to Cora. She'd be fearsome as the businesswoman in charge of the *Lady Air*. I had no doubt the entire CAB line would profit under her direction. Before I could reply to Georgiana, the ship lurched to the side, and a collective shriek went up from the passengers. The faintest rumble of thunder echoed outside.

The storm was getting closer.

Georgiana put a delicate hand to her mouth. "I must beg your leave. It seems air travel is perhaps less gentle than I was led to believe." The ship righted itself, swaying slightly and sending my gut dipping to my toes with the movement. Georgiana turned positively green.

"My lady, let me get someone to escort you to your quarters." No one wanted to see that lovely dinner regurgitated. My eyes scanned the liveried servants and attendants stationed at the edges of the room. Catching the eye of a porter, I nodded to the sick woman. The porter immediately understood and fetched a lady's maid.

"Here, miss, let me help you," the maid, a tall woman with dark hair and eyes and a voice deeper than I would have expected, offered quietly as she led Georgiana away.

Tilly sighed, looking bored with the whole thing.

"My lady is displeased?" I asked, an edge creeping into my voice despite my efforts to remain polite.

"Some people just don't know when to stop," Tilly said with a dismissive flick of her eyes toward the door where Georgiana had exited. My eyes snagged on orange silk. Cora was also in the line of Tilly's dismissive gaze. I bristled. Forcing myself to relax, I watched Terrance and Cora as they chatted amiably with two of the actresses. One of whom had been chatting with Phee and Dawson Davies moments before.

My heart picking up speed inside my chest, I glanced around, vaguely aware that Tilly was saying something but ignoring her until my gaze landed on Phee. The tight ball in my chest released some of its strangle hold. She was still with Dawson Davies, but they were yet surrounded by peers and the troupe. But from my vantage, it looked like he was edging her toward the door.

That would not do.

"You are uncommon distracted this evening, my lord. Surely I am not boring you?" Tilly asked, laying a gloved hand on my arm. I stared at it stupidly for a moment before giving myself a mental shake.

"Of course. My apologies. I fear I must shortly retire for the night. Have a lovely evening, Lady Remlaude."

I gave her a quick bow and went to collect Phee. I'd had enough excitement for one day. My eyeballs were practically on fire from lack of sleep, and I was done playing games for the night. I wanted Phee where I knew she was safe.

"Pardon the intrusion." I inserted myself near them. Phee glanced up and all but rolled her eyes. "It is time we retire for the evening. Lord Dawson Davies," I said as Phee reluctantly put her gloved hand on my arm and curtsied to Dawson Davies.

"It was an absolute pleasure today, Lord Dawson Davies."

"Truly, Lady Davenport, the pleasure was all mine."

I tugged my cousin along before she could bat her lashes at the man and incite another invitation for the morrow.

"Your timing is rotten, Nicholas," she hissed between clenched teeth and lips arranged in a polite smile.

"It's late," was all I said. It wasn't late by society standards, but even my bones felt weary.

We approached Cora and Terrance. Of their own accord, my eyes slid down the silk draped around Cora's trim waist and the appealing curve of her hips before jerking back to my brother. I cleared my throat. "Terrance, it grows late, and I fear I must retire. I wanted to let you know we were going."

"Oh, would you mind terribly if I retired too, my lord?" Cora asked Terrance.

"Of course not. Shall I escort you back now?"

Cora smiled up at Terrance. Heat expanded in my chest as I took in the gentle twist of her lips. Admiration crept in next to the heat.

I gave myself another mental shake. I must be more tired than I thought.

"I do not wish to take you away from your passions," Cora started, momentarily looking unsettled and unsure of herself. It was strange to see her so after she'd fearlessly stared down Captain Cordello the night before.

Terrance glanced back at the troupe, and my lips thinned. As a gentleman and a fiancé, it was Terry's job to see to Cora's comfort. Had he taken all leave of his senses? Maybe the altitude was wreaking havoc on his brain.

"Not at all, my dear." The words lacked conviction, but Terrance patted Cora's hand as he indicated we should exit together.

We deposited the girls, and I waited until I heard the tumblers click before retiring to our own chambers.

"I think I might go have a brandy with a few of the Crackford chaps in the smoking lounge," Terrance said as he adjusted his bow tie in the mirror above the washstand. "You're turning in?" He met my gaze in the mirror.

I nodded and scrubbed a hand down my face.

"Terry," I started, but what could I say? "Just be careful you don't drink too much," I finished with a weak smile.

Terrance grunted with a sheepish smile. "I've learned that lesson, I hope." He gave me a jovial wink and popped back out the door. I sank onto the bed, grateful our manservant wasn't currently in the room. The silence was a balm.

But only for a moment.

Because in the silence, visions of the mangled woman—Mary Albright—came floating to the surface. For one moment, I was tempted to ignore my own advice and head to the smoking lounge for more than a few brandies, but quickly banished the thought. I needed all my wits about me.

And sleep. My body begged for it.

Tossing my dinner finery across the back of a chair much like Dawson Davies must have done last night, I fell into bed and let exhaustion claim me.

CHAPTER 31

Cora

A single ray of morning light lanced through the porthole and landed directly on my face. Squinting against the brightness, I rolled over. When a peal of thunder rumbled, my eyes flew open, and my heart thundered with it.

Disregarding my burning eyes and the crick in my neck, I dashed out of bed and to the small window. I couldn't see well out of the tiny opening.

"What is that noise?" Phee mumbled as she sat up, her night cap askew.

"The storm," I said breathlessly as I legged it into the washroom.

The much-larger window allowed me a better look at the horizon, though part of me wished I hadn't looked at the deepening black of the cloud banks blooming against each other, vying for placement to dump their heavy watery contents and thrash anything in their path with their deadly lightning.

My stomach tightened. The storm hadn't worn itself out as I had hoped it might. It continued to follow us, closer behind now than it had been. There was still some hope. Sunlight danced merrily on the other side of the dark roiling mass. I stood in the frothy light, soaking in the warmth even as I shivered at the storm's proximity.

"Cora?" Phee poked her head in the wash closet.

"Mm? Sorry. I was distracted by the clouds." I tried to offer her a smile.

A knock sounded at the door.

"It must be Rose. Time to be up and about." Phee disappeared. I took one last look at the angry clouds before crossing my arms over my chest and going back into the main chamber.

"Is Charith not available?" Phee was asking Rose as she entered the room. The tall, dark-haired woman dipped her head and deposited a tray of breakfast and tea on the sideboard.

"Charith has fallen ill, ma'am. It seems several of the maids have been taken with airsickness. Vah theek ho jaayegee. I'm sure she'll be right as rain in a day or two."

I blinked, surprised to hear foreign words drop from Rose's lips when she'd only ever spoken in a proper British accent before.

"Gracious, I hope she recovers shortly—but that phrase, what is it?" Phee said, eyes alight with the possibility of new slang.

Rose blushed prettily and dropped a curtsy. "Forgive me, my lady. It's merely a Hindi phrase I picked up working for a memsahib before joining the staff of the airship."

"You've been to India!" Phee crowed. "Tell me all about it!"

Rose smiled as she opened the box containing Phee's hair pins as Phee seated herself at the vanity.

"The air is warm, and the flowers are beyond compare."

"How romantic!"

I rolled my eyes good-naturedly as Phee all but swooned. I left them talking of India and exotic spices as I examined the wardrobe's offerings.

"Oh, miss, one moment, I'll help you," Rose called as she finished putting a jeweled comb in the back of Phee's dark, curly hair.

"Thank you, Rose."

What did one wear when investigating a murder? Choosing a deep-blue skirt and serviceable wine-hued jacket, I pulled them out and laid them on the bed.

"That doesn't speak of gaiety," Phee said, lifting an eyebrow as I added an unadorned white blouse with a fluff of lace at the throat to the ensemble.

My cheeks heated. "Well, it's not as if I'm on board to attract a husband, now, is it?" I teased, hoping to distract her.

"Phillip is utterly dreamy." She scowled. "Nicholas stole me away far too early last night. I do wonder—dare I say—even hoped Phillip would ask me to attend another function or outing today. Alas. I shall never forgive my cousin if his desire for an early bed forces me into wedlock with a dribbling old man," she muttered darkly.

"I'm sure he had his reasons," I ventured.

Phee grumped.

"Breakfast, misses, or shall I help you dress first?" Rose asked us.

Warm cinnamon scones slathered in butter and cream scented the air as Rose cracked the cloche open for our perusal.

Another knock sounded at the door. Phee and I glanced at each other in confusion as Rose answered.

"Forgive the early hour, but the captain wishes to speak with Miss Beaumont as soon as she's ready." Nicholas's voice came muffled from the other side of the door. My heart tripped into double speed. Time for me to dress, then.

"How are you faring this morning?" Nicholas asked as we fell into step beside each other on the way to the captain's quarters.

"I think most of the shock has worn off, leaving only the dread behind," I admitted, stuffing a bite of scone into my mouth in a rather unladylike fashion. I assumed Nicholas wouldn't mind much. He'd already seen enough of my eccentricities to be unduly concerned over an error as small as a scarfed bite of breakfast. Nicholas shocked me silly when he reached over and plucked the last morsel of scone from my fingers and popped it in his mouth.

"A fair assessment." He gave me a wry smile around the pastry. "I confess I used the captain wanting to speak to you as a ruse to get you out of the room without arousing Phee's suspicions. I apologize, as it's not my intention to mislead you."

I nodded, lips pursed as I considered how to react to the theft of my last bit of breakfast but still appreciating his transparency. "I figured as much when you came to the door instead of one of the captain's staff." I brushed a stray crumb from my jacket. "You owe me a scone later."

"You don't miss much, do you?" Nicholas said with a grin.

"I try not to," I replied, matching his smile.

I did not miss the way Captain Cordello's expression blackened as his gaze landed on me. He jerked his head for us to enter into his quarters, the head porter already waiting as per Nicholas's instructions. Breaking into Dawson Davies's quarters, then the careful look at Mary's quarters, had eaten too much time yesterday. To keep up appearances, we'd had to move interviewing the porter until now. With a disgruntled growl, the captain exited the room and turned back to the bridge and his instruments near the great steering wheel and left us to our own devices with the sweating man.

The door snicked closed behind us, shutting out most of the mechanical whir of the control room. The head porter, James McIntyre, was seated in a wooden chair, his Adam's apple bobbing as his gaze raked over Nicholas, fear touching his eyes before confusion took over as his gaze slid to me.

"How can I be of service?" The man's stilted American accent cracked.

"We wish some information about the woman you escorted from second class back to her third-class accommodations," Nicholas began.

The man's eyebrows scrunched. "The suffragette?"

I nodded. "Yes. Dark hair, yellow dress."

"I'm not sure what I can tell you," he started, fidgeting his fingers against the seat of the chair. He cleared his throat. "I found her out of her class boundaries, and when she would not go back after my direct instructions, I took her there. Back to her quarters."

"How so?" I asked. I needed to hear him say exactly what he had done so I could catalog which injuries were from what offense.

"I swear, I did nothing improper."

"No one is accusing you of any improper offense," Nicholas broke in.

Mr. McIntyre swallowed again. "I took the miss by the arm. She put up quite a struggle. I had to move her bodily, you see." He blanched, probably fearing the impropriety of the situation.

"We understand. Please, go on." I nodded, trying to sound encouraging.

"I managed to get her back to her compartment. I . . ." He tugged on the collar of his starched white shirt, wincing slightly as he did. "I had to hold my arm against her, pinning her to the wall, like, to check my records book. Had to be sure to take her to the right cabin. I would have turned her loose once we reached third class, but she was putting up such a ruckus, I was afraid she'd just up and return. She was loud enough she were disturbing folks. They was popping out of doorways, checking in on the commotion." The further he got in his story, the more his proper accent broke down into something decidedly Irish.

I felt for the poor man. He was clearly rattled, likely afraid for his employment. Without knowing why we wished to speak with him, who knew what reasons he'd concocted for this odd treatment.

"There were people that saw you struggling to get the woman back to her room?" Nicholas asked, even as I opened my mouth to ask the same question.

Mr. McIntyre nodded vigorously. "Several."

"Very good. When you found her cabin, what did you do then?" Nicholas continued the questioning. Mr. McIntyre seemed less nervous when the questions came from Nicholas, so I remained quiet. Nicholas was asking everything I wanted to know anyway.

"I tried to unlock it, but by this time, she was screamin' fit to bust glass. One of the other staff heard and came to help. Buckley is his name. He came and got my keys, unlocked the door, and we forced her in. She fought like a hellcat." He unbuttoned the top button of his shirt and tugged the stiff collar down. "Beg pardon, miss, but she scratched me like a she-devil, she did." He craned his neck back, and sure enough, three jagged scratches went from his bushy muttonchops down below the neckline of his shirt.

"She was screamin' and clawin'. Caught me right on the jaw. When I jerked back, she kept right on goin'. Scratched me so hard, the button tore from my collar."

"Were you angry with the woman?" Nicholas asked softly.

"Of course I was angry. I was relieved when we finally got her packed off into her room. I told her in no uncertain terms if she came out like that again, I'd confine her to quarters for the duration of the trip." Mr. McIntyre nodded emphatically, wincing again as the deep scratches rubbed at his collar as he buttoned it back.

"Did you see her again that night?" I asked when Nicholas remained silent.

Mr. McIntyre shook his head. "I did not, and I don't wish to see her again if it can be helped. I've had my staff keep an ear out for any more disturbances, but no one 'as reported anything."

We were quiet for half a beat. If he did not wish to see her again and none of his staff had reported any more issues to him, then it seemed her death had not become known. I was grateful for whatever bribery Nicholas had undoubtedly resorted to in order to keep the airshipmen who had been with us silent about the affairs that had transpired.

"Do you know Lord Phillip Dawson Davies?" Nicholas asked.

Mr. McIntyre blinked and swallowed again. "He's a member of the peerage aboard the *Lady Air*. I sent a telegram on his behalf yesterday."

His accent had receded, his words formal once more. Interesting. Did that mean he was lying, or that he had nothing to hide? I honestly didn't know.

"I . . . I don't mean to be impertinent, but . . . but am I in trouble? Captain Cordello made it sound like it was best to tell you what I knew." The porter was visibly shaken.

Nicholas shook his head. "No. You've been very helpful, Mr. McIntyre. That will be all for now, but could you please have Buckley sent to the captain's quarters here?"

"Course, sir. Miss." He stood shakily, righting himself and bowing at the waist to us before exiting.

"Wait," I said. He hesitated and turned to us. "Did a lady's maid come to you about being assaulted?"

His face clouded. "Aye," he said slowly.

"Would you tell us what transpired?" I asked, trying to keep my expression open.

Mr. McIntyre rubbed the back of his neck. "She come to me, flustered and scared. She'd been attacked in the corridor, but someone came to her aid. She wasn't sure who was who. I took down her scant descriptions and have had my most trusted airshipmen keeping an eye out. We don't want to disturb none of the passengers." He cleared his throat, and his more polished accent slipped back. "No one can find the man through quiet channels."

Of course not. That would have been convenient.

"I've been keeping an eye out for the girl. Charith is her name. Charith Mount. She took airsick, though, and I relieved her of duties." He nodded.

Drat. Nothing new or useful, but at least there was confirmation of Charith's story, and of her sickness—not that I had doubted it.

"Thank you," I said. Porter McIntyre bobbed his head and turned again for the door.

"One moment." Nicholas reached a hand to the man's arm. He whispered into Mr. McIntyre's ear. The porter raised his head, surprise etched into the wrinkles of his brow.

"Of course, my lord."

Mr. McIntyre bobbled another bow, glancing questioningly at me as he left.

I lifted an eyebrow at Nicholas.

Nicholas smiled, winking at me.

"What do you think?" Nicholas asked me softly once Mr. McIntyre had exited. The clank and whir of machinery blanketed the room in noise with the door left open.

I leaned in so as not to be overheard. "I think it strange none of the servants who stood guard at the door have reported anything to Mr. McIntyre," I whispered, curious if he'd tell me what he whispered to the porter. "They've kept their silence. Your instructions must have been fearsome indeed."

Nicholas grunted. "If they keep their mouths shut, they'll leave this voyage wealthy men."

I glanced up at him. Bribery? Was that really all it took?

He shrugged. "It's effective enough."

"Effective for Mr. McIntyre too?"

Nicholas smiled and nodded.

"Thank you," I whispered again.

"It is for the Tristan name as much as for your benefit." Though his words were passionless, his tone was warm. I knew he'd taken my benefit into account, and I deeply appreciated it.

CHAPTER 32

Nicholas

Buckley was able to corroborate the porter's accounts, and while we didn't learn anything new, we were at least able to rule out several possibilities as we interviewed different members of the staff.

We interviewed Cora's maid, Charith, who did indeed look ill. Her pale, sweating features were drawn and pinched. She was unable to tell us anything beyond what she'd related to Cora the night of her incident.

Additionally frustrating, no one aside from Charith had seen anyone like the short, dark-haired gentleman Cora had last seen with Mary Albright. And Charith wasn't sure if he was rescuer or attacker.

"Have you disturbed things long enough?" Captain Cordello asked, a growl in his voice, as the last of the morning's interviewees left, leaving us with the skeleton crew and the captain in the bridge. Cora glanced out the window on the far side of the rounded room.

"You'd best mind your tongue," I said, pinning the man with a glare as iciness coated my soft-spoken words. While my initial opinion of the captain had been favorable, his prejudice and general distaste for Cora and her instructions was wearing thin. I was glad she wasn't within earshot.

My fierceness softened as I suddenly realized my initial opinion of Cora might have been similar. A murder inquiry was surely no place for a lady, yet Cora had managed things supremely well. She hadn't balked, hadn't wavered. Simply taken things in stride and sought to bring justice for Mary Albright.

"Miss Beaumont has things under control," I said quietly but firmly, trying to reassure the captain while reminding him that Cora had every right to take control of the investigation.

"You oughtn't encourage her. This will foul things irreparably."

My anger returned, and I decided I was done. "Enough." I turned my face from the captain. "Miss Beaumont, are you ready?" I called.

She jerked slightly, her shoulders going rigid, as if she'd been lost in thought. She took one more lingering gaze out at the wide expanse of ether and turned to face me. "Of course, Lord Tristan. Forgive my tardiness."

"Not at all," I assured her as her heels clicked dully against the polished wood of the floor.

"Captain." Cora turned to address Cordello. He quirked an irritated bushy brow, his lips thinning under his mustachios. "You should increase the ship's speed by three knots."

Captain Cordello harrumphed and grunted as we took our leave.

"Something wrong?" I asked once the door to the ship's bridge was closed behind us. Cora glanced around, pausing by the door to the crow's nest observatory.

"I hope not. Come look."

We stepped inside the small chamber, and electricity suddenly buzzed up my arms as I realized how alone and secluded we were in this tiny room with windows on all sides. We could see everything surrounding us, yet we were at a place on the ship where no one else could see us. It wasn't that we hadn't been alone at other intervals in this heinous mess, but this felt . . . much more intimate. I wasn't sure Terry would like it.

And I was concerned that I did.

I was taken from my musings as Cora pointed to the horizon.

"Oh," dropped gracelessly from my lips. A jagged bolt of lightning dashed across the far reaches of the sky, and the hairs on my arms stood on end, crackling with an entirely different sort of electricity.

Cora bit her lip. "It's bad. Will be very bad if we're caught in the middle." She sucked in a breath through her teeth. "If that storm and all its electrical energy catches us, it won't matter if we catch the murderer or not. Because it's completely possible we won't survive it."

Far beneath us, the Atlantic frothed and churned, winds from the storm tearing across its surface at speeds great enough to make the waves visible from our tenuous position in the sky.

Her blue-green eyes clouded. My fingers brushed her arm of their own accord. She startled, her gaze pulling back to mine.

"Worrying about it won't make the ship go faster," I said, even though a chill crawled across my shoulders as thunder rumbled faintly across the distance. "Let us focus on the task at hand. If it comes to all that, we'll take it in stride as it comes." I held her gaze, trying to reassure her, something indefinable and magnetic between us.

Finally, she nodded. "You're right. If nothing else, the investigation will distract me from the storm, and at best, we'll catch a killer and outrun the storm."

Suddenly, the ship lurched forward. Cora fell against the glassed wall behind her as I pitched with the motion of the ship, my hands catching myself against the same wall on either side of Cora's head. For a full moment, we stared at each other. I swallowed heavily, every inch of my body aware of the woman bracketed within my arms. Her rose and lemon scent filled my senses in the small enclosure.

I cleared my throat, desperate to distract myself. "Are you well?" Why did my voice sound so hoarse?

A thin smile ghosted over Cora's lips as she tilted her head up to better meet my gaze. "The captain must have agreed with my assessment and increased our speed. There may be hope for us yet." She inhaled a heavy breath, her chest innocently brushing mine and sending fire through my extremities. She squared her shoulders and jutted out her chin. "Right. I'm ready. Let's go catch a killer."

"Yes. Let's."

Why was it so hard to move away from her?

CHAPTER 33

Cora

I was still thinking about the way my insides curled when the ship pitched Nicholas nearly straight into me. He'd caught himself, but we'd been so close together. I didn't quite understand the little flutters that danced and tingled through my middle.

Speaking of my middle, I was hungry. As if on cue, my stomach rumbled as we descended the stairs back into the body of the ship. Mortified, my eyes widened as my hand flew to my belly.

Nicholas lifted an ever-expressive eyebrow. "Perhaps we should stop for lunch before continuing investigations."

Heat radiated from my cheeks as I cleared my throat. "It would appear that this morning's scone—that someone stole, might I add—wears thin."

"Hmm, that last bite would have made all the difference," Nicholas teased.

"Scalawag," I muttered.

Nicholas snorted. "Tell me you learned that word from Mrs. Beesly and not my cousin," he goaded.

I turned, doing my best to keep a straight face. "You, sir, are incorrigible. We are in the middle of something serious, and all you can do is steal my scone and crack jokes?"

He slowed, though mischief still glinted in his green eyes. "It has been said that laughter *is* the best medicine. And if ever a situation called for it, I'd say this is it."

My mouth dropped open to retort, then snapped shut. "I can find no rebuttal to that," I conceded.

Nicholas smirked.

"Shall we see about collecting Terrance and Phee and attempting a normal lunch before proceeding?"

"That's as good an idea as I've ever heard."

It didn't take us long to find our way back to our first-class corridor.

Nicholas left me at my door to collect Terrance while I collected Phee. I quickly unlocked my door and stepped into my chambers but was surprised to find them quiet. Glancing around, I saw no Phee, and the washroom door was ajar. One of her dresser drawers was open. Ophelia was spirited, but I hadn't noticed any slovenly tendencies. Crossing the room, I made to shut the drawer but noticed the corner of a yellow rosette poking out from beneath a silk stocking.

Face burning, my fingers acted of their own accord and lifted it from its hiding place.

It was a suffragette badge.

I nearly dropped it like it was on fire. Regaining my wits, I studied it. Was Phee a secret suffragette? Did this have any bearing on the murder investigation? Questions shot across my brain in rapid fire and burned where they lodged.

Lost in thought, I startled visibly when Rose walked in from Mrs. Beesly's adjoining rooms, feather duster in hand. I jerked, nearly colliding with the statue of Athena adorning Phee's chest of drawers.

Quicker than a stampede of newsies selling papers hot off the press, I dropped the rosette and shoved the drawer shut, catching the end of my finger in the process.

"Oh, gracious, miss." Rose's husky voice cracked as she dipped a quick curtsy. "I was tidying up while you and the other miss were out. I beg pardon, I didn't hear you come in."

"The other miss?" I glanced about, coming back to the present and realizing with a sinking heart that Phee was indeed gone from our quarters. "Where did she go, Rose? Did she tell you?" I swallowed down the panic that bubbled up as all my curiosity and thoughts of suffragettes mingled with thoughts of Dawson Davies and Mary Albright and dire dread that politics might truly be at the forefront of things. Ignoring it all, I focused on my friend. Finding Ophelia had to take up all available gray matter.

"The tall gentleman, the one with the blond mustache? He came and fetched Lady Davenport for a picnic, I believe."

"A picnic. Did either of them say where? And did she have a chaperone?" *Please, please let her have taken a chaperone!*

"They took the memsahib too."

The *memsahib*? If I hadn't been in such a rush and had such concern for my friend, I'd have smiled at Rose's choice of words.

"They took Mrs. Beesly?"

Rose nodded enthusiastically. "Yes. They took her out in a wheeled chair. She complained the whole time, but the young lord said it'd be good for her to get some air. Lady Davenport coaxed her into it. I helped dress her myself, made sure she was bundled up securely under a nice throw blanket."

"Thank you, very kind of you," I mumbled. "Where did they go?"

"To the gardens, I think, ma'am. They did not tell me directly, but it was mentioned."

"Thank you, Rose." I dashed back into the hallway, nearly colliding with Terrance as he approached the doorway.

"Miss Beaumont, steady on. What's all the rush?" Terrance caught my elbows but dropped them as soon as I righted my hurried footing.

I gulped, trying to calm my stampeding heart rate. "Lady Ophelia has taken lunch in the garden with Lord Dawson Davies," I managed to say without shouting or bursting into a thousand pieces. My heart drummed a frantic, staccato rhythm that echoed up my backbone. I was certain at any moment I'd fly into a thousand pieces. I pressed my sweating palms against my skirts and took a slow inhale. It would take very little to tip me over the edge. Especially now that I'd found that suffragette rosette in Phee's drawer. It was another odd-shaped puzzle piece to add to the pile of misshapen puzzle pieces of this crime.

Nicholas straightened behind Terrance and pasted on a smile. "I think it'd be an excellent time to visit the gardens."

Terry shrugged and offered me his arm.

I gulped, immediately calmer with a direct course of action. Well, I had wanted to see the hothouse gardens anyway. So long as no dismembered bits were hiding among the foliage.

CHAPTER 34

Nicholas

"They've taken Mrs. Beesly with them as well," Cora said as we took off down the hallway, quickly enough that Terrance tripped trying to keep up with the pace Cora set.

Not that Mrs. Beesly would be any real kind of deterrent, but at least it was better than nothing.

"Well, I'm glad she at least had the decency to have someone accompany her. It would look monstrously bad for her to go on about unchaperoned," Terry said. "Glad your chaperone was feeling less ill as well."

I grunted my agreement as guilt niggled in my gut. I was all but Cora's brother, which allowed for certain legalities of society's rules to be ignored; it was the *but* that was the hang-up.

She and Terrance weren't married yet.

Which did lend a questionable air to my traipsing around the ship with Cora unattended. I swallowed down the anxious feelings that rose in my throat. So long as no one found out, there'd be no harm done. Even so, we couldn't afford to be connected to any dead body either, which was double the incentive to keep our noses clean—or at least unseen.

"Lady Cora, you are uncommonly quick today," Terry mentioned with a chuckle.

"Forgive me. I didn't mean to rush," Cora said. I could tell it vexed her sorely to lessen her pace. I knew how she felt; urgency also pounded through my veins.

At last, we came to the leaded glass doors that led into the hothouse gardens. Even from the outside, bright-green fronds and pokes of garish color were visible behind the transparent doors.

"I am continually surprised by the things I've found on this ship," Terrance said, a strange expression on his face as he gallantly swept the door open and let Cora step through. Warm, moist air tickled my nose, and I wanted to sneeze.

"Where do you suppose Lady Ophelia might have gotten off to?" Cora asked, craning her neck around a particularly impressive sort of tree I'd never seen. PALM read the plaque at its base. Interesting, but as time was of the essence, I ignored the greenery and stepped forward onto an evenly cobbled pathway that wound through leafy bowers and plumes of gold, vibrant pink petals, and flashes of purple flowers. A titter sounded off to the right. Cora flashed me a look, and I shared her concern. She glanced back at Terry as she arranged her face in a smile and hooked her arm through Terrance's.

"Let's try to the right, then, shall we?" she asked a tad too brightly.

"Of course," Terry replied with slight bewilderment.

We all but charged down the path, rounding it, and stopped collectively in surprise at Mrs. Beesly wreathed in wrinkly smiles as she sat in a wheeled chair. The old woman was leaned down, patting Dawson Davies on the shoulder while giggling like a schoolgirl, presumably at something he'd just said. Phee sat on his other side, an adoring expression gracing her face as she took in her stupidly mustachioed hero.

Relief nearly buckled my knees. Even so, this merry scene sent my brain into a proper state of befuddlement. Here I was, desperate to ensure my cousin's safety, only to find Phee and her near-ancient chaperone in peals of girlish laughter, practically fawning over the man who could very well be a scoundrel and a murderer.

"Cora!" Phee squealed. She jumped up and dashed over, grasping both Cora's hands in her own. "I'm so delighted you've found us. You don't mind if Miss Beaumont and my cousins join us for our picnic, do you, Lord Ph—Dawson Davies?"

My blood pressure spiked again. Was Ophelia Hortense already attempting a first-name basis with this man? No one had asked my opinion on this matter. And on this voyage, at least, I *was* the authority for Ophelia.

"Not at all. Please, sit." Dawson Davies motioned to the colorful blanket embossed with the CAB symbol spread out on a grassy patch that could only have been designed for just such an excursion. Clearly, Cora came by her penchant for the details quite honestly.

"This young man has kept us properly entertained. This is the best I've felt since stepping foot aboard this great ship," Mrs. Beesly said, wrinkles still showing her pleasure.

"I'm so glad to hear you're feeling better," Cora said as she, Terry, and I sank to the quilt.

"I wouldn't have left the bed if not for Lady Davenport's most boisterous perseverance in her petition. While her vigor may have been a touch effusive, I am glad she insisted."

"Ah, Mrs. Beesly, ever one for compliments," Phee said with a hint of saccharine to her words. Dawson Davies coughed into his fist, eyes crinkling at the corners like he was amused. Mrs. Beesly's slitted as if she wasn't sure if she'd just been insulted or not.

"Is that salmon spread with capers?" Cora said, breaking the mounting tension.

"It is, and it's mouthwatering." Phee wiggled her eyebrows once. Mrs. Beesly lifted one of hers, all gaiety forgotten as she eyed her charges with all suspicion.

Altogether, it would have been a pleasant picnic had I not been attempting to overanalyze every minute twitch of the man's perfect mustache and every furtive glance my cousin shot at him. Additionally, I found I was increasingly distracted by a fragrance of roses with a faint hint of lemon—which, as I'd discovered earlier in the crow's nest, was emanating from Cora's hair. A fact that only furthered my diversion.

Cora turned and met my gaze. I swallowed, startled she'd caught me staring. I hoped no one else had picked up on my inopportune distraction. She gave the slightest nod of her head toward the door. I dipped my chin back. We needed to continue investigating.

But just as I made ready an excuse to leave the merry, tension-ridden party, Tilly Remlaude and Georgiana Nyland rounded the corner of the pathway.

The hackles on the back of my neck stood on end as their collective eyes zeroed in on us and their pace increased.

CHAPTER 35
Cora

If Mrs. Beesly wouldn't have had me stoned, flogged, and tossed over the side of the airship for such unseemly behavior, I'd have rolled my eyes to the highest heavens and gagged as Tilly and Georgiana plopped themselves right down at the edge of our blanket. I stuffed a sigh of long-suffering down.

"Oh, what a grand picnic," Tilly cooed.

"A *private* picnic," Phee muttered too softly for anyone else to hear. I glanced at her sidelong, and she returned my glare. We had solidarity in our irritation, though for vastly different reasons. I chafed to continue things—and also chafed in general in the presence of Tilly Remlaude. I didn't want to leave Phee with Dawson Davies, but the need to uncover the mastermind behind the nefarious happenings aboard my ship was overwhelming. We had other leads to continue in the form of interviews, and we still had a murder weapon to find. I supposed Tilly's leech-like personality might come to our rescue again on that account. But it almost made me feel beholden to her, and I didn't care for that sensation one jot.

"Ladies," Dawson Davies said politely. Stress lines showed at the edges of his eyes. I harrumphed to myself. At least he had better taste in women. Unless he was the murderer—in which case I'd much rather him pay his attention to Tilly or Georgiana.

I mentally chastised myself. What a horrid thing to think. Even if it was the truth. I pulled my mind back to the scene before me.

"These are lovely little quince tarts," Georgiana said, eyeing them.

"Won't you have one?" Phee said icily.

"Why, I wouldn't want to intrude, but since you insist," Georgiana replied, her brown hair curled and falling delicately over her shoulder.

"Lord Tristan," Tilly began.

"Yes?" both Terrance and Nicholas answered.

Tilly tittered. "I apologize. Is it too early to use the title *Your Grace?*" She batted her eyes at Nicholas as my pulse thundered behind my eyeballs. What was it about this woman that set my teeth on edge? Terrance busied himself with a cold cut of roast beef on zwieback with some sort of pungent cheese and, as I was uncharitably coming to expect, was no help at all.

Nicholas cleared his throat. "As my father is very much alive and well, *Your Grace* would be premature."

Phee nudged me. I glanced at her as Tilly prattled on at Nicholas. Phee tipped her head to Mrs. Beesly. The poor woman was dozing in her wheeled chair. Maybe this would be a good excuse to escape.

Just then a porter dashed down the cobbled path, stopping in front of us and bowing at the waist. "Beg pardon, Lord Nicholas Tristan?" the man asked.

"I am he," Nicholas said, standing, wide shoulders stiff with tension. Could shoulders be attractive? I blinked away the absurd thought.

"A telegram for you, sir. I believe it's urgent. Shall I take you to the telegraph room? You may send a reply directly as it suits," the porter said with another bow.

Nicholas scanned the missive, eyebrows rising. "Do excuse me. I'll be back momentarily." He nodded to the group of us, meeting my gaze for a fleeting moment before following the porter down the walkway.

We were quiet a moment, nibbling or fidgeting. Terrance glanced down the pathway opposite where Nicholas had disappeared.

"Miss Beaumont, tell me, what is it you perceive to do here? We're all a bit more nob than you—several steps above your . . . *American* societal station?" Tilly examined her fingernails, long neck extended to its greatest advantage.

Phee grunted beside me, and Dawson Davies's eyes went wide. Mrs. Beesly snored softly, and Terrance Tristan, who should have been my champion at this critical moment, still stared off down the pathway, fascinated by who knows what. Mayhap there were fairies vying for his attention.

Silence descended on our party as dread clawed up my back. When it was clear that Terrance would say nothing, I turned to Tilly and met her gaze. "Don't you know, Lady Remlaude? *Lord Tristan* and I are engaged. I am surprised news of it has not reached your ears." I did my best not to grind the words out between my teeth, but I wasn't sure I was successful. I was so angry with Terrance, I didn't even bother to include his Christian name or his full title. Instead, I arranged my hand, my engagement ring winking in the filtered sunlight, so that she might see it clearly for what it was.

Tilly blinked. Perhaps she *hadn't* known. Or hadn't believed the rumors I knew were swirling. It didn't take her long to recover her tongue. "*Engaged?* Miss Beaumont, you are the daughter of an *American businessman.*" She nearly spat the words. "Surely you cannot mean to form an attachment with the son of a *duke?*"

"Indeed, I do not mean to. It is already done."

Phee nodded emphatically beside me.

"Excuse me." Terrance interrupted all thoughts and barbs ready to fly as he got to his feet and deliberately set off down the path that led deeper into the hothouse.

If looks could have maimed, Terrance wouldn't have been walking anywhere the rest of the voyage. My incredulous stare burned into his broad back.

"Well, I never," Georgiana murmured.

"Do shut your mouth, Lady Nyland," Tilly quipped.

"Perhaps you should do us all a mercy and shut yours." The words were out of my mouth before I could censor them. With rage roiling through my bones, I got to my feet and left the group, uncaring that my words might lead to social suicide.

CHAPTER 36
Cora

Though the rational side of my brain was loathe to leave Ophelia with Dawson Davies, my anger blinded me to everything but the intense need to put space between me and Tilly Remlaude before I tore her eyes from her sockets. As I stormed down the path to the entrance of the hothouse, the implications of my words began to sink in, and regret curdled in my middle. I also latently realized that not all my anger should be directed at Tilly. I was *furious* with Terrance.

Regardless of where my anger should be directed, I'd still said those ugly words.

Too late for it now. It was out in the world. I shoved it aside, focusing instead on the interviews we needed to continue to ascertain what had happened to poor Mary Albright.

I glanced up, and heat flashed through me as Nicholas rounded the hallway.

"Cora?" He increased his pace toward me.

I cringed, thinking about my venom-laced words and my abrupt departure from the picnic.

"I found I needed space from . . . a certain member of the upper crust," I admitted sheepishly, hoping he didn't ask who exactly. Both Tilly and Terrance were members of the peerage, and truthfully, I needed a break from both of them.

I chanced a look at Nicholas, surprised to find his gaze already fastened on me. For a moment, I was tempted to give in to the desire to let my eyes trace his squared jaw, his straight nose, the curve of his bottom lip.

But, of course, that was utter rubbish. Instead, I gestured to the corridor he'd just come from. His green eyes widened, and he acknowledged my silent request. I racked my brain for a polite nothing to fill the silence, and how to once more formulate words, but catching Nicholas's intense stare directed at me had unnerved me.

And not entirely unpleasantly.

"I understand." His fist clenched.

"What has happened, Nicholas?" I asked, suddenly aware of the tension in those broad shoulders.

"It is nothing."

I lifted an eyebrow, silently reminding him of our agreement of honesty. He smiled ruefully.

"Merely a note from my father about a potential business arrangement. He sought my opinion. It was not so urgent as the porter made it out to be."

"Well, I'm glad to hear it's not more sinister news aboard the *Lady Air*."

"Indeed. I apologize, but I need to speak to Terrance." Nicholas's brow wrinkled. "If you are so aggrieved that you left the picnic, why is he not here with you?"

I cleared my throat uncomfortably. "Something snagged his attention, and he left the group . . . prior to my exit," I finished lamely.

Nicholas frowned. "I see. I'll only be but a tick. Please don't feel you must come if you'd rather take a moment."

I glanced over my shoulder through the glassed doors of the hothouse and sighed. "I should face things. It does no good to run forever." Besides, if I was being honest, reentering the scene of my unwieldy words with Nicholas at my side was bolstering to my confidence. Let Tilly Remlaude make what she would of *that*.

"Very well, then." He extended his arm, as any conscientious gentleman would. Gratefully, I slipped my hand atop his arm and tried not to be aware of the taut muscles of his forearm.

I steeled my nerves as we walked the same path to the picnic area. Tilly's eyes went round as she noted my arm resting on Nicholas's. It was most gratifying. Even if he wasn't the brother I was engaged to. My ring still sparkled, faceup, resting on the arm of a powerful man.

I kept my face carefully neutral as Terrance ambled back up the pathway he'd escaped down. He looked momentarily confused as he looked at the spot where I'd been sitting, but then he caught sight of us and his head canted to the side, as if he were trying to figure out what he'd missed.

Bitterness and irritation snarled inside my belly. We stopped at the edge of the blanket.

"May I speak with you a moment?" Nicholas asked his brother as he lowered his arm. I took my hand back, clasping them both ladylike in front of me.

"Of course," Terrance said, his tone implying the question his words did not. The two of them walked a few paces from the group to speak without being overheard.

"Miss Beaumont," Tilly began.

"Have a mince pasty," Phee interrupted with an overly sweet smile.

"They are most tasty," Dawson Davies interjected. He leaned back on one arm, closer to Ophelia, in silent support of her and distinctly not in favor with Tilly. As much as I feared he could yet be connected to the murder, at the present moment, I appreciated his quiet support. Tilly's eyes narrowed as she took in the three of us. Mrs. Beesly snored lightly still from her chair.

Even Georgiana stared at Tilly, her expression hovering between slavering over a scandal in the making and abject horrification.

We were saved yet again by another porter rounding the bend of the hallway. He stopped in front of our blanket and bowed to our party.

"Begging pardon, but this just came for you, sir, Lord Dawson Davies."

"Thank you," he said as he accepted the paper and scanned its contents. His face paled. He fished out a coin from his pocket and handed it to the porter. The younger man bowed and left back down the path.

"Lord Dawson Davies?" Phee said carefully.

His blond head rose, and he met her gaze. "I must apologize. It seems business of my own has come up that needs my immediate attention."

Was that regret that flashed across his face?

"But I do hope we might continue our socialization this evening at dinner and the play?"

Phee's expression morphed into one of exquisite anticipation. Tilly could have been sucking on a lemon for all her face puckered at his words.

"Most assuredly. Do have a pleasant afternoon," Phee said.

"And you as well," Dawson Davies replied as he stood. "And do tell Mrs. Beesly for me that she must take care. Thank her for joining us today."

"You may tell me yourself, young man." Mrs. Beesly's eyes fluttered open, and she blinked at the tall man.

He smiled at her, and Mrs. Beesly's face melted. Her typically severe expression was nowhere to be seen. She was positively charmed by Phillip Dawson Davies. She extended her hand magnanimously toward him. With the greatest chivalry, he took it and bowed over it. He did not touch his lips to her knuckles, though he did discreetly wink at Ophelia.

"Well, don't let us keep you," Tilly said haughtily as she rose from the blanket, nearly dragging Georgiana with her.

"Pleasant afternoon," I deadpanned, not quite willing to apologize for my earlier words. While I regretted saying them out loud, I couldn't bring myself to feel sorry for the sentiment. Because I meant it.

It was probably another societal strike against me.

The two aristocrats flounced down the path, and another sudden snore from Mrs. Beesly had my shoulders twitching. When I glanced over, she appeared to have completely dropped off again. Nicholas and Terrance were still deep in their hushed conversation, and I decided to look for some answers of my own.

"Phee," I whispered.

She leaned her head in. "If he asked me to marry him tonight, I'd say yes," she whisper-squealed back. Good gracious, that was moving quick.

"I do want all the details, but I fear I must confess something to you, Ophelia." My heart rate picked up and my palms perspired as I readied myself to say just the right words and ask my friend for forgiveness while also fishing for information.

What a rotten friend I was turning out to be.

"Whatever is it, dear?"

I bit my lip. "When I was last in our chamber—to see if you wanted to come to lunch—one of your drawers was open. I did not mean to pry, but as I went to shut it, I saw a suffragette rosette tucked between the leg of some silk stockings. Are . . . are you affiliated with them?" I kept my voice as low as I could for fear of being overheard.

Her eyes went wide as her lips dropped into an O. "Oh, blazes. That's not mine; that's yours!"

My brows furrowed. "I beg your pardon?"

She shook her head, dark tendril curls flitting over her shoulders. "No, no. That first day aboard ship. A woman came to our door. I thought it odd. She didn't look like she belonged in the first-class corridor. At first, I thought maybe she was a maid you'd brought, but she had on a yellow dress—not servant's attire. She was pretty, dark hair—"

I sucked in a breath.

"She asked for you specifically. Said the rosette was yours and that she had a message for you. Cora, I'm so sorry. I completely forgot to tell you with all the excitement of the first day and the ball and—oh, blazes—with Dawson Davies too. What a dolt I am!" she lamented. "I even remember wanting to ask you about it, because, well, you know, the politics. She came in while you had stepped out to get a book from the first-class lounge. By the time you came back, my brain was all focused on finishing getting ready for the ball. Will you forgive me?"

My blood chilled.

Mary Albright had sought me out. To give me a suffragette rosette. The *C* carved into her belly. My name underlined in her book. Was she marking me somehow? What was my connection to these murders?

"Cora? Do say you'll forgive me. I couldn't bear it if you didn't."

I glanced up sharply to see tears standing in Phee's eyes.

"Oh, Phee, of course I do. If you'll forgive me for unintentionally riffling through your things."

"You may riffle at will, so long as we may remain friends." She gave me a watery smile.

I forced a chuckle. "You are one of the best friends I've ever had, Ophelia Hortense."

She clasped my hands, her face melting into a smile. "The best of chuckaboos."

We both jumped as Mrs. Beesly whacked her cane down on the arm of her wheeled chair.

"A lady does not use slang," she growled.

"My apologies," Phee stammered, her hand at her chest, still startled from the sudden, unexpected crack.

The noise had also drawn Nicholas and Terrance—who looked decidedly unamused—back to us.

"Mrs. Beesly, do you require assistance?" Nicholas asked politely, scanning Phee and me, his brows puckering in concern.

"I fear I must go back. Girls, let us go. You mayn't be out and about like harridans without your chaperone." Mrs. Beesly's tone brooked no argument. Clearly her charm had left with Lord Dawson Davies.

If only the woman had the first clue what was really going on aboard ship.

Nicholas caught my eye as he personally took charge of Mrs. Beesly's chair, and the rest of us fell into a group around them. Two liveried maids were already approaching to pack up the remains of our picnic.

I tried to tell Nicholas with my eyes that we needed to talk.

His pace increased. I assumed he had gotten the message.

CHAPTER 37

Nicholas

I was frustrated. There was no other word for it. Cora had just finished telling me about the suffragette rosette. I had to agree; it much more solidly seemed to tie Cora into the middle of the murder mess.

And I didn't like that at all. Despite my frustration, I also felt a surge of protectiveness that couldn't be ignored.

We'd spent the rest of the day following various trails to no end. The interviews turned up nothing new. We'd analyzed Dr. Bellson's findings fourteen ways from Sunday, and still we had nothing. We'd attended dinner and the play. We'd put up our good society front. And we had nothing new to show for it.

I blew out a hot breath.

"I concur," Cora said.

We were headed to the first-class lounge. While the observatory was left open for any first-class member to use at any time, Cora had declared the lounge to be locked at ten o'clock, encouraging patrons to take advantage of the exclusivity of the observatory and its exquisite gilded finishings if they needed a place to congregate after the evening activities. I applauded the business decision. But more importantly, it gave us a private meeting space where we could discuss the case. I applauded this as well.

Even so, I dragged a hand tiredly down my face as we glanced down the hallways. Seeing no one, Cora slipped her master key from her pocket and softly unlocked the door. As we had requested, a pot of tea and two cups were steaming gently on the edge of a table, ready for us to sink into the upholstered chairs, to sip and discuss at our leisure.

Only murder wasn't such a leisurely discussion.

We sat.

"Shall I pour you a cup?" Cora asked as she gracefully picked up the porcelain teapot, the CAB logo glistening in its blue tones across the sides.

"Please."

The shadows lengthened and flickered in the wavering gaslight as the ship sailed through a patch of turbulent winds. I felt old. Far older than my twenty-three years. The past days had aged me. I let my glance flick over Cora, lingering over the curve of her cheek, the tendril of hair curled against her neck. We hadn't stopped to change out of our dinner finery, and we'd probably have to make up an excuse for Phee, but as such, Cora's dinner dress left her neck and the tops of her shoulders exposed. Her smooth, creamy skin was pale and . . . enticing. I swallowed. She held delicate hands around her cup of steaming tea, the amber liquid fragrant against the tang of metal and grease that always seemed somehow present on the airship. Her expression was one of turmoil.

I cleared my throat. "Cora, are . . . are you faring well enough?" The words sounded hollow, and I wished there were something else I might do for her—might give of myself to ensure her comfort. It was an odd sensation. A sensation of duty tinged by something more.

Cora blinked and looked up at me, her lashes framing her deep blue-green eyes like a thick fringe against her smooth skin. "I suppose I am lost in thought," she confessed.

"About the murder?" I ventured carefully.

Cora huffed and took a sip of her tea. "It's always there, in the back of my mind. I suppose it will be until it's resolved, though I'd not be surprised to find I carry some part of this wretched business always." Her words were practical, though I could plainly see hurt lurking in the corners of her eyes.

"There is something else?" My voice sounded less hollow—filled now with purpose—purpose to care for Cora through the duration of this nightmare.

She was quiet a moment, biting her lower lip before she glanced up at me through her lashes again. "Weren't you once engaged, Nicholas?"

My eyebrows shot up my forehead at the unexpected question.

"I'm so sorry. Forgive me. That was a . . . not a question I should have asked." She clumsily put the cup back on the saucer, the china clinking together and nearly spilling the tea.

Before I thought better of it, I covered her hand with mine, surprised to find a slight tremor working through her fingers.

"No. You are free to ask me what you will. I merely did not anticipate the question. Your mind does move at a frightfully quick pace. Sometimes it takes me a moment to catch up." I smiled at her, trying to put her at ease. A pretty blush stole up her cheeks, but she timidly smiled back.

With some reluctance, I let my hand slide from the top of hers and leaned back in my chair. I took a sip of my own tea, which was now cooled enough I could drink it without scalding my throat. "I was engaged to Susannah Faircott; she was a lovely girl, from all accounts. I did not know her well. Indeed, we'd only met formally a few times. Her father is well connected, a peer of the realm, as I'm sure you know."

"I was on archaeological digs with my father a goodly amount. There is much I missed. Something some people like to frequently bring to my attention," she added, an acerbic undertone to her words.

I raised an eyebrow, but when she demurely looked down to take another drink of tea, I continued, realizing she still felt awkward.

"Society thought we were a wonderful match. We had all that breeding could hope for on both sides of the family." Like a fist curling in my chest, memories crowded into my mind. Guilt that didn't rightfully belong to me pressed against me, sharp and confusing. "Susannah had come to visit at Debensley Manor. She and her friend who had come as chaperone came in an open-top buggy. Though the weather was fine when they set off, they got caught in a downpour on their way back to Faircott Manor." I swallowed as memories of her funeral tore at my mind. It had been a harrowing affair. Susannah's mother had needed to be removed from the wake and the doctor fetched, as the woman was in such deep throes of grief. "Susannah developed lung fever and died scarcely a week later."

"Oh, Nicholas. I'm so sorry." Cora's words were struck with genuine concern. Her eyes were large in her face, tears beading on her lower lashes. She looked so distraught, I found myself wanting to reach out to her again. Reminding myself that it was not politely acceptable, I left my arms at my sides.

"Thank you. I suppose I have always felt some degree of guilt that it happened on my account, and that I did not truly know her though we were to be married."

Cora huffed another sigh and swiped under her left eye. "Sorry. I'm not usually such a mess."

I smiled. I'd never seen Cora less than fully in control of her mental faculties. Digging out my handkerchief from my pocket, I handed it to her.

"Thank you," she sniffled. "Oh dear. I fear now that one has escaped"—she hiccupped—"the rest won't be contained. Do forgive me." Her voice wobbled as water leaked from her eyes. She ducked her head away from me, and the reaction in my gut was visceral. I didn't want this woman turning from me. The urge to protect her—as her brother-in-law, surely—rose in my chest.

"Hang propriety. Come here," I said as I gently gathered her in my arms, drawing us to standing and her to my chest. She resisted only a moment before melting against me, her tears silent, her frame shuddering with unheard sobs at intervals. I let my cheek rest on the top of her head as my thumb traced soothing circles on her shoulder.

CHAPTER 38

Cora

Nothing in my young life had ever felt as exquisite as the comfort of a man. Never had I been cradled so carefully, never had I been so distraught and in need of another's comfort—not even when Father died and my mother and I had clung to each other. Somehow the weightiness of the atrocities that had happened aboard my airship combined with the awkward rejection from Terrance and the anger I still felt against him inflicted a deeper pain that needed to be shared.

Nicholas's steady chest beneath my cheek was a balm to my frazzled nerves. The tears were unleashed, and I couldn't call them back. After a moment or two, I gave up trying and just let them come, soaking into the soft wool of Nicholas's dinner jacket as his hand gently moved from my shoulder and rubbed up and down my arm.

I'd never been so free in the company of another besides my parents. The relief that letting go brought was astounding. Eventually the tears ran out, and embarrassment threatened to creep in. As if he could sense it, Nicholas held me firmly when I would have pulled away. My tired muscles relaxed, and I drew in a shuddering breath, scented with Nicholas's mint and cedar smell.

We stood in silence for long moments, the quiet only interrupted by one or two lingering sobs that came out unexpectedly.

"Thank you," I finally whispered against the dark wool of his lapel.

"You're welcome. Are you well?"

I nodded, pulling back slightly, though as soon as I did, I wished I were still pressed against him. Nicholas . . . surprised me. He'd quickly become a confidant, an equal, a friend. Swiping Nicholas's handkerchief under my eyes as I once more took my own seat, I tried to take the vestiges of my tears, though I feared I resembled a mottled tomato.

"I think so." I glanced at him, suddenly shy. He slowly drew his hands back, folding them into his lap as he sat again.

"I know no other lady who could have borne what you have with as much aplomb."

I smiled weakly.

"It's not weakness to let the dead affect you. I think I should be worried if it didn't."

I met his gaze then. Kindness radiated from his emerald eyes, and a sliver of contentment wiggled into my heart.

"It has helped tremendously to have your support in this . . . wretched affair. Unpleasantness indeed. I am still determined as ever to see it through to the end, but"—I hesitated, daring to meet his gaze again—"I did not know how badly I'd need a friend."

Nicholas smiled and dipped his head.

"Nicholas," I started, hesitating again. I swallowed a quick sip of tea.

"Mm?" The familiar sound rumbled deep in his chest and sent prickles dancing over my skin. He picked up his own cup, the blue logo with my father's initials emblazoned on the side.

I licked my lips, unsure how to give voice to my inner thoughts. "Do . . . do you think I please Terrance?"

Ever expressive, Nicholas's eyebrows rose. "Why would you ask such a thing? Has he given you reason to think otherwise?" Concern crinkled at the edges of his green eyes, and insecurity surged in my middle. Suddenly, now that the words were out of my mouth, I wished I could take them back. I didn't want my insecurities laid bare before this man whose good opinion I sought. Though I had just literally cried my eyes out in front of him. It was unlikely I could make things much worse than they were presently.

"No," I said slowly, not completely convinced of my own words. "But I do fear that he may find me . . . lacking. At the picnic, Tilly made a rather biting remark . . . of a nature I would have expected to elicit some sort of reaction from my intended," I confessed as irrational shame coated the back of my throat.

Nicholas sighed heavily, his teacup plunking back onto its saucer. "It's likely he was so distracted by other things in the hothouse that he simply did not hear her. Terry has a tendency to overlook things if his mind is occupied elsewhere. Would you like me to speak to him?"

"Oh, no," I replied quickly. I didn't want to cause trouble, but concern regarding my upcoming nuptials still lingered. "I do not wish to cause any division. I merely wanted to ascertain if . . . if Terrance will be pleased with me. Forgive me. This is a conversation I should have with him." I blew out a guilty breath, marveling that it felt so much more natural to explain these things to Nicholas than it would to broach the subject with Terrance.

"How could he not, once he gets to know you more?" Nicholas smiled, though I detected the barest hint of strain around his eyes. The tea curdled in my stomach. "The truth of the matter is that the two of us have spent so much time together in such precarious circumstances, it's only natural to feel the discrepancy with Terrance, simply because you've not spent much time together yet."

"I'm sure that's all it is."

"Surely," Nicholas repeated, his eyes sinking back to his cup of tea.

I took another sip of mine. Before the soothing liquid even had a chance to slide down to my stomach, the offending organ growled loud enough it echoed in the small space.

I gasped, utterly mortified to my bones. My gaze flew to Nicholas, whose lips were twitching.

I rolled my eyes, my cheeks flaming, and his twitching lips broke out in a full chuckle. "Did you not eat anything at dinner?" he asked as he set his tea and saucer down.

"I swear I did. Veal and roasted potatoes are one of my favorite dishes," I protested. My stomach growled again, and I flinched in embarrassment.

"Clearly all this investigating is burning through your normal requirements. Let's ring for a snack, shall we?" Though his eyes were still dancing, his tone was kind.

"I suppose that's the only thing to do." I rose from my padded seat and crossed to the door, where a bell pull was mounted to the wall. Anyone could pull it and a staff member would immediately come to attend them. I gave the delicate chain a gentle tug.

The whole chain dismounted from the wall. I frowned, looking at the silver chain in my hand, then peered back at the wall mount. This was not acceptable aboard my ship.

"So much for ringing for a snack," I said, tossing the chain irritably on top of the nearest bookshelf.

"It's likely late enough likely even the cooks are abed. Ringing the bell would have only brought whatever porter is on duty, then he'd have had to fumble his way through the kitchens anyway. Why don't we just sneak in and grab some fruit or cookies? You still have your master key, yes?"

A grin tugged at my lips. "Nicholas Tristan. You used to do this at Debensley, didn't you? You were a little rascal that sneaked around after you were supposed to be abed and ate forbidden cookies, didn't you?"

One of his eyebrows quirked.

"Now, now," I found myself teasing. "We have sworn a sacred oath that only the truth will prevail between us. You must confess."

"It's possible."

I snorted a laugh, then found that more bubbled up behind it. What was wrong with me? First, I'd sobbed all over the man, then my stomach turned into a ravening beast, and now uncontrollable giggles were welling up and I couldn't make them stop. I clapped a hand over my mouth, only to realize that Nicholas was laughing too.

"It's also possible the cook still leaves a plate of cookies out for me," he said as he wiped the corner of his eye.

Some of the heaviness lifted from my chest, and I embraced the situation. Laughter *was* the best medicine, after all.

"I'm glad my grumbling stomach is not alone."

He stilled, mouth still tipped up but his eyes sincere. "Never alone. Now, let's get you fed before your appetite gets cranky."

—◈—

Stealing down the darkly lit corridors was beginning to feel absurdly normal. We descended the servants' staircase, my dinner dress *shush*-ing against the baseboards. I should have changed. After dinner and the play, it seemed we had both felt too tired, but now I was regretting it.

Once we exited as near to the kitchens as we could, we walked softly and slowly. A loud thunk jarred my nerves, and my heart leapt into my throat. Hushed voices sounded from behind the door closest to me on the right. My gaze tore to Nicholas. His expression was grim. We stood near the kitchens—all the doors near here were either for storage, the butler's pantry, or extra housekeeping supplies. There was no reason anyone should be behind any of these doors at this hour.

A trill of anxious words—a woman's voice—issued from behind the door. Another loud thunk, and she cried out.

I shared a look of horror with Nicholas.

We had to know what was going on behind that door.

CHAPTER 39
Nicholas

With one last glance at Cora, I turned the knob and flung the door open.

A muffled shriek sounded, and golden curls whipped through the air as one of the actresses clutched the neckline of her banyan wrap closed, her cheeks bright with color, lipstick smeared slightly across one cheek, a bucket upturned at her feet.

And with her stood Lord Philip Dawson Davies.

Thunder roiled through me as my eyes took in the man my cousin had plainly set her hopes on. The man who had entertained her under the veil of informal courtship. Anger clenched my jaw even as my short nails bit into my palm and two knuckles popped.

He gaped, clearly at a loss for words. Regret flashed across his features as red hazed my vision.

"Lord Tristan, this . . . this isn't what it looks like," he said, hands flinging helplessly to his sides and nearly knocking into a broom leaned against the wall.

I lifted a disdainful brow. I was not interested in his excuses. "What this is or isn't is no longer any concern of mine or of those under the protection of the Tristan name," I replied curtly. "You," I turned to the woman. "Remove yourself."

She fled, golden hair streaming behind her as she dashed past.

Presumably feeling the full import of my words, Dawson Davies's shoulders wilted. I'd never knowingly let Phee get tangled up with such a libertine, regardless of his breeding or standing in society. A man of honor kept his promises. Even if he hadn't formally declared any intentions toward my cousin, his taking her to luncheon and then to a tour of the gardens aboard ship—not to mention his flirtations at today's picnic—shouted his objectives quite clearly. I'd put a swift end to that.

Before anyone could say anything more—indeed, before anyone else could even move an inch—I slammed the door shut, only to realize I was shaking.

Anger coursed hot and righteous through me, and for a moment, my vision wavered. Shaking my head, I took hold of myself, glanced at Cora, and took off down the hallway to release the tremors from my limbs.

"Nicholas," Cora whispered a few moments and two corridors later.

I clenched my jaw.

"Nicholas, stop," she said softly. Her hand fell on my arm, and I came to a lurching halt, her hand like a brand. "Speak to me."

I took a moment and glanced at her face. Her eyes were large, her skin pale. Concern etched a wrinkle across her forehead. I swallowed.

"I am well," I said gruffly, trying to rein in my emotions.

She stepped back and assessed me. "You are *not* well. Come now. We swore not to lie to each other." She pinned me with a look and crossed her arms over her chest, waiting.

I blew another breath out, irked, but starting to calm.

"I apologize for my outburst. It was ungentlemanly. I find lubricous cads to be among the most detestable creatures."

Cora's eyebrows rose.

"You disagree?" I challenged, still half of a mind to argue.

"Of course not. But it's refreshing to hear, just the same. Though I ache for Phee when she finds out. She'll feel so betrayed." Cora glanced down, a frown tugging at her lips.

I ran a hand distractedly through my hair, tangling the pomaded strands. "As do I. But at least we have proof and reason for her to keep away from him."

"What a mess. What a horrific, magnificent mess," Cora muttered.

"Indeed." I checked my timepiece. "Did you still want a snack?" I asked, mildly chagrined.

"No. Lord Dawson Davies has taken all of my appetite."

I frowned. "We should return to quarters. There's nothing more to accomplish tonight, and it's very late."

Cora nodded and we turned back.

"Will you break the news to Phee?"

Dread settled in my middle.

"Yes. In the morning."

CHAPTER 40
Cora

We were trudging down the corridor toward the stairs that would take us back to first class when a sudden whiff of eau de cologne assaulted my senses. I stopped, pausing to sniff the air again. We were still in the belly of the airship, in the industrial servants' areas, only down the hallway from where Dawson Davies and his mistress actress had been discovered. I knew some of the woodwork was polished using orange oil, and that was a scent I'd expect to find down here, with the cleaning closets being along the corridor. But this was a different orange scent, distinct and largely out of fashion save among the grand-mothers who still liberally dabbed it on their handkerchiefs and always carried at least three or four of the doused cloths with them.

"Cora?"

"Something isn't right. Do you smell that?" My head canted as I tried to discern the direction from which the scent emanated.

Nicholas wrinkled his nose. "Yes I do. It smells like my great-aunt Gertrude."

The scent was stronger toward one end of the hallway. There, beneath the crack in the door, was the tiny white edge of a handkerchief. Foreboding tingled at the base of my spine. Slowly, I lowered to the ground and tugged on the material. It gave as a dull *whump* sounded from within the room. The edge of the white lace was stained with a splotch of blood.

Dots danced before my eyes, and my breath came in tight pants. Nicholas's hand landed on my arm and broke the macabre spell hanging over me.

"We must find out what's behind this door." Determination banished the hysteria threatening to bubble up. I would not succumb!

"At least do me the courtesy of standing back while I open the door," Nicholas said, resignation heavy in his tone. I nodded warily and stepped back.

Nicholas knocked softly on the paneling. When there was no response, he turned the knob. Slowly, he inched the door open. But about five inches in, the door stuck. Nicholas groaned and pulled back. Immediately, heedless of the consequences, I poked my head into the opening.

Blood pooled on the floor around the mutilated body of Lady Cadieux. Her arm—which had clearly been holding her eau de cologne–soaked handkerchief—lay wedged against the door. But most horrifying was the *A* carved clearly into her bared midsection. A heavy bruise marred the middle of her forehead.

Bile rose in the back of my throat.

Nicholas grasped my arm and tugged me back, shutting the door on the hateful scene. He was breathing hard.

"Nicholas, we . . . we must. We *must* get to the bottom of this!"

He nodded tightly. Motioning me back a few paces, Nicholas swallowed hard, twisted the knob, then pushed the force of his body against the wood. A sickening hiss slithered over my ears as he shoved Lady Cadieux's arm away from the door so we could gain entry.

Gingerly, I stepped into the room, shivers rippling to my fingertips. The blood was fresh. So fresh it was still wet upon her person. Much like Mary Albright, Lady Cadieux's dress and corset had been slashed away, a carved *A* reaching from between her breasts to end at the sagging folds of flesh surrounding her navel. A ring of dark skin circled her neck. The killer must have strangled her before hacking into her.

"Oh, poor Lady Cadieux," I murmured as I took in all the carnage afresh.

Nicholas was staring critically at the woman's forehead, and I drew my gaze to the bruise. It was unquestionably the imprint of my father's airship emblem. I bit the inside of my lip as the room seemed to chill ten degrees.

The *C*, the *A*, the CAB logos . . .

"We'd best call for the doctor again," Nicolas said softly, eyes heavy with concern.

The metaphorical noose tightened around my neck.

CHAPTER 41
Cora

I slept late the next day. Far later than I intended, but it was much needed. Nightmares of knives, yellow dresses, and bloody handkerchiefs had assaulted me half the night until exhaustion had taken me fully in its grip. With dread and trepidation clinging to me, I dressed for the afternoon, wondering when I could escape to see if there were any more clues that Dr. Bellson had discovered on Lady Cadieux's body. I'd just sat down to eat with Phee when there was a knock at the door.

It was Nicholas, who had come to speak of the scoundrel who would break Phee's heart. I held Phee's hand as Nicholas delivered his verdict.

He paused, looking for the right words, glancing helplessly at me. But this was better, for now, for if I broke the news, then we'd have to divulge my involvement in the murder investigations. I suppressed a shiver. *Divulge the murders*. And that did not seem wise either.

"I have every possible confidence that Phillip Dawson Davies is a man who would not treasure you, were the two of you to make a connection." Nicholas's expression bespoke his regret at hurting his cousin.

Phee's eyes filled with tears, and my heart twinged in sympathy.

"Speak plainly, Nicholas," Ophelia spat.

"He has a mistress."

"Blast," Phee wailed softly.

"I'll call for tea," I whispered, squeezing her hand. Before I got up, I gave her a quick hug. Phee sniffed but put her chin in the air and steeled her expression.

"Yes. Well. Thank you for this information. We'd best get ready for this evening." Phee dismissed her cousin.

Nicholas nodded and slowly rose to take his leave.

I reached the door ahead of him and popped my head out to Rose, who was stationed outside the door so Nicholas could speak to Phee in private.

"Rose, would you please fetch a tray of tea?"

Rose dipped a quick curtsy and marched down the hall in the direction of the kitchens.

"Wait for us here. We'll collect you for dinner," Nicholas said softly as he stepped by me, his hand accidentally brushing my skirt over the curve of my hip. He jerked his hand back like my dress was lava. "My apologies for my clumsiness," he stammered.

My cheeks heated as a flush fell over my shoulders. "Of course, think nothing of it," I blurted before shutting the door in his face.

Though guilt niggled at me for giving it enough thought to cause a blush, Phee was too distraught to notice my cheeks, which were as red as I'd feared, as I confirmed with a quick glance across the room to the mirror hanging by the wash closet.

"Phee, dearest. Is it so very bad?" I asked, turning all my sympathy and attention to her.

She stood, shook out her skirts angrily, and stomped to the porthole, where dark clouds were ever encroaching.

"Was I a fool to think he could care for me beyond an advantageous match?"

"Ophelia Hortense, you will stop thinking such nonsense this instant," I demanded. I went to stand beside her. "You are worth a dozen of any other high-society girls. Any man would be fortunate indeed to take you as his wife."

"I'd certainly hope I'd be worth a few Tilly Remlaudes," Phee said dryly.

I snorted before I could censor it. Phee lifted an eyebrow, mimicking her cousin's mannerism. "You're worth a dozen Tillys alone," I told her seriously.

Phee cracked a grin, though fine lines lingered around her eyes. She took a fortifying breath. "I shan't waste any tears on the man now. Heaven knows I must now go on the hunt again, and I can't have tear splotches ruining my complexion for the performance tonight." She dabbed at the corner of her right eye and tossed her dark curls. "There. He's behind me. At least for the moment."

I squeezed her hand. "In that case, what shall we wear?"

"Fashion always lifts my spirits."

"I have noticed this."

She snorted.

"Miss Beaumont, you are a picture," Terrance said as he and Nicholas stood on the other side of the door, both looking dapper in their dinner tails.

"Thank you," I said, willing a proper blush to appear in my cheeks. Nothing happened. I glanced quickly at Nicholas standing behind Terrance. He nodded, nearly imperceptibly, and my cheeks lit up like bonfires.

I cleared my throat as Terrance led me into the hall, the train of my deep-blue silk overlaid in black lace and black sequins brushing against the doorframe with a tiny clinking as the beads and sequins on the trim fell against the wood. The puffed sleeves ended just above my elbows, but I'd opted for black silk gloves and my black lace shawl. The lights would dim as the actors took the stage, and I wanted to watch, rather than be watched, if I could. I hoped the dark shades of my dress might aid me.

"Phee, you look lovely," Nicholas complimented quietly as Ophelia exited our chambers, back straight, chin up, and clad in a gown of red velvet one shade away from garish. Her dark hair was done up with elegance and style. A large ruby pendant flanked by double rows of pearls graced the open neckline of the dress.

She had dressed to conquer. This was the battle dress of the elite, and Phee wore it well.

"Thank you, Nicholas," she answered primly, accepting his proffered arm. My engagement ring winked at me from atop the shiny satin of my gloves. The green gem seemed to mock me as my hand rested lightly on Terrance's arm. I couldn't keep my eyes from its shiny surface as we moved through the hallway and to the grand staircase that would lead us into the ballroom after properly showing us off as we promenaded down the steps.

Dragging my eyes from my engagement ring, I caught sight of Dawson Davies at the far corner of the room as I took care not to trip on the hem of my gown on the next stair. He stood, handsome but inconspicuous in evening dress and standing to the side, behind a collection of young men from the peerage.

A pained expression crossed his face as his gaze landed on Phee and Nicholas two steps ahead of us. Nicholas's jaw tensed. Dawson Davies looked down and swept into the ballroom.

The ballroom glittered in all its golden glory. With the long banquet tables all arranged in a wide U formation so that the patrons faced the stage, the entire room truly took on a completely different air. There was a hush of mystery, and a whiff of dread, as I walked beside Terrance to our seats, the name cards at each place elegantly scripted with our appellations. As the ranking peers, the Tristans, and me by extension, were seated in the prime location at the center. Lady Cadieux's seat would remain empty next to Terrance. I forced my eyes from the vacant chair and back to the front of the elegant space. The ranking peers had a full view of the stage. But more important to me, with the curvature of the tables and seats, I'd be able to observe most of the peerage without much effort as the performance carried on.

I didn't know what I was looking for—any clue that might lead me to the murderer—and that frustrated me to no end. I hated the not-knowing. The feeling that I was no closer to solving this than when we'd first discovered Mary Albright, and then last night when we'd found poor Lady Cadieux. I smiled politely as we moved through the throng of people.

At last, we were seated, the same as we had been at the earlier banquets. Terrance was to my right, Nicholas to my left.

Ophelia was quiet and ramrod straight on Nicholas's other side. The muscle in Nicholas's jaw clenched and unclenched. I had forgotten in the upset of Lady Cadieux's empty spot that Dawson Davies would naturally be seated beside us. And there he was, settled on Phee's far side.

A few times I caught him out of the corner of my eye, leaning toward Phee, presumably to whisper something. Each time, Ophelia blatantly turned to make conversation with Nicholas. My belly clenched. I hated this for my friend. Hated more that Dawson Davies could still be a person of suspicion. He'd been in the same hallway only paces away from the murder. He'd had access. He was certainly strong enough to incapacitate and strangle old Lady Cadieux. His jaw clenched as he chewed harder than necessary on the delicate jellied shrimp appetizer.

Searching for something to occupy my mind besides the frustration growing between my friend and her former desire, I glanced around the patrons, noting nothing out of the ordinary. Not that I'd expected to find respectable members of the peerage wielding axes and concealing knives behind their fans.

"Cora, are you out of sorts?" Nicholas asked in a hushed voice meant only for my ears, as he did not use the formal *Miss Beaumont*.

I daintily held my napkin to my lips. "Forgive me. Yes. I am wretchedly out of sorts. I have observed nothing helpful." Anxiety chewed at my backbone.

He leaned farther in, a hairbreadth from impropriety, to whisper into my ear. "Likewise. I wanted to tell you, too, that Dr. Bellson found nothing beyond what we'd already ascertained. I shall keep tabs on Dawson Davies. See if you can relax and enjoy this one evening. At least while you can." Nicholas leaned back and gave me the barest tip of his head, lending me his encouragement and support.

My toes tingled in appreciation. Resolving to attempt to enjoy myself, I turned to Terrance. As I gently put a gloved hand on his arm, he startled from his trancelike stare at the double doors nearest the dais.

He blinked once at my hand laid on his arm. My cheeks heated. It wasn't improper for me to touch him in such a manner. Why did my insides squirm?

"M-Miss Beaumont," Terrance stuttered. He cleared his throat. "How has your day been? I regret we did not see each other today."

"It was well, my lord. I fear this trip has been overtaxing. Did you meet more with any club members?" I took my hand back, letting it rest with the other in my lap, the shiny silk swishing as my fingers knotted against one another.

Terrance's eyes lit up. "As a matter of fact, I did. Jolly good fun, the lot of them. Oh, and speaking of the club, one of them mentioned an archaeological dig starting up. Something about some mountain cave in which they've discovered . . ." He hesitated, leaned close, and dropped his voice. "A mummy was found petrified in all its ceremonial wrappings. Most peculiar. Dreadfully macabre." He sat back up in his seat while my heart raced with the thrill of it.

"Do you remember any other details?" I asked, my interest immediately piqued.

"Somewhere in the Alps."

"That's not so very far, as the train or airship goes, from your grandmother's ancestral properties, is it?"

Terrance pursed his lips. "I suppose it would be a short journey compared to this, going all the way from America to England rather than from England to Germany." He shrugged. "Grandmama does not keep to the German residences much. She far prefers her British estates and never misses a season in London."

I wanted to lose myself in the happy memories of archaeology with my father, but before the rosy hue of remembrance could overtake me, CAB-liveried waitstaff entered bearing beautiful silver trays covered in elegant cloches.

Quickly, I looked up and made an observation of the staff I could see.

There. That dark-haired man at the end—the build was right; the coloring was too. My heart pounded as adrenaline flashed through me at an alarming rate.

Just as I was about to alert Nicholas, the waiter turned. My heart fell, both with relief and frustration. The man's nose was enormous. So large that it would overshadow any mustache he sported. Which had not been the case with the man I'd seen with Mary Albright.

Willing my heart to settle once more in my chest, I skimmed the rest of the staff. Nothing seemed amiss. The waitstaff finished depositing the soup course, and the lights dimmed. Terrance leaned forward next to me, eyes riveted to the stage.

The first spoonful of delicious, rich, tangy, warm consommé slid down my throat as a shrouded figure appeared on the stage. For the next fifteen minutes, I enjoyed the soup course and the opening segment of the play. As the first scene ended, the lights came back up and the waitstaff took our bowls, replacing them with tiny pots of stewed eels in a savory sauce.

"Magnificent," Terrance murmured, leaning toward me.

"The eel or the performance?" I asked, still unsure how to interpret my intended's fascination with the theater.

"Oh, I'm not wildly keen on eel, but this troupe of actors is just sublime. Sublime, I tell you."

I nodded. "What is it that so captivates you about the play?" I asked, attempting conversation.

He sighed, a wistful expression overtaking his face. "The ability to transport oneself to be someone other than the person you can't escape."

That wasn't cryptic at all. "You . . . you are unhappy, my lord?"

He blinked as if pulling himself from a trance. "No, no. Indeed not. Just a passing fancy." He shrugged and waved his hand about, as if to dismiss the notion of unhappiness.

Unease curled in my stomach. His words disquieted something within me—something that touched too close to my heart. The actors took the stage once again, and Terrance all but forgot his fish. His eyes followed a trio of women, one blonde, two brunettes, all three with dark-red stain upon their lips. They stole across the stage, gossamer skirts trailing ethereally behind them like ghosts.

An expression of sheer longing swept over Terrance's face. It was only there for a moment. But in that moment, my heart ached. I didn't know what his longing was for—was he really so frustrated with his life as the spare son of the Duke of Exford and Debensley? Surely such an exalted life could not prove to be a massive hardship. He had his freedom. He was not burdened with responsibility for the family business and inheritance like his elder brother, nor restricted to the dictations of society in the same way women were.

Flashes of Mary Albright's yellow suffragette sash danced behind my eyes. For just a moment, I let myself seriously imagine what my life would be like if I did not have the restraining shackles society put upon women.

What would I change? I bit the inside of my lip. With the exception of marriage to Terrance, the part of my dowry I kept would give me that freedom I so desperately craved. Even so. I glanced sidelong at Nicholas.

Being with Nicholas—letting him care for me as we carried out our horrid investigation—had not been the hardship I might have imagined. Nicholas had seen who I was on the inside, the me I hid from society. He hadn't tried to squelch me. He had certainly been shocked, and likely concerned more times than either of us cared to count, but once he realized I was not so simple as many women were made out to be, he'd accepted me as I was. I'd even seen respect lighting his green eyes. And that had filled me with a sense of satisfaction I'd never experienced.

Perhaps Terrance would be the same. Terrance and Nicholas were of the same stock, after all. Once we were off the *Lady Air* and back on land where we could properly get to know each other without a murder hanging over my head, maybe he'd respond to my eccentricities as Nicholas had.

That would make my freedom all the sweeter.

◆◆◆

The play continued, and twenty minutes after the fish course, the lights came back up and the servers came back in, delivering dishes of steaming mutton cutlets in sultana sauce with a side of compote of pigeon. After the next segment of the play, the lights came up fully, signaling the intermission before the cheese and dessert courses.

"I must beg your pardon. I'll return momentarily," Terrance said with a glassy smile as he rose from his chair. I bit the inside of my lip.

My own glass of water and goblet of wine were making themselves known, and a trip to the powder room might offer more information along the way. As I rose from my own chair, Phee quickly stood, her back facing Dawson Davies. Catching my eye, she quickly stepped behind Nicholas and looped her arm through mine.

The last sight I had of the tables was of Nicholas and Dawson Davies staring daggers at each other before Dawson Davies lurched from the table and walked heavily toward an exit.

"Phee, are you holding together well enough?" I asked, keeping an eye on Dawson Davies.

"Aside from the acute torture of sitting next to the lecherous cretin I wanted to marry this morning, everything is just ducky."

I patted her hand. There wasn't much I could offer, but I did very much want to follow the lecherous cretin to see where he went and what he did.

"Phee," I began, glancing back at Dawson Davies's shoulders as they disappeared through the side entrance.

"I'm nearly bursting, but part of me desperately wants to know any other information. I . . . this macabre desire to know why her and not me. If you wanted to follow him, you'd have my blessing," Phee offered with a chagrined smile. Her chin wobbled.

"I'll be back in a jiff."

It was easy enough to ignore my own bladder at the prospect of finding more information that might bury Dawson Davies under the mountain of his own guilt. I hated to admit it, but currently all information pointed to him as the likeliest suspect. Truthfully, I had only Dawson Davies and the mysterious man I'd seen holding Mary Albright on my suspect list at all. I ducked down the hallway, smiling politely at the few peers I passed.

Dawson Davies's blond mane was yet ahead of me. He glanced back, and I ducked behind a decorative pillar. He abruptly turned down a darkened hallway that I knew led to the actors' quarters.

Wretch. Hadn't he had quite enough of actresses already today? Oh, if I could give him a sound lashing right now. Anger burbled beneath my skin as I took a few more steps in his direction.

Footsteps clicked briskly against the parquet floor of the hallway. Before I had a chance to duck behind yet another pillar, the last person I expected appeared from the gloom of the hallway leading to the actors' chambers.

"Miss Beaumont? Whatever are you doing over here?" Terrance asked. He briskly tugged his waistcoat down and fiddled with his cravat, which had become slightly untidied.

"I . . ." My voice sounded hollow. No other words came out.

"Come. It's nearly time for the intermission to finish. We cannot be late."

With my ability to form cohesive sentences momentarily missing, Terrance grabbed my hand and placed it on his arm, walking us quickly back down the hallway and into the ballroom.

What had Terrance been doing in the same darkened hallway as the lecherous cretin?

For that matter, Terrance had several unexplained absences over the course of the past few days.

A cold pit formed in my belly.

Chapter 42
Nicholas

Though the performance was well executed—I flinched as that word stuck in my brain—I chafed for it to finish. There was a restlessness that crawled into my bones and settled. Phee gasped beside me as the music crescendoed and the lead actor flung his arms out.

Dawson Davies had not returned after the intermission. I stewed on this as the play reached its climax. On my other side, Cora sat pensive. We had not had another moment to converse—I assumed she'd made some sort of discovery, given her fixation on everything but the play. I hoped she'd learned *something*. The only thing I'd learned was that Dawson Davies's proximity raised my blood pressure.

Terrance leaned down and whispered something in Cora's ear. Did his lips brush the side of her face? Blood pounded in my temples.

Clearly Phillip Dawson Davies wasn't the only person capable of exacerbating my regular flow of blood. I gripped my linen napkin under the table. I needed to calm down. I was not normally so given to excitement. Not until Cora reentered my life.

Giving myself a mental shake, I turned my attention again to the performance. The trio of actresses who had trailed across the stage earlier had taken position to the left. But wait. I squinted in the dim light. The blonde one. She was not the original actress. I was fairly certain there were now three brunettes onstage and the third was wearing a wig to mimic the appearance of the character from earlier. We were close, but with the rays of the colored spotlights on the three women, the finer details of their faces were lost.

Quickly, I scanned the rest of the players. None of them appeared different—just the one. Of course, I wasn't an excellent judge of faces, but I'd been on high alert, and I'd been trying to pay attention between being so wretchedly aware of Cora on my right and Phee and Dawson Davies on my left.

At last, the play ended, and the lights rose to full strength again. Chatter and exclamations of praise rose around us like a swarm of starlings from a field, blanketing us in a haze of noise.

Before Terrance could drag Cora to the front to mingle with all the actors and actresses, I leaned down, under the guise of picking up my napkin.

"Be ready at midnight," I whispered to Cora. She gave me the barest nod of her head as she glanced at me.

I wanted to know if there was anything else I should be aware of in order to better protect her. Because my heart stopped in my chest at the mere thought of something happening to Cora.

Or Phee. I glanced again, finding no sign of Dawson Davies. At least I could ensure she arrived at her quarters in one piece. I didn't need to fear her impulsivity and that she'd attempt to sneak out to find him later. My cousin was an upstanding woman, though she had a wild streak that didn't belong to our society.

I smirked; Cora did too. But Cora at least seemed tempered by some modicum of sense. I nearly snorted to myself. Though it was Cora who had sneaked out to examine the third class by herself, Cora who had swung down a cable and into her chambers through a window. Maybe I didn't know the first thing about the fairer sex in general.

"Forgive me, my lord, I'll be just a moment. Do go on without me," Cora said to Terrance.

The group of us stood, Terrance smiling as he nodded to Cora, then disengaged himself and moved with the throng going toward the stage, where a line of actors and actresses stood waiting like celebrities.

"Tonight," Cora breathed as she skirted me to get to Phee. Tingles raced over my scalp.

"Phee, care to accompany me to the powder room?" Cora turned to my cousin.

"Of course."

The two walked toward the back of the room, and I fought the urge to tear after them. Taking a breath, I told myself I was being ridiculous. If I'd learned anything on this voyage, it was that Cora Beaumont could take care of herself. But the compulsion still niggled, refusing to let go.

A prim sniff sounded behind me. "I suppose some will be impressed at such a mediocre display of playacting. Tell me, you must have seen much grander schemes than this on your travels across the continent?"

I didn't quite quell the eye roll, but at least I finished the gesture before I turned.

"Lady Remlaude, good evening. I thought the performance was quite admirably done. Possibly the best traveling entertainment I've had the privilege of viewing," I said with just a touch of ice in my tone.

She blinked lazily. "Would you do me the honor of taking me to meet some of them? I fear I wouldn't know what to say, I've traveled so much less than you. Would you be my instructor in how to approach those of a lesser state?" She looked at me coquettishly from beneath her lashes. Ah. There was that typical lady-of-the-peerage attitude so many women displayed. Were women specifically instructed to act stupider than their wits would allow them?

I admitted to myself as I automatically extended my arm, cursing myself the moment her claws latched on to me, that I'd been as guilty as the next man. The younger me had been flattered when a lady asked my opinion or required my instruction. But after attaining a small amount of wisdom with a few years of experience, not to mention spending more time with Phee and, lately, Cora, I was beginning to appreciate a lady who respectfully voiced her own thoughts and opinions. Glancing at Tilly in my periphery, I knew she had her own opinions, and likely a complete agenda, in which I refused to factor, as she just wasn't accustomed to anything other than subterfuge.

In a way, I pitied her.

CHAPTER 43
Cora

"Tell me you have some diverting scandal to tease me with after suffering through that impossible dinner next to the most wretchedly handsome man in the room," Phee whispered.

Since she'd been sitting next to Nicholas, I couldn't argue with her. Blast. I shouldn't think things like that. Though the embarrassment coming on the heels of that thought did cool my ire somewhat.

"Did he attempt conversation with you?" I asked softly. I *needed* to get to the powder room. Since Terrance had found me—or rather, maybe I'd discovered him—coming from the actors' hallway earlier, I hadn't had time to relieve myself, and I found the need quite acute.

Phee sighed heavily, flipping her fan out and wisping it in front of her face to hide her words.

"He attempted to tell me it was all a mistake. But of course he would say that, wouldn't he? I come with a sizable dowry. Not as impressive as yours, mind you"—she gave me a sly gaze—"and I'm not completely blind to my own looks. I am the cousin of the great and powerful Tristans—half a Tristan myself. I am a desirable match." She sighed heavily. "I really thought he was different. I've had a string of suitors, none of whom have met my father's expectations. But I really thought Phillip might." She shook her head. "Never mind. I shan't waste another thought on him."

"I am sorry, Phee. Truly." I put a hand on her arm. She gave me a watery smile.

"His absence during the second half was the only peace I've had this evening." Her face clouded, and I knew she was wondering if perhaps he'd gone to be with the other woman.

After taking care of much-needed business, we ambled our way back through the clusters of society matrons and gentlemen, a few couples, and the waitstaff as they finished clearing away the pudding dishes. I watched people as they moved about, in and out, almost as if in a lazy dance. All seeing who could fetch the best connection, who could impress the other, who could broker the best deal. A bunch of strutting peacocks, the lot of us.

I shook my head, clearing the acerbic thoughts. Terrance and Nicholas—that cat Tilly Remlaude on his arm—stood among the trio of actresses. I wanted to hiss at Tilly's intrusion into my circle. I felt . . . protective of Nicholas. Tilly was the greatest peacock of them all; a rotten mollisher, as Phee would call her. She had no business dallying with Nicholas Tristan. For that matter, what could possibly have induced Nicholas to escort Tilly in the first place?

CHAPTER 44
Nicholas

Tilly dragged me to the cluster of troupe and peers. I steered her toward Terrance, who had ensconced himself among the triad of actresses—including the one I thought had replaced a different player at the intermission. Sure enough, as we gained ground, I could tell that she was wearing a blonde wig.

"And you all danced so marvelously. I could have sworn the three of you were apparitions," Terry said as we joined his side.

"Mere mortals, I'm afraid," Tilly broke in with a saccharine smile. Her fingers pressed lightly against my forearm. So much for her wanting my instructions. I nearly snorted to myself.

"Oh, but Lady Remlaude, you are mistaken. Such grace, beauty, and command of the stage could never belong to mere mortals," Terry interjected.

The brunette actress with the heavily kohl-lined lids lifted her red lips into a shy smile. The one in the wig tossed the flaxen locks over her shoulder.

"Forgive me if this is impertinent," I said, the words tumbling from my lips before I completely thought through the wisdom of them. "But was not another actress doing your part before the intermission? I do not mean to speak ill, but I only noticed as you appeared lighter on your feet in the dance number, and it struck me that you might have switched at the break." I willed my neck to keep from bursting with red as my inane statement thudded to the ground like lead.

I breathed only slightly easier when no one made comment on my clumsy question.

"Oh, yes. Normally Collette does the whole number, but she vanished at the intermission," the wigged woman said.

The middle one, who had been silent until now, whipped her prop fan from her deep sleeves and waved it in front of her face. "Some say she's taken a lover while aboard the *Lady Air*," she said, her voice surprisingly low and seductive as she batted her eyes at Terrance and dipped her shoulders toward him, emphasizing the low cut of her frock.

To his credit, he backed up a step, his cheeks blushing. "My good woman, I really don't think that's proper," he stammered.

She quirked an eyebrow and let her gaze lazily rove over him. The woman with the kohl eyeliner subtly kicked the brazen one in the ankle. She winced but held her tongue.

Taken a lover, had she? My money was on a certain aristocrat who had formerly been paying his attentions to my cousin.

"My lord." Cora's voice broke into the awkwardness descending on our little clump. Terrance twitched, his cheeks burning hotter. I'd never taken Terry for the nervous type, but perhaps engagement and a pending marriage could do that to a man.

"Ah, Miss . . . Miss Beaumont. You're back."

"Indeed, though I fear Lady Ophelia Hortense is unwell. Would you be so good as to escort us back to our chambers?"

The actress with deep-kohled eyes snagged Terrance's attention, softly asking him something. He leaned down to hear her better before answering Cora.

"I should think she'd be unwell. All this senseless pitching and rolling about in this great blimp. I've never ridden transport this ridiculous in my life," Tilly commented, still hanging on my arm.

Anger singed beneath my skin as Cora's jaw set, and I waited for Terrance to break away from the minor conversation he'd picked back up with the actresses and say something. As Cora's fiancé, it was his duty to defend her honor, even if it was the honor of her ship. Tilly Remlaude had spoken plenty loud enough for Terrance to hear her.

When Terrance remained silent, I cleared my throat. Disengaging my arm from Tilly's, I took a step nearer Cora and Phee.

"It's what happens when you're caught in a storm. Little to nothing to be done about it." Without bowing, I turned, effectively snubbing her, which wasn't remotely polite of me, but I was past caring at that point. "Ladies, Terrance." My voice was sharper than I intended. He glanced up at me, chagrined, nodded to the actresses, then slowly extended his arm for Cora to take.

She took it without looking at him, her face set toward the exit.

CHAPTER 45
Cora

I was so angry, I might have had steam coming out my ears. How dare Tilly Remlaude say such nasty things? And how dare Terrance keep his silence! I huffed, stomping as hard as I dared with society matrons watching our exit.

Taking a breath, I took back my hand, smiled sweetly at Terrance, though I'd have rather growled at him, and sidled next to Phee. Nicholas hesitated a moment, then nodded and stepped close to his brother.

I dropped back and walked with Phee.

"The woman is a vazey, pigeon-livered strumpet," Phee bit out under her breath.

"You shouldn't say such things aloud," I whispered back. "Even if I agree with you."

Phee snorted.

The men escorted us back to our first-class hallway, where I was surprised to spy Rose at the far end.

"My ladies, you're back earlier than I expected; forgive my tardiness. Shall I attend you?" Rose asked, legging her way down the hall toward our chambers. She stopped and dropped a deep curtsy.

"Yes, thank you, Rose," I answered for us.

I glanced back at Terrance and Nicholas. Terrance gave a short bow and a small smile, igniting a fresh spark of anger. I gave him a tight-lipped curve of my lips. It's possible it more resembled a silent snarl.

Midnight, Nicholas mouthed as I caught his eye. Butterflies erupted in my belly as I gave him the briefest of nods in return.

"We'll bid you ladies a good eve, then," Nicholas said as I dug the key from my reticule.

Phee placed a palm to her forehead. "Good night. I think I shall retire quickly."

"Good night, Lords Tristan," I murmured as I unlocked the door, and the three of us entered. I shut the door, clicking the lock back in place as Rose turned up the lights, and I immediately kicked off my pointed slippers. They pinched my toes most dreadfully.

Turning, I glanced back and gasped. "Rose, your nose—there's blood on your upper lip."

Her eyes widened in shock, and she quickly whipped out a handkerchief and dabbed at the single drop of blood beneath her nostril. "Oh, forgive me, my lady." Her husky voice was hoarse with surprise.

"Are you well, Rose?" Phee asked.

"It's the altitude. I . . . it has happened before. Just before I came back here. Forgive me, I thought the bleeding had stopped."

"Should we fetch the doctor?" I asked. It wasn't uncommon for nosebleeds to happen this high up. And by my calculations, we were higher up than we might have been, trying to stay ahead of and avoid the storm.

We sent Rose to the washroom to clean up.

"My head aches. I think I must retire quickly," Phee moaned.

"You've had a difficult day," I commiserated. It was possible the altitude was being unkind to Phee's head as well.

"I am recovered, ladies. How may I help?" Rose said as she exited the washroom, the corner of her apron spattered slightly with red.

Rose made deft work of unbuttoning and unlacing us from our dresses. The relief was instant the second my stays were loosened. I was ready to be done with them. I so wished I could tell Phee of my rebellion against fashion, that I'd be traipsing the hallways unchaperoned with her cousin, and minus my corset. But on second thought, when things were phrased as such, it was probably best I didn't mention anything of the kind.

We dismissed Rose afterward, and she left quickly. I brushed and braided Phee's hair, and we spent the time in companionable silence. Anxiety niggled at me for sending Rose off early. A lady of status did not ready herself for bed. But I couldn't have her suspecting anything when I didn't *stay* dressed for bed.

"Thank you, Cora, for being such a jolly good sport, not to mention a bosom friend in all this mess. Likely not what you expected when you accepted Terrance's hand."

"Finding you as a friend has been more than I dared hope for. Sleep well, dearest." I meant it, too. Phee was one of the best friends I'd had in years.

It didn't take her long to drift into a deep slumber, exhausted as she was.

And then I set to work.

I raided my closet and dug out a serviceable, loose-fitting, navy tea dress and black wool jacket for warmth. Deliciously smooth against my skin, the tea dress was gloriously loose around my middle, bare of confinement. Bending easily, I retrieved my black suede slippers. The lower heel made for quieter espionage. My thick jacket was a comforting weight against the chill. With the altitude, even with a fire going in our warming stove, the air was cool. My hair was still down and unpinned from the chignon I'd worn at dinner. I quickly braided it down to the ends and wrapped it in a crown around my head in a style a lady's maid had taught me on a dig in Egypt. With my dagger in my pocket, I was ready and waiting, anticipation thrumming, for Nicholas's coming.

CHAPTER 46
Nicholas

I paced in front of the small coal heater in my sitting room. I couldn't stand to sit still, with nerves jangling inside me like beads in a baby's rattle. I had another twenty minutes yet to wait before the clock would strike midnight. Terrance had made an excuse about promising to meet one of the fops from the Crackford Club and had taken his leave. I wasn't wild about him traipsing over the ship by himself at such a late hour, but unless I told him what was afoot, what could I do? He was a grown man.

I sighed and checked my pocket watch again. Fifteen minutes. I shivered. Both from anticipation and the cold that seemed to have stolen over the airship as the storm grew ever nearer and we maintained our scant lead on it. With another shiver, I crossed the room to the wooden armoire and reached in to grab my overcoat. My hand closed over the woolen material as my eyes landed on the black cape, so deeply hued it blended with the shadows of the armoire. On second thought, I let go the coat and reached for the cape. The heavy material draped around me, bringing a sense of ridiculous mystique.

I snorted to myself. All this intrigue had addled my brain.

Ten minutes.

Close enough.

With one last sigh I glanced at Terry's empty bed, grabbed my room key from the nightstand, shoved it in my pocket, and turned toward the door.

My blood froze as a knock sounded, echoing softly in the silence of my chambers. Carefully padding across the thick rug, I cracked the door.

"So sorry to disturb you, Lord Tristan. Cap'n told me to bring this to you straightaway." A liveried airshipman held out a thick cream-colored envelope, sealed with navy-blue wax, the CAB logo stamped in it.

"Thank you," I said, taking the missive. The airshipman sketched a quick bow and bounded down the hallway.

Breaking the seal, I opened the envelope and drew out the paper. In a thick, bold scrawl, the message read simply:

Actress missing. Whereabouts unknown. Blood drops found in troupe practice room. I leave it in your capable hands.

It was signed by the captain. I sighed. I could practically hear the sarcasm dripping off the missive as I reread the last line.

But an actress was missing. Was it the one from tonight's play who had absconded at the intermission? It seemed she'd be the likely candidate.

I hoped with everything within me that we didn't have another murder.

I quickly made my way to Cora's room and knocked softly, three taps, on her door. While I was utterly revolted at the prospect of another murder, a missing actress, and the situation at large, I found my nerves twitching for an entirely different reason as the wooden door creaked quietly and Cora's face appeared on the other side.

She stole from the room like a ghost, clad in all dark colors, much like me, ready for another night of espionage and hopefully some answers.

"There's news," I whispered. Her eyes widened, the gaslighting catching on her teal orbs. I nodded toward the stairwell, and we moved away from the doors. I unfolded the note from my breast pocket and handed it to Cora.

She gasped. "Oh, this is not good." Glancing up, she met my gaze. "What do you suppose the odds are that she's not dead?"

"The sooner we find her, likely the better her odds."

"Where should we start the search?"

"I'm not an expert at this, but I figure we have roughly ten hours—until tomorrow morning—before the other actors start talking in earnest about her missing. If we don't find her"—I gulped—"or her body by then, it's going to get ugly. I think we need to prepare ourselves for the possibility that word of Mary Albright or Lady Cadieux is going to break, hinging on what we discover about our actress."

Cora nodded. "My thoughts were running much the same." She grimaced. "We'd better get on with it, then."

"Right. If you were going to hide a body, where would you put it?"

CHAPTER 47
Cora

The passage from the third-class quarters to the storage bay was long, narrow, and lit by a gaslight only every fifteen feet, leaving the hallway between lights nearly pitch black.

"I truly hope the actress is abed with some man, causing scandal, rather than rotting in some forgotten alcove of the *Lady Air*," I whispered.

"As do I," Nicholas said, close enough behind me that his breath tickled the fine hairs on the nape of my neck.

A thump sounded on the stairs behind us. We froze.

A muffled curse and a voice, too low for us to pick up words, whispered back. Nicholas and I stared at each other, panic written on his face as it surely must have been etched into mine. I glanced around, looking anywhere for a hiding spot. It was too far to the end of the corridor; whoever it was would round the bend from the stair landing before we could reach the door leading to the storage bay. There were two additional hallways, but as I was about to tug Nicholas toward one of them, a man's voice echoed again, closer—too close.

"Forgive me," Nicholas breathed against my ear. As if he grew wings, he swirled his great cape around us both, shrouding us in the black silk, while pushing me back into the shadows. My back hit the wall, and Nicholas pressed against my front, shrinking us into the darkness.

His hand was hot against my side, and my uncorseted middle practically lit with flames as Nicholas's fingers closed around my waist. My breathing came in silent, shallow inhales, nerves, awareness, and no small degree of pleasure at Nicholas's touch making me light-headed. My own hands pressed, one against his chest, the other smashed against his thigh—both trapped against his body as he shielded us from prying eyes.

This was so wildly improper.

I didn't want it to stop.

On some absurd level I realized this must be part of what was so enjoyable about marriage—why society warned against men and women touching beforehand. The brush of a man's hand on my waist was sending me through all flights of fancy and befuddling my brain. Even as a murderer stalked the corridors of my airship. Possibly scant feet away from me.

Confused by my own thoughts and the reaction my body was having to Nicholas's, I still felt terror leeching around us, leaking into the scarce space between us as the heavy footsteps grew nearer.

Nicholas's heartbeat thundered beneath my hand. His other gripped my waist tighter as the footsteps dragged closer to where we were hidden away in the shadows.

Closer. Closer. A loud thud made me twitch.

"*Tarnation!*" a female voice muttered.

My pulse pounded. A woman was out at this hour? My mind flashed instantly to the actress we'd caught with Lord Dawson Davies. Could she be his accomplice? I gave myself a mental shake. For all we knew, it was a female crew member coming down the corridor hauling things to be laundered.

Curiosity ate at me. Silent as a ghost, I angled my head and ever so carefully shifted the hand that was pressed against Nicholas's leg. His whole body tensed even more as my fingers, mashed against him, trailed across his muscular thigh to tease his cape the barest fraction of an inch away from the wall so I could peek out into the bleary darkness.

I couldn't see much, just shadowy shapes. The first had to be a woman with her hair in a bun, then a long, thick roll—of carpet?—then a larger shape, presumably a man. The woman must be going backward and must have dropped her end of the roll.

The light didn't hit where I needed it to for me to see anything else more useful as they moved away from my line of sight and disappeared down the corridor.

We stood, pressed together, utterly still, breathing, chests moving against each other, hands as they were. His thumb brushed over my bottom rib once, and my breath caught. There were mere folds of fabric separating his hand from my skin, no corset to offer any protection against the onslaught of tingles his fingers elicited. My hand reflexively clenched into the material of his shirt. I felt more than heard him swallow and realized my own breathing was uneven. The danger had likely passed, but still we stood, locked together, neither of us moving.

At last, Nicholas slowly moved back, glancing both ways down the hallway.

"I . . . I think they're gone," he whispered raggedly. "Forgive me for the impropriety. It was the only thing I could think of in the moment."

"No, quite . . . quite right," I stammered as cold air rushed to fill the heated space between us.

The heat of his body left mine, and I realized something with a start as Nicholas refused to completely meet my gaze.

It wasn't the touch of a man that had made me feel so deliciously on fire.

It had been *Nicholas's* touch.

Oh, blast.

Chapter 48
Nicholas

My heart galloped in my chest, so hard it was painful. I knew there were potential dangers afoot, and the adrenaline from nearly being caught had to be clouding my judgment. So help me, I couldn't make my mind focus on the important things at hand. All I could think about was my hand on Cora's waist, her chest against mine, and her hand against my upper leg. How each of those things had felt.

How none of those things should make me as addled as they had.

"There were two of them, carrying something large between them. We should try to follow them," Cora whispered, even her soft words breathier than usual.

I nodded, not trusting my voice and, as sense returned, not wanting to lose this potential lead.

We crept down the corridor, light on our feet, my nerves alight with awareness of the woman next to me. Unsure which way the load-bearing couple had gone once we met a fork in the hallway, we stopped.

"You said they had a large load," I said. "This branch leads to the third-class lounge, and this one—where does this go?"

My forehead crinkled as I tried to keep the maze of hallways straight in my mind.

"The boiler room," Cora replied. She shivered beside me. I clenched my fist to keep from putting my arm around her and drawing her to my side. That was an impropriety I could not afford. I feared touching her again would be like setting a match to gasoline. Separate, both things were perfectly functional, useful, and safe. But when they were combined . . . I gave myself a mental shake.

Lot of places to hide something in a labyrinth of pipes and water heaters.

Her hand brushed against mine as the ship tipped slightly.

"The storm is getting closer."

"Not good," I said.

"Not good at all. Nicholas, what if we don't find the murderer before we land in Southampton?"

"At that point, I don't think we'll have a choice but to have everyone detained, call the authorities to investigate on the ship herself, and pray that the killer—killers—don't dispose of the evidence before then."

She sighed heavily. "I was afraid of that. We must find him—them? I cannot let the murderer get away with this. And I cannot lose the *Lady Air*," she added, sounding guilty.

I paused, reaching for her against my better judgment. "Cora," I said softly, letting my fingers caress hers for one moment as I touched her hand. I would have said more, but a door opened down the hallway leading to the lounge. It was time to move.

Before I realized what I'd done, we were shooting down the corridor toward the boiler room, Cora's hand still firmly tucked inside mine.

CHAPTER 49
Cora

Nicholas's hand wrapped firmly around mine, and though I knew it was improper, at that moment I didn't care. Terror slapped at my heart, footsteps behind us for the second time in the past fifteen minutes. It was the middle of the night. How many patrons were up to ill intent? Surely there must be some committee where they all met up. That was the only reasonable explanation for this many ominous goings on at this disreputable hour.

Ahead was a door I was reasonably certain led to a small storage bay. I fumbled my master key from my skirt pocket, and we blundered our way into a room filled with brooms, a mop—and my foot unceremoniously found the bucket that went with said mop. Blessedly, the bucket was no longer full of water.

We waited awkwardly, trying not to touch each other in the tiny confines of the closet. I was aware every time Nicholas brushed against me. It was like webs of that newfangled electricity flashing over my skin.

Thunder rumbled quietly from outside the ship, chilling my extremities and jumping my nerves into an even higher form of awareness. Gears clanked, and I could faintly make out the hiss of a spray of steam from one of the boiler rooms.

"If we wait any longer, we'll likely lose our chance at catching this lead," Nicholas whispered.

"Agreed. We'll have to risk it." Because I refused to lose the murderer—maybe murderers—again.

We quickly made our way as quietly as possible from the closet to the outer boiler room. I silently placed a hand on Nicholas's arm, stopping us. I pressed my ear to the door but heard nothing. I hoped we weren't too late. Nicholas motioned for me to open the door and stand back. I nodded, understanding that he wished to enter first. While I loved that Nicholas treated me as an intellectual equal, all the ladylike parts of me still loved that he wanted to protect me as best he could.

Gripping my knife in one hand and the metal knob in the other, I attempted to turn the cool brass. It was unlocked and rolled smoothly in my fingers. My heart hammered in my throat as I silently turned the knob all the way, then gave the door a push.

Weak light streamed out into the corridor.

"You!" Nicholas snarled.

Poised over a body still half rolled in the bloody carpet stood Lord Phillip Dawson Davies.

CHAPTER 50
Nicholas

I lost all reasonable control as Dawson Davies jerked up, his pale eyes fixed on my face, blond hair forming a devilish halo around his head in the weak lantern light.

Red swam before my eyes as thoughts of Phee and this wretched blackguard—what he might have done to her, what could have happened because of my negligence—enraged me.

I flew at him, fist connecting to his jaw before I hardly realized I'd entered the room. Phillip grunted, his head jerking back as he stepped back with the impact. Ignoring my smarting knuckles, I swung my left fist, though he dodged, catching my punch on his shoulder rather than his nose.

Pain sliced through me as he landed a hit to my gut, the wind leaving me in a sickening rush.

"What are you doing, Tristan?" Dawson Davies panted.

With a growl that reverberated in my chest, I launched myself at him, plowing into his middle. We landed hard on the floor, bashing into a row of pipes as we skidded with the lurching of the ship.

Cora squeaked in the background, and my focus was momentarily torn between the fiend pinned beneath me and the woman standing at my back. Dawson Davies took the opportunity to land another fist low on my side. An ache bloomed along the bottom edge of my ribs. Pain was no deterrent. In that moment, rage clouded all. I had him pinned, and I swung again, fist landing with a satisfying *whump* against his flesh. He grunted and lurched, rolling us against the pipes, their cold and hot metal alternating through the material of my jacket.

"Tristan! Peace! I didn't kill the woman!" he cried.

"As any murderer would say," I ground out between my clenched teeth. Dawson Davies kneed me, nearly unmanning me, but a quick dip of the ship sent us sliding two feet the opposite direction. His knee bashed against my hip, and a growl of pain sounded at the back of my throat.

"I am no murderer. Listen to me!" His words were muffled as we rolled again, his teeth catching a mouthful of the shoulder of my coat. He bit down, and an involuntary yelp escaped my lips. The heavy wool of my jacket did little to blunt his bite.

"The devil take you," I muttered.

"Stop it this instant!" Cora shouted.

The both of us were so startled by her vehement words that we paused, my hand at his neck and his forcing my chin up at an uncomfortable angle.

Cora's face quivered red as she clenched the tip of her knife, arm cocked back and poised to throw it.

Was there no end of surprises to this woman?

"Lord Dawson Davies. I really must insist that you cease fighting, or I shall have no choice but to impale my blade through your skull and split it like a ripe cantaloupe."

"She can't be serious," Dawson Davies muttered, his voice betraying his shock and confusion.

"She is, and she will," I replied, hesitantly getting off him as some of the red haze cleared from my vision. I wasn't certain if

Cora was telling the truth or if she was bluffing about splitting the man's skull. But more importantly, I believed she *could* if she so desired.

"Get up." I spat the words at the blond man.

He rose stiffly to his feet, favoring his right side. A twisted part of me took satisfaction in that.

"I am no murderer," he repeated, holding up a hand imploringly while his other braced about his ribs.

"Move three paces to your left," Cora instructed. Her eyes and her knife aim trailed his obedient movements. "Now. Prove that you are not the murderer. We found you all but finishing the deed as we walked in the room. Was it not you and your lady friend that carried the body down the hallway? Or perhaps you merely carried the carpet, killing your accomplice once you reached the boiler room, hoping it would be far enough out of the way that no one would find you nor disturb you."

Cora's chin gave the faintest of tremors. I moved to stand beside her, my side and hip groaning angrily at me. I'd have to come up with a good excuse as to how I'd gotten the bruises I was sure were forming.

Dawson Davies straightened, holding both his hands in the air. "I did not kill this woman. I have killed no one!" he amended quickly. "I was following a pair. I thought maybe I had found a lead."

"A lead to *what*?" I pressed. My breathing calmed as the adrenaline began fading from my system.

Phillip tipped his head back, his eyes sliding shut as he blew out a hot breath, his shoulders dropping as his eyelids drooped. He cleared his throat. "It is not a discussion to have in the presence of a lady."

Cora snorted. "Yet standing about corpses in the middle of the night is perfectly acceptable."

"Not to mention the knife throwing," Dawson Davies retorted, eyeing the blade still poised in her hand.

"You were saying?" I arched an eyebrow and crossed my arms over my chest.

"My . . . my sister is"—he swallowed again—"is in a delicate condition. I was attempting to ensure the well-being of my family."

"By going on a murder spree?" The sarcasm fairly dripped from my tone.

"Hang it all. Tristan, in the right side of my suit coat is a hidden pocket. You'll have to rip the seams, but inside are three letters that prove what I'm about to tell you is the truth. I swear to you, I am not about nefarious purposes—at least not of the murdering nature," he said, indicating the body still mostly concealed by the carpet.

"Cora, keep your knife trained on him," I said, utterly unconvinced.

"Here, I'm taking my jacket off and handing it to you." Dawson Davies took off his jacket slowly. He grimaced, "Blast, Tristan, you haven't gone soft, have you?" His grimace turned into a wince as he shrugged the right sleeve off and tossed the jacket to me. Assuming Cora was a better shot with her knife than I would be, I rummaged in Dawson Davies's coat rather than handing it to her while I kept Dawson Davies in place.

Sure enough, there was a cleverly stitched pocket. I clawed the seam open with my fingernails, ripping the material with it but caring little. My eyebrows lifted as I saw several folded letters poking out of the inside of the secret pocket.

With fingers and knuckles that smarted as they bent, I plucked the missives out and opened the first. My eyes grew large, and I couldn't keep my mouth from dropping open. This was the last thing I'd expected.

"Nicholas?" Cora asked, nerves in her voice.

I cleared my throat and read from the scrap of cheap paper. "'Leave ten pounds in a sealed envelope marked with *DD* on the upper right corner. Address it to Lady Buckingham and leave it at the bar of The Albert pub on Victoria Street. Do this by Friday or the world will learn your sister is with child,,'" I finished softly. My gaze riveted on Dawson Davies, still standing where Cora told him to.

"What are you about, man?" I asked, as my brain churned.

Phillip swallowed. "I pray I may rely upon your silence and discretion?"

"I hardly see you have any choice but to trust us, and we've already assumed the worst, given the blatant nature of the letter," Cora said with a nod at the knife still poised to fly into the man's chest.

Phillip nodded miserably. "Yes. But please, for the sake of all my sisters, I beg of you to listen and keep silent about the matter. As you heard"—anguish drew his brows together—"my younger sister has . . . has become involved with a man. A man she cannot have." He swallowed hard, his Adam's apple bobbing. "She is indeed with child. We received this note. With regret, I left the ten pounds, and even stayed in the vicinity to attempt to find our blackmailer. No one ever came to retrieve the missive, and I hired a private investigator. We wanted to know whom we are paying, for obvious reasons, but also so that we may come to a final arrangement of sorts."

"A permanent arrangement like your blackmailer's death?" I couldn't help but ask.

Dawson Davies vehemently shook his head. "No. I may be many things, but I've always striven to be an honorable man. There are other forms of payment. Passage to another country, for example."

"Is that why you're here?" Cora asked, wheels practically turning behind her eyes.

He nodded miserably. "I hired a private investigator in England, as I mentioned, but he refused to leave the country. He traced the letter we received to a London address. There, he found an empty tenement and a name. Pauline Swift. Around that time, we received a second letter." He nodded to the missives still in my hand. "This one requested an outstanding one hundred pounds within a two-day timeframe."

I whistled. That was a year's rent for the upper working class.

Dawson Davies continued with a nod in my direction. "You see, I have *four* younger sisters at home. And my sister's condition progresses. The ruination of one would be ruination for them all. I thought perhaps the one large payment was satisfactory enough." He huffed a long-suffering sigh. "Then the"—he cleared his throat, casting a hesitant glance at Cora—"the father of Della's baby contacted us, seemingly half-mad, and warned us to put an end to such machinations that were threatening his own security and good name. He had been on the receiving end of some rather less-than-polite letters himself. I ascertained he was not successful in dealing with the problem, so he made it ours.

"This gentleman is not a kind man. How my sister ever ended up in his thrall, I will never understand." He looked like he wanted to spit just thinking of the cad, and his face clouded in anger. "I knew we had to do something. The only thing I knew to do was to go after the blackmailer. The trail had gone cold in the meantime. I crossed to America on the faintest whiff of information, and here I am on the *Lady Air*, following the last-known possible whereabouts. I've already checked the manifest, though—there is not a single Pauline or Swift aboard ship, but one day before the *Lady Air* launched, I received a wire that another letter, postmarked from America, had been delivered to my family's home in England. The wire was sent from aboard the *Lady Air*. It was another demand for one hundred pounds. You'll find the telegram in the third envelope." He sighed once more. "I've done my level best to find this Pauline Swift, but the only thing I seem to have found are dead ends, and"—he gulped—"a dead body."

CHAPTER 51
Cora

Lord Philip Dawson Davies was in a most regrettable position.

He swallowed hard, and I realized the hand that held my knife had lowered slightly. I searched his face in the dim light. Earnestness shone from his expression like a beacon, and though I wasn't entirely certain I trusted him, I did believe his story.

"I had been trying to track down one of the actresses. She mentioned she might have information for me regarding Pauline. I spoke with her once before, the night of the first ball, but we were interrupted. We happened upon a man attacking a maid in the hall. We chased him off, but Collette was spooked, and reasonably so. I had only just convinced her to speak with me again when you found us and assumed the worst." Dawson Davies's face contorted. "I was so hopeful of getting a lead. I tried to meet with Collette—the actress—once more tonight, but she was not there at the designated time, and then I saw the pair hauling this carpet down the hall. It just . . . struck me as odd. So I followed them. And then you found me." Dawson Davies shrugged.

Oh, how utterly, deliciously, horrifically scandalous. Phee would be in raptures to be on the sidelines of such opprobrium once she found out—if she *could* find out. I desperately hoped joy for my friend, and a large part of me was intensely relieved that perhaps Dawson Davies wasn't the scoundrel we all currently took him for. At least, it was possible he wasn't.

"You think for certain Pauline is here?" My wits cleared, and I tried to focus on the matter at hand.

"As I said"—Dawson Davies slowly lowered his hands all the way to his sides—"the wire to my family came from aboard ship the day before she sailed. I dropped everything and purchased the last first-class accommodation from the London office. I'm fortunate my name made the ship's booklets at all. I traveled through the night in order to board on time. I've been scouring for any possible connection. I thought for certain it must be someone of the peerage who was close to my sister—perhaps Tilly Remlaude—but I'm less sure of that course of inquiry now. She's attempted attachment, and she would not if she knew of Della's predicament."

"And you've used Lady Davenport as a convenient excuse to navigate among the peers while you gathered information," Nicholas said icily.

Dawson Davies hung his head, and an unseen fist squeezed my heart.

"I won't lie and say that her attentions haven't helped, but truly, it is not my only reasoning for wishing to spend time with Lady Davenport."

Nicholas made a dark noise at the back of his throat, then raised an unyielding brow. "You were found hovering over a dead woman."

I glanced between the two men as some unspoken communication seemed to pass between them. Nicholas was more discerning than I had realized. My already heightened respect for him moved up yet another notch.

"I love my sister. All of my sisters," Dawson Davies implored.

Nicholas's shoulders lost some of their tightness, though Della's situation burned in my chest.

"So you see," the young marquess continued with a weak smile, "I really had no choice if I wished to save the family reputation. As we're both well acquainted with the perception of society and our comings and goings, surely I needn't explain myself further."

My arm lowered. His face was shrouded in pain and discomfort, but the lines around his eyes and the way his nails were clenching little half-moons into his palms told me he spoke the truth.

As my brain registered these things about Dawson Davies and my hackles smoothed, I became aware of the very dead body not more than five feet away. The heavy carpet was still partially rolled, obscuring the dead woman but for a hand and the matted golden tresses sticking out of the end. I swallowed back the bile as my eyes locked on the body.

"I suppose that leaves the body, then," Nicholas said. Dawson Davies sagged and nodded.

Carefully, he took a step nearer me. By some unwritten rule, the three of us exchanged a mutual trust, suddenly allies against the grisly murders taking place aboard my airship.

"I was following a pair; there were two of them. I had been snooping in the actors' area, trying to find Collette, the"—his face blushed red, even in the weak light—"blonde actress in whose room you found me. I swear there was nothing untoward occurring. She was acting as an informant to me. Keeping her ears open for additional information I might find useful. I swear, that was all. I was moving into the room where they store the troupe's things when I heard muffled scuffling and quiet steps in the corridor. I hid myself, then determined to follow.

"I would have caught them in here, but there was a noise in the hallway as I was trailing them. I feared being discovered myself, so I hid for a few moments, then continued. I found the carpet with the . . . deceased there. You came in before I could learn anything more."

Guilt gnawed at me. I glanced at Nicholas. He'd come to the same conclusion, judging by his pursed lips and slight nod. It was likely that Nicholas and I were the noise Dawson Davies had overheard. I sighed, trying not to grind my teeth together. It was disgusting and disheartening to think that our hiding from Dawson Davies might have led to the killer—*killers*—walking free. Again.

I shook my head to clear the ironic thoughts, then stopped.

Killers. Plural. We were dealing with a pair of murderers.

"Best we see what we're about," I said. I bit the edge of my lip as fear and anxiety started clawing up my spine. Flashes of Mary Albright's slashed torso and the horrified expression left behind on Lady Cadieux's face blasted behind my eyelids. I swallowed and blinked them away as best I could. I crouched on the floor near the carpet. Nicholas knelt beside me with Dawson Davies on the other side as I gingerly pulled the flap of carpet back and gasped.

"Collette." Dawson Davies breathed the painful word.

Her face smeared with blood and ashen white, Collette, the blonde actress who had been feeding information to Dawson Davies, lay dead as a doornail before us.

CHAPTER 52

Cora

"I never dreamed when Collette vanished at the intermission that I'd find her like this," Dawson Davies said, regret heavy in his tone.

"There was another actress—I remarked upon the blonde wig—that took her place," Nicholas murmured quietly.

Bile rose in the back of my throat as my eyes trailed the dead woman's blood-spattered face, her once-beautiful golden hair plastered to one side of her head and caked with drying blood and what might have been part of her brain. My stomach heaved and I turned quickly, breathing a few times through my mouth.

"Cora, are you well?" Nicholas asked. His hand familiarly grazed my arm, lingering until I nodded.

"Well enough." I took another fortifying breath and drew the carpet the rest of the way from Collette's body.

Another depraved carving adorned Collette's lifeless body.

Ice rushed through my veins as terror clawed at me, seeking a foothold.

"This was clearly done by the same assailant that killed Mary and Lady Cadieux," Nicholas said, his hand covering his mouth, eyes anguished.

"Who is Mary?" Dawson Davies asked. "Lady Cadieux? The poor old bat who doesn't realize she can't hear? Wait, she— they're both expired?" He covered his mouth with his fist, turning away, shoulders heaving once. He took several inhales, collecting himself.

I groaned. "There was a murder before this . . . before Lady Cadieux, and before Collette." We quickly filled him in on the bare details we had.

"They were cut?" Dawson Davies's face showed his horror. I followed his troubled gaze to Collette's midsection. As before, her blouse had been torn asunder, her skirt slit from the waist to midthigh, leaving the poor woman completely exposed. Every inch as gruesome as the first two murders, the letter *B* was hacked into her flesh in one long sweep along with two jagged, clumsy curves joining directly across her navel.

"Is he trying to be fancy?" Nicholas asked as he stared in disgust and discomfort. He indicated a curl starting between her breasts and ending at the point of the *B*. The right leg of the letter also had a slash under it extending down into her pelvis.

My blood seemed to stop flowing altogether. *B*.

I swallowed past the painful lump in my throat. First a *C* carved into Mary, then an *A* into Lady Cadieux. Now a *B* carved into Collette. My name underlined in Mary's book.

CAB.

Clarence Abner Beaumont, but also Cora Alexandria Beaumont. Was this truly a murder focused around my father— around me? Around the *Lady Air*? What grievous injury could either of us have caused to warrant this level of brutality in retribution? And what could I *do*?

"Cora, look. Her pin." Nicholas nodded toward Collette's shoulder, where a bright-yellow suffragette ribbon corsage was pinned, half of it stained from the ooze of her head wound. It hung askew from her ruined dress. Right next to a bruised imprint of the CAB Airship emblem.

The sight of that bruise, then the bright-yellow ribbon, arrested the terrifying free fall of my thoughts. Could these murders yet be politically motivated?

"But what of the letters? The . . . initials?" I whispered. "Lady Cadieux?"

"What do you mean, initials?" Dawson Davies asked. His face was white, nearly as ashen as the dead woman's.

"The *B* carved into her belly. Mary Albright had a *C* cut into hers. Lady Cadieux had an *A*. I . . ." I glanced at Nicholas. The ship pitched again, and thunder shuddered in the distance. Without meaning to, I wavered and reached a hand out to steady myself against his shoulder. The sculpted muscle tensed beneath my touch but did not pull away.

"We are in this together now, are we not, Dawson Davies?" Nicholas asked, his voice grave.

The blond man nodded. "You may count me as your confidant. You know enough to ruin me, so I fear I must trust you as well."

"You may count on our discretion," Nicholas answered for both of us. Realizing my hand was still against his nicely rounded shoulder, I quickly removed it.

The men exchanged nods, and Nicholas continued as I let my eyes catalog details.

"We fear the carvings and murders may have something to do with Cor—Miss Beaumont." Nicholas switched to my formal name midsentence, and I was glad of the dim light that hopefully hid the heat rushing to my cheeks. If Lord Dawson Davies marked it unusual, he did not let on but kept his face impassive as he listened intently to Nicholas. "We found a bruise in the shape of the CAB Airlines logo on the first victim, and Miss Beaumont's name underlined in Mary Albright's passenger book. *CAB*—CAB Airlines. We do not know if someone has a vendetta against Clarence Beaumont, or Cora," Nicholas explained, enunciating the initial sounds in the names.

"Clarence Abner Beaumont, Cora Alexandria Beaumont, and CAB Airlines." I said my earlier thought aloud.

"We are taking precautions." Nicholas nodded gravely. "There is also the matter of the suffragette sash. Mary Albright was an outspoken women's vote advocate. It appears Collette shared her thoughts on the matter. It's possible these killings could be politically motivated, though we don't have an immediate connection to Lady Cadieux."

Dawson Davies was quiet as he studied the grisly scene before us. His brows, bushy and blond, drew together. Truthfully, I was impressed with his not being completely disturbed at the sight—or at least with his ability to hide his feelings. This murder was every bit as grotesque as the others, but in some ways, seeing Collette was easier than seeing Mary and Lady Cadieux. It was still shocking, but not as much as it once might have been. Likely, I'd just been desensitized to this level of macabre.

"I may have another theory. Do you know Mary Albright's profession?" Dawson Davies said.

"In the record book, it states she was to be employed as a domestic upon her arrival in England," Nicholas supplied.

"What are you thinking?" I asked.

"This may be far out on a limb, but what if these *are* politically motivated? You have three women with no apparent connection save the possibility of the women's vote. What if that *is* the connection?

CHAPTER 53
Nicholas

All the air seemed to hang suspended in the room.

I glanced at Cora.

"I don't mean to pry, Miss Beaumont, but do you or your father happen to have any ties to the suffragette movement?" Dawson Davies asked.

Cora's brows were drawn together. "I *do* think women should be allowed to vote," she started hesitantly.

I was in no way surprised by this information.

"But I do not have any formal ties to the movement."

"Did your father?" I prompted, finding that to be unlikely but feeling the need to voice the question anyway.

Her brows drew together. "The closest thing I can recall is a singular memory of Father sending money to his foreman, Harry Francis, who was overseeing some of the construction for the *Lady Air* over in India. Several of the mosaics and some of the handcrafted woodwork were done in India, then shipped and assembled in New York. But the money was intended to be given to support the Kalikrishna Girls' School. It was a free school for girls. For their education." She blinked away a sudden tear, and I wanted to comfort her.

"Anything else?" Dawson Davies asked gently.

Cora shook her head. "The money never even got to them. Harry Francis gambled with it. Lost it over the course of one fateful weekend. Father fired him immediately once he found out."

Something akin to guilt twinged in my middle. Was it so wrong of these women to want a say in their own lives? Thinking of the caste system in India, I supposed it wasn't so different from British class society. In which I *was* the top. Perhaps I should reevaluate how I conducted myself and my affairs.

"I think politics should be put back on the docket for motive," I said quietly.

"We should alert the doctor," Cora broke in.

I nodded. We needed as much information as we could get. I also wanted an army surrounding Cora to protect her. Though I thought I trusted Phillip Dawson Davies, I wasn't about to leave him alone with Cora and test that trust so early.

"Dawson Davies, I assume the head porter is in your pocket?"

Phillip blinked. "Yes. But how did you know?"

"I saw him slip you a note the night of the first ball. In the smoking room."

Phillip shook his head. "And here I thought I was being discreet. It seems my attempts at subterfuge have come to naught."

"I would not have been watching you so closely had my cousin not been on the receiving end of your attention," I admitted.

He smiled weakly. "It always comes back to a woman, doesn't it?"

Guilt niggled at me as Cora's presence burned beside me.

"Go fetch Porter McIntyre. Have him retrieve Dr. Bellson to come here. We'll need to alert Scotland Yard—the porter can send the message—then we need to arrange a transport to move

Collette to the refrigeration chamber as well. I hope there is enough ice."

Cora grimaced but nodded.

"I shall fetch McIntyre and the doctor. Is there anything else I should do as I'm on the way?" Dawson Davies shrugged helplessly.

"Don't become the next victim," Cora said.

"I'll do my best," Phillip said as he rose, dusting off the knees of his breeches. "Tristan, you should take up boxing." He gingerly rubbed his shoulder.

I grunted, starting to feel ashamed of my ungentlemanly behavior. "Yes, well, if I'm limping tomorrow, you'll know why," I admitted with a rueful smile. Phillip returned the gesture, nodded to both Cora and me, then quietly exited, shutting the door behind him.

It was just Cora and me and the dead woman.

Still crouched next to Cora, I drew my attention back to Collette's body. Cora leaned over, examining something on the floor.

"Nicholas, hand me the lantern?" she asked, a tremor in her voice. Without rising, I reached over to snag the metal-and-glass box and held it aloft.

Cora gasped, the light shining on her widened eyes as she fumbled with something in her fingertips. She turned to me, her other hand going to my chest, and my heart galloped beneath her touch, unsure what she was doing but aware that I was having an entirely inappropriate reaction as her fingers traced the buttons on my waistcoat. I swallowed as she skimmed every button on my vest.

"Cora?" I hedged, my voice on the edge of cracking.

"Nicholas." Her voice broke, a sliver of terror leaking in.

Her hand against my chest lightly circled over one of the silver buttons. They were custom buttons, adorned with a likeness of Debensley Manor and a hawk in flight over the top. Not that I was currently thinking overmuch about buttons, as I was more focused on breathing with her rather intimate touching along my chest.

Her deep-teal eyes met mine. Leaving her hand against my chest, she slowly drew her other up, a glint of silver shining in the palm of her hand.

It was a matching silver button. Suddenly, my attention was riveted on *buttons*.

"Nicholas." Her voice wavered. "You've been with me all night, and all your buttons are accounted for," she said fearfully. "Unless you have others just like this."

Terror and horror gripped my chest like a vise, painfully squeezing all the oxygen from my lungs.

"I do not. Only this vest."

And only one other person on this ship had the right to wear the buttons of Debensley Manor.

Terrance.

CHAPTER 54

Cora

I sat dumbly, alternately staring at the button in my hand and the matching buttons on Nicholas's waistcoat.

In some ways, holding that button that had lodged just underneath the corner of the rug was more shocking than finding another mutilated body.

"Surely," I stammered, "surely he can't be involved." I couldn't wrap my brain around it. The man I was to marry could not be a murderer. Not the boy I'd played with as a child. The man who smiled considerately at me. He could not—simply *could not*—be involved in such a heinous crime.

Nicholas's chest heaved under my hand. I snatched it back as I realized how inappropriate touching him was.

"It would seem he must be involved." Nicholas's voice was hoarse. My eyes flicked to his, finding anguish and confusion swirling in their green depths.

"Nicholas," I breathed. "I saw Terrance in the hallway leading to the actors' quarters at the intermission this evening." A heavy pause weighted the air between us. "What do we do?" I whispered.

Nicholas was silent a moment, his body rigid. He swallowed. Once. Twice. "We wait for the doctor. Then we find Terrance. *I* will find Terrance."

I couldn't help reaching out to carefully touch his hand. He was hurting. So was I. Our collective fates hung in the balance of what Terrance might have done. Nicholas gripped my fingers in silence.

***

Dr. Bellson puffed in nearly twenty minutes later, Porter McIntyre opting to stand at the door and take down our message to send to Scotland Yard. Nicholas and I had recovered from our shock enough to examine things as best we could while waiting. There wasn't much more to discover. Collette had no marks or bruising on her hands or arms, and her fingernails were kempt. So she hadn't struggled with her assailant. Did she know him? Had she, Mary, and Lady Cadieux all been taken in by a charming, homicidal maniac?

My head spun with ideas, none of them helpful, but all of them centering back to Terrance.

"This does not look good. Not at all," a rumpled Dr. Bellson commented as he motioned for Dawson Davies to come in behind him and hold up another lantern. Dawson Davies looked the worse for wear, his jaw discoloring, his clothing no longer neat, tidy, or tucked. His tie was askew and dangling round his neck. I absently wondered what Phee would think of him if she were to see him presently.

She'd probably stroke his poor, limp mustachios and bring him a soothing cup of tea.

Poor Dr. Bellson was in a similar state. His maroon silk dressing gown had been thrown on over his rumpled linen pants, and he had on house slippers as well. I cringed, thinking how those would soak up blood should they get too close.

"I shall do a cursory examination and report my findings as the last two times," he said as he squatted down near Collette's body and adjusted his spectacles, mustache twitching disdainfully. "Eh, what's this?" He paused his cursory examination and pulled the edge of Collette's dress back, wiping at some blood and revealing more of her hip. There, on the newly exposed flesh like embossing on a card, was the imprint of the CAB logo. Just like on Mary Albright's temple and on Lady Cadieux's forehead.

I gasped, and the doctor shook his head. My eyes found Nicholas. His lips were set in a grim line, and he gave the slightest indication toward the door. I took his expression to mean we should go find Terrance. I nodded. He tipped his head to Dawson Davies, who came over to us at the side of the room, giving the doctor room to work.

"Are you able enough to stay and monitor the doctor? Keep a watch and make sure the body is transported in disguise?"

Dawson Davies blinked. "Of course."

"This is what you need to do to have the body moved," I inserted quickly. I had not gone to all the trouble to keep Mary's and Lady Cadieux's bodies a secret only to have Collette's alert the ship and cause panic just before we docked in Southampton.

I shivered. Two days. I had two days to apprehend the murderer and stop this madness.

Or to discover if my fiancé *was* the murderer. And watch my life disintegrate.

I swallowed and quickly explained how we had moved the others through the hallways.

"I'll see it done." Dawson Davies nodded gravely after hearing my instructions.

"Have Porter McIntyre help you organize the food carts if you need. We'll need to completely involve him at this point so you can access the kitchens," Nicholas said. "There is another connection we want to check for relevance. We'll keep you updated as we find out more." Dawson Davies nodded again, and my heart fluttered as Nicholas put his fingers to the small of my back, quickly steering me from the room.

"What are we really going to say if . . . if things are what we fear?" I whispered as the door to the boiler room shut behind us.

"I don't know yet," Nicholas said, eyes closing momentarily. He swallowed even as my mouth dried. Too much of my future hinged on Terrance Tristan. Invisible spiders skittered over my skin, and I fought down the rising panic.

"We have to find him first," Nicholas rasped. "I . . . would feel better if I knew you were safely ensconced in your chambers," he admitted, meeting my gaze. His green eyes blazed with concern that warmed my heart.

"Please, Nicholas. Let me come with you. I need answers in this as much as you do." We stared at each other for long moments.

At last, he straightened, tugged his waistcoat down, and readjusted the black cape still hanging from his shoulders. "You stay behind me at all times. Do you understand?"

I nodded, relief that he wasn't shutting me out relaxing my shoulders even as my stomach tightened with apprehensive nerves.

"I cannot believe my brother a murderer, yet I cannot deny his involvement—either with Collette or her demise. Somehow, Terrance *is* involved."

I nodded, unsure what to say—what I *could* say—that might possibly improve this situation.

Nicholas checked his pocket watch and sighed. "It's nearly three thirty in the morning. Surely he's asleep in bed," he said unconvincingly.

"Then let us check there first," I said, willing it to be so. Nicholas nodded, and we set off down the corridor that would lead us to the servants' staircase.

CHAPTER 55
Nicholas

Dread squeezed my chest, and I felt ill. The ramifications of what Terry's involvement in a murder would bring made the breath seize in my lungs. Such despicableness would touch every corner of our lives, and the Tristan name would never recover.

Moreover, betrayal burned in my gut, at Terry's actions as they directly related to me but also extending to Cora. It was as hard to face the consequences Terry's actions would have upon her as it was to consider the consequences to my own life.

I wanted to reach out and clasp Cora's hand, as much to comfort her as to feel her skin against mine. Though she made my heart race, she also calmed me. I swallowed and fully admitted it to myself. I . . . did not feel *brotherly* toward her. It was yet another issue I needed to address. But not in this moment.

We stepped from the servants' staircase and into the first-class hallway. The plush carpets emblazoned with their blue CAB logos running down the hallway reminded me of fresh blood swirling around the bruised letters impressed into the victims—which only reminded me of the murdered women. I took a breath through my mouth and fished my key from my trouser pocket. The door to my chambers was just ahead. Ten more paces. We halted.

Cora's fingers drifted over my forearm, raising every hair on my body. I glanced down at her. The gaslight shone on the side of her face, showing me her steady deep blue-green eyes. She stared back up at me, resolute, lending me some of her unflappable courage.

I loved her for it.

She nodded gamely.

I took a breath and turned the key.

The door swung open into darkness.

Heart in my throat, I reached into the blackness and fumbled for the knob that would bring the gas lamp on the wall to life.

My fingers twitched over the knob, and light whooshed into the room.

Motioning Cora to stay behind me, I crept into the sitting room of my chambers and moved toward the bedroom. The breath rattled in my chest, competing with my thundering heart rate. This was my brother. My brother whom I loved. Whom I'd grown up with. With whom I shared blood and family.

My brother who might have murdered Collette.

I stood at the door, hesitating. Fear squeezed the back of my throat. The heat from Cora's body standing behind me gave me the courage to open the door.

Light from the sitting room flooded into the bedchamber.

Two made beds stared back at me.

Terrance was not here.

CHAPTER 56

Cora

Anxious fear rattled my bones.

Terrance was gone. My fiancé could well be the murderer.

Hysteria bubbled up in my throat, but I swallowed it back down, determined it would not get the better of me. A pair of white gloves rested on the nightstand. The barest hint of red crept over one finger.

Dashing across the room, I snatched the offending garments up and held up the stained finger to the light. It was red. I couldn't tell if it was blood or something else, but it looked like Terrance had swiped the edge of something bloody, a tiny swath of red dancing across the pointer finger of his glove.

I thought my stomach might rebel right there on the Turkish rug.

I took a deep breath, willing my rebellious stomach into submission.

"Surely there is a logical, rational explanation for this," I whispered into the empty room. I met Nicholas's gaze, forcing the panic to stay behind my teeth.

"The sooner we find Terrance and hear it, the better," Nicholas answered, his voice raw. He took the gloves from me, looked hard at them, then flung them on the bed.

Disregarding propriety again, Nicholas grabbed my hand and spun us back toward the door. He dropped my hand quickly to shove his key in and roll the tumblers with a click. Pocketing his key, he grasped my hand again, and I realized it was as much for his benefit as it was for mine. We were both distraught, terrified at what we might yet discover this night but determined to uncover it, no matter the cost.

I squeezed Nicholas's fingers. He blew out a ragged breath as we descended the first-class hallway. Pausing at the end of the corridor, I peered around Nicholas's broad shoulders. No one was in the hallway. Sneaking to the servants' passage at the opposite end, we slipped in like shadow wraiths.

"Where are we looking first?" I whispered as the door snicked shut behind us. Nicholas paused, and in the darkness, I bumped into his back. I didn't step away but let my body remain against his, needing the contact.

"The troupe's quarters. There . . . there would be a mess to clean up."

Ice shivered down my spine, but I didn't dare give voice to my fears.

"Even if he is not there, there may yet be evidence. Obviously, Collette was moved," he concluded.

I nodded, my cheek brushing his shoulder blade. "All right," I agreed softly. "Ooh," I moaned softly.

"What?" He turned in the tight confines of the hallway, his hands cupping my upper arms.

"When I met Terrance at the intermission—when Dawson Davies disappeared, I followed after him—" Nicholas frowned, likely at my going off alone. "I followed Dawson Davies to the actors' hallway behind the stage. There I lost Dawson Davies, but Terrance found me. He was coming back from the direction of the troupe's area." I bit my lip. It was one more nail in the coffin lid of Terrance's guilt.

Nicholas swore. Then crushed me to his chest. "We'll figure this out," he whispered, though I wasn't sure if it was for my sake or his own. I inhaled the manly scent of him, my belly pitching wildly at his nearness. I squeezed my eyes shut, and of their own accord, my arms twined around his back.

Motionless for several heartbeats, we took what solace we could of each other, then wordlessly let go to continue with our heinous mission. We crept quickly and quietly down the stairs until a splash of paint let us know the door we'd come to would lead us into the second-class corridor.

Silent as church mice, we held our collective breath and stole into the hallway. A clatter and a tinkle of laughter sounded from the second-class lounge not far from where we stood. The troupe was all quartered in a cluster of rooms located next to a ready room and the prop storage chamber near a doorway that led directly above into the grand ballroom.

Nicholas paused and clenched his jaw, nodding back toward the servants' stairwell. We slipped back in to hold a hushed conversation.

"If we go charging in there with people about, it will raise more questions than answers." He raked his hands through his thick hair, standing it on end.

I reached for his agitated hands, clasping them still in my icy-cold ones. "Then let us look with our eyes and remain unseen and unheard."

He nodded. "I did not expect to find people still awake at this ungodly hour. Well, except maybe the murderer," he finished darkly.

I had no words for that, as we shared the same intense fear that perhaps we were speaking of Terrance.

Once more, we crept through the servants' entrance and down into the corridor. Tingles raced up my arms as the tinkling laughter sounded once more, breathy, followed by the slosh of liquid in a crock.

Peering around the edge of the doorway, I noted a man and a woman sitting opposite each other, a deck of playing cards spread out on the tabletop between them. The woman picked up the jug, took a full swig, then wiped the back of her hand over her mouth. The man leaned forward, wavering. She giggled as he clumsily *thwapped* a card down, a stupid smile on his lips. They were both properly overcome with drink.

Without giving either of them pause, we moved down the hallway, scouring every inch of the empty prop room and the ready room outside the ballroom.

Coming up empty, we crossed the ballroom. All the lights were out. We kept to the edge as we cut across to the doorway on the far side. I shivered in the blackness.

Black, bleak, and desolate, like my prospects and my future if Terrance was the murderer.

CHAPTER 57
Nicholas

We searched high and low, every nook and cranny either of us could conceive of searching. Not even the engine room and storage bays remained unchecked. We traced our weary steps back to my shared quarters only to find them still empty. Though neither of us spoke of it, the fear of finding another body with Terrance poised over it, a bloody knife in his hand, hummed between us.

At last, exhausted and out of options, we sank into the pristine chairs of the first-class observatory. Thunder rumbled and lightning flashed—plainly visible through the bank of windows—sending electricity prickling over my skin at its nearness.

New fear rippled in my belly.

"This isn't good. Nicholas; the storm has caught us. We may have more than present circumstances to worry us," Cora said, her eyes flashing the same fear that rushed through me.

I chewed my lower lip as I stared at the two cups of tea we'd helped ourselves to from the urn kept for overnight visitors to the observatory.

Cora rubbed the heels of her hands against her eyes. Mine were so tired they felt full of grit.

"Nicholas," Cora said, her voice low. I raised my eyes. "What . . ." She cleared her throat. "What if Terrance wasn't the perpetrator? We've searched these past hours with no trace of him." She swallowed, a crease appearing between her brows as new adrenaline began pumping through my veins. She continued, "What if we found the button not because he was enacting the crime, but because he was another victim?" Cora's voice strangled over the last word.

Breath left my lungs in a whoosh as her words sank into my overtired mind.

"Oh, Nicholas," she murmured.

Emotion seized my throat, and I took my cup of tea and slung back the contents, wishing for all the world it was strong drink that would numb the pain and panic thrumming through me. "We must go to Captain Cordello at once. We must find Terrance. The time for secrecy may be over."

She nodded, gulped her own tea, and rose. She stumbled as the airship pitched and lightning cracked again. Cora whimpered. Extra mindful of lines I should not cross, as I'd already crossed several of them in the past hours, I did not touch her but hovered, herding us both out into the lashing rain in order to climb the steps that would lead us to the bridge of the *Lady Air*.

Whether Terrance was murderer or victim, I'd raze this ship to the ground if I had to.

I would find my brother.

⋅•⋇•⋅

Though it was yet early, Captain Cordello stood resolutely at the helm of the ship when we barged in.

"Your Lordship. Miss Beaumont," he said icily as we ascended the few steps to stand beside him.

"Captain," I said, slinging rainwater and too tired and fearful for my brother to argue with the man and call him on his rude behavior. "You must make a search for my brother at once. He has been missing all evening, and we fear something untoward may have happened to him."

Captain Cordello blinked twice before giving a snort of laughter. "*Untoward?* I suppose some might call matrimony *untoward.*" His eyes cut to Cora. She stood stock still as the blood drained from her face.

My brain was sluggish, and it took me a moment before the full import of his words struck me.

"Matrimony?" Cora whispered beside me.

Cordello raised an eyebrow. "One can hardly say no to the son of a duke when he wakes you in the middle of the night and makes demands. I married him myself, right here on this bridge, some hours ago."

Fully alert now, I did not miss the sting behind the man's tone, nor the way his gaze hardened as he watched Cora all but crumple beneath the heat of his words. Something inside me snapped, and I grabbed the man's lapels and spoke within three inches of his face.

"It's a pity you did not first consult the *heir* to the dukedom. I swear to you, you will never captain another voyage as long as you live. You have made an enemy far greater than the friend you thought you earned on this day."

The captain's eyes widened as fear flashed across his features. Perhaps he was only just realizing how deeply he had transgressed. While Terrance did hold a certain degree of power, I held more. By aligning himself with the lesser of the two of us, Captain Cordello had made a mortal enemy of the House of Exford and Debensley.

Thunder boomed and the ship rocked, as if in accordance with the blackening of my mood.

Terror danced through Cora's eyes as the ship roiled hard enough I lost my grip on Cordello and went skidding backward.

"Get this ship righted and through this storm, or so help me, I'll pitch you off the deck myself," I growled.

Shakily, the captain nodded, giving his full attention to the wheel and steering. He hollered orders to the airshipmen as the storm heaved around us, the glassed bay of windows dark with the angry thunderheads surrounding us.

"We need to leave here," Cora said, tugging on my hand.

"Wait." I turned back to Cordello. "Who did he marry?"

"An actress."

With one last oath under my breath, I wrenched the doors open and led Cora back through the pelting rain and into the hallway of the first class.

Had he married Collette? Before she was killed? Was Collette victim, sister-in-law, or something else?

And where was Terry?

CHAPTER 58

Cora

My life in society had as good as ended. My freedom, so close within my grasp, vanished like smoke. I stared despondently at the ring on my left hand, the dark-green jewel shadowy and dull in the light of the storm. Maybe it was cursed. Like the jewels of a pharaoh's stash.

The weight of failed expectations, of betrayal, disappointment, and an agonizing fear of what my future held threatened to suffocate me.

I shivered, gasping for air.

"Cora," Nicholas called, his tone implying he'd said my name a few times.

I blinked, biting the inside of my lip to keep it from quivering.

"We must wait out the storm. We both need sleep. We will resume once the storm blows itself out, or once we're not so tired we can stand up straight again," he said with a sad imitation of a smile. "Will you be all right in your chambers?" He swallowed, rainwater dripping down his face in little rivulets from his hair from the lashing we'd taken crossing the deck.

There was nothing to say. I nodded and turned numbly to my door, my fingers shaking as I inserted the key.

"Cora, I swear, I'll fix this," Nicholas whispered, barely audible over the storm. "I cannot believe Terry would do something so foolish, nor am I fully convinced that the captain legally wed anyone."

My gaze jerked to his face. Sincerity shone in his eyes, even as the ship swayed, and I clutched at the door. Even if Terrance wasn't legally wed to another, his rejection stung like salt and lemon juice over an open wound. Tears pricked the back of my eyes as I rocked with the motion of my ship.

"Go. Bunker down," he said with another weak smile. "We'll figure this all out once the storm blows over."

I nodded, heartened at his words but still skeptical. But on one count, he was right. There was nothing to do now but wait for the storm to pass.

If it didn't kill us first.

Slipping into my quarters, I first noticed the stillness. Not the quiet—the storm raged beyond the portholes and the wind was deafening. But the room was too still. It was approaching mid-morning. Ophelia should have been up, dressed, and chomping at the bit to get details of my whereabouts.

"Phee?" I said softly.

She groaned as a mound of blankets moved on her bed. She'd been so still; I hadn't even realized she was there.

"Phee, are you well?" I called louder, crossing the room.

She moaned again, her hand falling limply from the bed. Clutching it, I squeezed it gently, her pulse racing under her skin. "Phee, dearest, whatever is the matter?" Her skin was clammy and cool.

"Stomach . . . legs . . . ache . . ." A shiver racked her slight frame, and sweat broke out afresh on her forehead.

"I'll fetch the physician, Phee. Hang on," I promised.

Phee moaned weakly, her eyes rolled back, and she fainted dead away.

"Phee? Ophelia?" I called frantically.

"Ah, Miss Beaumont. I've just cut a piece of this decadent almond coffee cake all frosted in chocolate ganache and left it for poor Mrs. Beesly. Won't you come and have a slice? The cook assures me it's a special breakfast treat, served on account of the storm making passengers nervous," Rose said as she appeared in the doorway between my chaperone's adjoined chambers, holding a lovely chocolate-iced round cake. I could smell the chocolate and almonds from across the room. Tired, scared, wet, and weary beyond comprehension, I felt my patience snap.

"Rose, can you not see that Lady Ophelia is ill? Go fetch the doctor at once."

"Oh, miss, 'tis naught but a bout of airsickness. She but needs to rest."

Fear for Ophelia and anger, both at Rose's refusal to immediately comply and anger at myself for my impotence, rose in me like a tidal wave.

"Rose, go at once and fetch the doctor, or I will have you dismissed." My words were sharp and clipped.

Rose smirked, her brown eyes going hard and cold. Just then, the ship pitched. I stumbled as Rose lurched, the rim of the cake hitting her in the face and smearing chocolate ganache on her upper lip.

Aghast, I stared as she forcibly threw the cake down, the plate shattering, and righted herself.

"It would have been easier for you if you'd just eaten the cake."

Recognition slapped me across the face hard enough I stumbled a step back. The dark eyes full of hate, the chocolate icing making a perfect mustache on her upper lip. Lightning crashed outside the ship, and for one blinding moment, it wasn't Rose at all who stood before me.

It was the man who'd held Mary Albright.

Mary Albright in her yellow sash, her dark hair cascading around her lover. Mary Albright who'd been brutally murdered.

Who'd been held by no lover . . . but by my maidservant in disguise.

"You," I stammered, jerking back another step. Horror clouded over my vision.

Rose nodded knowingly, wiping the smear of frosting from her upper lip.

"No one ever expects a woman to do a man's job." Casually, she wiped her finger and then her upper lip on her white apron, leaving a dark smudge across the pristine fabric.

My stomach clenched. Shock gripped me tight, making my breaths difficult. Phee moaned again.

"What . . . what have you done to Ophelia?" My voice was weak, my brain racing to put the pieces together and form a plan of action.

"Well, I'm afraid it's not really airsickness at all. This chocolate almond cake really is superb. You should have a piece. I assure you, it would be far preferable to what I shall have to do to you now. I had hoped to pretty up Lady Davenport, what with her political ties and her support of the suffragette movement. I saw that yellow rosette in her drawer; she kept her secret well. I never suspected. It would have made things so much more satisfying to leave one more message for you. Have you

been terrified? Did you get all my messages?" Her eyes blazed
with a manic passion, a sneer of a smile curling her lips.

Oh, blast.

"But . . . but why?" I stammered as I backed a step away
from her. "Why are you doing this?" The ship rocked, and I
swayed, my hands flying out to help keep my balance. My pocket
thumped against my thigh with the roiling of the ship.

My knife!

Rose smirked before baring her teeth. "Your father took
everything from me. Do you know who I am? Who I really am?"

I shook my head, at a complete loss as terror and bile rose in
my throat.

"You will. My father was Harry Francis." She waited, crossing the room so that she completely blocked my exit.

"My father's foreman who oversaw parts of the airship construction in India?" I said, breathless and desperate to keep her
talking. As slowly as I dared, I let my arms fall to my sides,
closer to my knife.

"A brilliant man who your father sacked and then doomed—
and me with him—to the dregs of society. Your father *ruined* my
father, and then ruined *me*!"

"Rose," I pleaded, "your father stole money intended to fund
a girls' school. He stole it, then lost it all gambling and drinking."

"No!" Rose seethed, venom dripping from her voice. "No,"
she said again, more controlled. "Father liked to drink and gam-
ble on occasion, but he'd never go so far."

Casually, she picked up the beautiful cast-iron statue of
Athena. *Goddess of wisdom indeed,* my inner cynic quipped. *She'll
look ever so wise with my brains splattered upon her.*

"My father was a good man. An honorable man. Clarence
Abner Beaumont put him in an early grave when he destroyed

my father's reputation and stole our livelihood." She hefted the statuette, letting Athena's head smack her palm once, twice, three times, as she stared at me with hungry eyes.

"Is that what you did to Collette? Smash her over the head?" I gulped, inching my hand to my pocket.

"Ruined a good apron with her mess. At least the first one went quickly and quietly. My hands around her pretty little neck." Mania blazed off her in waves. "I confess, I did expect my work to be more publicized. It would have been nice if it had been given its proper due. Instead, you had to keep things quiet." She curled her lip like a toddler who has been told he cannot have another sweet. "That first girl? She was a domestic. I had to be a domestic, too, once Father drank himself to death." She sniffed. "I had planned to kill a seamstress on board next. I tried to work as a seamstress too. They didn't like it when I got blood on their clothes. Wretched needles." She grimaced. Thunder pealed, and the ground tilted enough my arms windmilled. Rose was anchored to the floor, Athena at the ready once she finished her monologue.

Keep her talking! I needed to stall! Something, anything, until I could gain the upper hand.

"Why did you kill Lady Cadieux?" I asked.

A truly devious smile broke over her features. "That was a stroke of luck. Do you know who the memsahib was that dismissed me from her house? Yes, she made me call her *memsahib* to make herself feel exalted." Rose took a step toward me.

"Who was she?" I asked quickly.

Rose halted, smiling again. "It was Lady Cadieux's own daughter. So when I found the old lady aboard ship, that was a sweet little piece of revenge I hadn't counted on. I've never had so much fun as I did pressing my father's CAB token to her forehead and smashing it down to make sure it would leave a calling card. Wasn't that a nice touch? I wanted you to be sure that all these deaths were your fault."

"And Collette? The actress? Why kill her?" Was she Terrance's wife? Was he a widower—or Rose's next victim? Nausea chafed against my innards.

"She was an accident. She saw me poisoning the cake last night. That wouldn't do, so I had to do away with her." Rose frowned. "Why were you in her quarters? I left her where she lay in the middle of her floor between the two beds." Rose cocked her head to the side, puzzling it out.

"She was moved." I gasped as the floor angled again and lightning crashed outside the porthole. I bit the inside of my cheek hard enough it drew blood.

Rose shrugged. "So long as you found her. Finally, since Clarence Abner Beaumont is dead, I shall kill Cora Alexandria Beaumont in his stead, and I shall have my vengeance for my father and for my stolen life."

"Rose, please. Listen to yourself! I had nothing to do with your father or his losing his job. I'm sorry for your suffering. Put the statuette down, and let's talk more. I can give you money," I pleaded.

Rose snorted. "Money. I'd rather see you rot." She advanced, Athena raised in her grip. Glee crossed her face, and I gave up on subtlety and grabbed my knife. I wished my threat against Dawson Davies hadn't been a bluff. What I wouldn't give in this moment to have accurate knife-throwing skills.

Rose raised an unimpressed eyebrow. "A knife? Have you not seen my precision with your precursors?" Rose was too close now. If I backed up, I'd only hit the wall to the wash closet. I circled as best I could nearer the door. Rose swiped with the statue, growling as it narrowly missed me.

"Rose, you don't need to do this. I have nothing to do with this," I panted desperately. Icy sweat trickled down my spine.

"Your family is the reason for all my misery. I've waited *years* for this. I'll kill you with my bare hands, and I'll relish every drop of your blood that flows from your broken body."

"You're insane!" I gave up any pretense of subtlety. Rose lunged, and I sidestepped again, feeling the whiff of air the statue created.

"Be still," Rose grunted, her movements teetering as a gust of wind blasted into the side of the *Lady Air*.

"And let you bludgeon me to death? Thanks ever so much for the offer, but I'll pass." I had no idea where such bravado came from, but it bubbled up and out before I could censor it.

A feral noise ripped from her throat, and this time, Rose sprang at me. I had no hope of deflecting it, and we crashed to the ground. The statuette dented the floor beside my head as I frantically squirmed, desperately trying to find purchase against her with my blade.

I screamed for all I was worth, praying it could be heard above the storm, attempting in vain to use my knife against my enemy. The ship rolled, and we tumbled with it. I wiggled out from under Rose, only to receive an excruciating blow that ripped open the flesh of my arm. My upper arm took only half the intended blow, but even so, blood soaked through my sleeve instantly, my grip on my knife growing limp.

Shoving the rising panic down, I rolled away, only to find my skirts trapped beneath Rose's heavier frame.

"Ha!" she gloated, and it was moment enough for me to switch my knife to my less dominant hand. Kicking out, I caught her square in the nose. I wished I'd had my heeled boots on instead of my slippers.

Rose keeled back and howled as blood streamed from her now-mishappen nose. Nausea churned in my gut at what I'd just done, but self-preservation quickly covered any remorse I might have suffered.

"You'll pay for this," she uttered, blood streaming over her lips and bubbling at her words.

Forgetting Athena, she lunged again, hands like claws, ready to slice me to ribbons. I rolled away, but not before she grabbed the bun at the back of my head.

I screamed again, as much in terror as in pain as hair ripped from my scalp and brought me to a sudden halt.

A crash against the door brought a growl from Rose and a startled yelp from me.

"Cora?" Another bang on the door.

"Nicholas!" I shrieked. "Help! The—it's Rose. *The murderer is Rose!*" I screamed.

A crash of thunder boomed, shrouding my words, but the tempo of thumping at the door increased and the metal clanging of the doorknob jangled in time with my frenzied nerves. Nicholas shouted from the other side, but I couldn't focus on the words. Rose yanked me by my hair, eliciting another scream of pain from me.

Suddenly, Rose's hands were at my throat, cutting off my air. Desperately, I flailed as black dots swam at the edges of my vision. Stabbing back blindly with my left hand, I prayed my knife would find purchase somewhere.

It swished through the air as Rose bodily hauled me to my feet and braced me against her chest. Her fingers cut into my neck as my body, starved of oxygen and weak with blood loss, flailed. I stabbed again, and this time, my knife made contact.

Rose jerked wordlessly, loosening her grip enough that I shifted my weight. Kicking back with my heel, I caught her in the shin. She released me with a grunt and staggered back toward the doorway between our adjoined rooms. I stumbled forward, gasping for air like a fish on land, my knife dropped in the fray.

Dazed as oxygen flooded my system even as my vision wavered, I became dimly aware of two things happening at once. Like a phantom wraith, Mrs. Beesly, white as a sheet and as insubstantial as a ghost, appeared behind Rose.

The door crashed open, spraying splinters into the room.

"Cora!" Nicholas shouted as he charged into the chamber.

Glass and amber liquid exploded behind Rose's head. Seemingly in slow motion, Rose's eyes went vacant, and she dropped like a stone to reveal Mrs. Beesly standing like a queen, the neck of a broken decanter clutched in her bony hand.

"Wretch," the old woman croaked as she tottered back into her quarters.

"Phee," I rasped, one hand braced on my knee, the other weakly pointing at Ophelia's prone form. "Get the doctor." The words scraped themselves like nails over my bruised vocal chords. My arm trembled and dropped uselessly to my side, blood slicking my skin and sticking my shirt to my arm. Dizzy spots hazed my vision.

"Fetch the doctor, now! You, secure that woman," Nicholas commanded. I was vaguely aware that several CAB-liveried attendants were grouped about the door. Two of them peeled off, and their heavy footfalls echoed down the hallway until another crash of thunder and flash of lightning sent us all swaying. The other two men wrenched Rose from the floor, dragged her bleeding form to a corner, secured her, and stood guard.

I sank completely to the floor, willing now for the storm to take me. Rose was responsible for the murders aboard my ship. Even if the winds raged and tore us to pieces, better that than that evil woman stalking her next victim.

"Cora? Cora! *Cora*," Nicholas said as he crouched in front of me, the urgency of his tone pulling my gaze to his. His warm hands cupped my face as his eyes scoured over me, snagging on my bloodied arm. "Come." It wasn't a request but a command. Without waiting for my shocked brain to respond, Nicholas rose from his squat, bent, and scooped me into his arms. My head fell against his shoulder and my eyes closed of their own volition. I felt the softness of my mattress beneath me and let the darkness take me under.

CHAPTER 59
Cora

My arm hurt like the devil himself had set it on fire. I glanced down, my shoulder and arm bare but for the thin strap of my chemise. White bandaging circled my upper arm, a faint line of blood welling through the stitches Dr. Bellson had put in to hold my skin together.

I'd attempted napping. It hadn't taken. I was cranky, angry, and more than a little depressed. But I wanted answers more than anything else. Nicholas had left once Dr. Bellson had arrived, largely because propriety demanded he do so. It was gratifying to know he hadn't wanted to leave us. He'd gone, swearing he'd search room to room if he had to, in order to find Terrance and . . . anyone else he might be with.

My heart dropped at the thought, and dread crawled up my spine. I shoved the thoughts away. I would not speculate. I would not focus on what could be the collapse of the rest of my life. Instead, I looked across the room to Phee, who was sleeping, blankets still clenched in her fists.

Dr. Bellson had induced Phee to vomit, and she was currently reposing, her face still wan and pale, but she seemed to be resting easier at least. Arsenic, he'd later confirmed.

He'd stitched my arm up—I was sure to have an impressive scar that would ever remind me of this harrowing journey and the crash of Athena against my flesh. Maybe it would remind me to use a bit more wisdom in future, though I wasn't sure what I'd have done differently, given the chance.

The relief of knowing that Rose Francis was done with her escapade of horror lifted the burdensome weight from my shoulders. But again, it left room for all the nasty doubts about my uncertain future to creep back in. I put off contacting my half brother. There was no need to involve him before I had to. He'd take any opportunity to steal my dowry or my inheritance and package me off to the first available man who would take a tainted woman. That thought, too, was nearly enough to induce vomiting.

Growling at the futility of my thoughts and my frustration with life in general, I threw back my coverlet and spun around, throwing my legs over the side of the bed. When no dizziness assaulted me, I stood and crossed to the wardrobe. I swayed as thunder boomed and the ship shivered. I was so disgusted with the state of things that I was too tired, even, to be realistically scared of the storm. Now that it was upon us, it felt useless to worry about it. There was nothing more I could do. If we were struck by lightning, we'd perish. No action of mine could prevent it.

Hissing as pain sliced up my arm, I kept it close to my chest as I awkwardly grabbed a teal silk faille tea dress that I thought I could do up with one hand. My corset was out of the question. And if ever I deserved a day without its confines, today was it. A tea dress really was not appropriate attire for this time of day, or for marauding down the airship corridors, but propriety could go sit on a tack today.

It took far longer than I cared to admit to struggle into my clothes. After the debacle with Rose, I didn't want another lady's maid helping. I'd had enough. I threw a warm cape over my shoulders—both for the warmth and to cover my lack of expected underclothes. There was nothing to be done for my hair. I bit my lip. Finding a tortoiseshell two-pronged comb, I awkwardly twisted my hair up in it with one hand and secured it at the base of my neck. It wasn't properly fixed, by any means, but it was good enough.

With one more glance at Phee, who was still sleeping, I marched to the door and slipped into the hallway. I knocked smartly on Nicholas's door. If he hadn't found Terrance by now, I'd tear my own ship apart if I had to in order to get answers.

Thunder pealed and a gust rocked the airship. I gripped the doorframe just as Nicholas opened it. The ship pitched again, and I crashed against his chest. His hands found my waist, and all rational thoughts fled.

For one brief, terrifying moment, I hoped Terrance *had* married someone else. The thought was banished as my arm bumped against Nicholas and I winced and sucked in a sharp breath against the jagged throbbing.

"Cora," Nicholas gaped, staring at me like I'd grown two heads.

I realized I looked a fright, but I hadn't thought it was all *that* bad. Clearly, I was wrong.

"Close your mouth, Nicholas. It's not as if I've sprouted wings," I snapped testily.

He snorted. "Not a feather in sight. But you shouldn't be out of bed. Not only is the storm still spitting its venom at us, but you've only been stitched up little more than an hour ago. Why aren't you asleep?"

I glared, my bad temper on full display. "Because I'm exhausted beyond sleep, in pain, and sick over what my *fiancé* might have done."

Nicholas's face gentled as pain lurked in his gaze and melted some of my ire. "Cora."

Just as he opened his mouth to say more, none other than Porter McIntyre rounded the corner. Nicholas immediately dropped his hand from my waist, though his other still hovered near my back should I waver.

"Lord . . . Lord Tristan," the man puffed as he braced a hand against the wall and tried to catch his breath.

"What is it?" Alarm sounded clearly in Nicholas's tone, and anxious knots began clenching in my belly. My fingers dug into the folds of my skirt.

"You brother. The other Lord Tristan. He's been found." The porter's eyes flashed to mine.

"Spit it out," I ordered as my teeth ground together.

"He's been found . . . in a delicate position."

Blood rushed from my head, and I swayed. Nicholas put his hand against my shoulder, and my blood suddenly started pumping again.

"Where?" Nicholas bit the word out.

"In one of the storerooms near the actors' quarters."

"Take me there at once," Nicholas said with no room for protest. "Cora"—he turned to me—"though I fear it's futile to even suggest it, but are you sure you won't rest and let me deal with this?"

I gave him a tired smile that probably appeared more like a grimace. "It *is* futile to even suggest it. But thank you for the consideration just the same."

Nicholas shrugged, then nodded toward the porter. "Lead the way."

We tripped and traipsed our way through the hall as the ship continued racing against nature.

I felt I was racing against my own fate.

CHAPTER 60
Nicholas

I was surprised to find Phillip Dawson Davies standing, still disheveled and unkempt and very much looking like he'd been in a brawl—I was doing everything I could not to limp on my own impressively bruised hip—standing like an imperial guard, arms crossed and a scowl on his face, outside the door where Porter McIntyre led us.

"Lord Tristan," Dawson Davies said with a sketched bow. "My apologies to be the one to inform you that we've found your brother." He turned to Cora. "And my apologies to you, Miss Beaumont," he whispered. Pain lurked in his gaze.

Cora's chin trembled, but otherwise, her face remained impassive. I knew her well enough to know she was likely mustering the last of her impressive courage, and I wanted to rip into Terrance all the more for it.

I glanced at Cora. Whatever we found on the other side of this door was bound to hurt her irreparably.

"Will you wait?" I asked softly. *Let me take care of this one thing for you so I can spare you some pain,* my brain screamed at her.

"After what I've seen on this voyage, everything I've endured in the past few hours, and what I've imagined because of it, I doubt anything I might find inside this room could be worse."

Disregarding the eyes watching us, I leaned down to whisper my next words. "If I asked you to wait and let me take care of this, would you?" I pulled back, searching her face.

Anger and hurt flashed over her features, then morphed into something else as I watched her.

She took a steadying breath. "I would."

My heart swelled at the respect in her tone.

"But I don't think you would ask that of me," she said softly.

I grinned ruefully. "As you would, then."

I met Phillip's gaze. He nodded, then cranked the handle on the door and swung it open.

The first thing my eyes landed on was my brother. He sat on the edge of a lump of blankets, his shirt askew, feet bare, hair disheveled, and eyes rimmed in red.

Cora gasped beside me, and my gaze flew to her before I could register anything else in the room. Cora's mouth was set in a hard line, anger, disbelief, and shock stamped across her face. I followed her line of sight and locked on to the other person in the room.

The beautiful actress—the one whose eyes had been lined in kohl the night Phee snubbed Dawson Davies. My heart stuttered to a stop.

"Terrance Tristan," I said, but no other words would come.

My brother blearily eyed me, a sloppy smile on his face. "Congratulate me, broffer. I'm a married man. No more forshed eng . . . engoog . . . wivesh on me. I picked my own." He leaned over and plastered a wet kiss on the side of the woman's head, his hand resting on her waist in a most intimate fashion.

"What is wrong with him?" I thundered, not sure who I was asking but certain I would have answers.

"He's drunk on absinthe," Cora said woodenly beside me. Sure enough, there were two glasses on the floor near one corner of the blankets. One was empty, the other still full of the lime-green liquid.

My stomach churned. Terrance was too drunk to do much of anything, let alone answer questions. My steely gaze landed on the woman. Her dark eyes were astonishingly clear, and though she wore a haughty expression, there was real fear lurking in her brown eyes.

"Who are you?" I bit the words out tersely. She was about to receive the full weight of the ire of the heir of Debensley.

"I am the legally wed wife of Lord Terrance Tristan, second son to the Duke of Exford and Debensley." Her voice was London accented and not the clipped vowels of the upper class.

"She's bloody *Pauline Swift*," Dawson Davies growled from behind me.

The blackmailer. Terrance had married Phillip Dawson Davies's *blackmailer*?

"You wretched fool," I muttered at my brother. "Why would you do such a thing?" I wanted to throttle him. Beat him until he came to his senses and realized the gravity of what he'd done.

"Becash I love her. Met in London, we did. At the theater. Bacshtage. Brokenhearted when she had to leave. Told her I'd protect sher, but she needed to leave. Bully." His head swiveled to Dawson Davies. "Are you the bully?" His unfocused eyes swung back to the woman beside him. "But then I founded you here. Couldn't believe my besht fortune." He smiled stupidly at his bride. She smiled back, though her expression was still tinged in fear. Terry's head bobbed on his neck, and he focused on Cora—perhaps only noticing her presence for the first time. "Oh. Cora. Shorry. You're shwell. But I don't love you. I love Lina. Lina Pearl ish my wife. I love her. I loved her in London. I love her now." He grinned, no reserve, no remorse, completely, utterly, smothering-the-parrot drunk on absinthe.

Cora inhaled sharply, putting pieces together while I still tried to determine the parameters of the puzzle before us.

"*You* are who he has been spending all his time with. Not at billiards, not with the Crackford men, not . . ." She paused. "It's *you*. It's been *you* this whole time. You who have stolen my fiancé and my future." Cora's voice cracked along with my heart. Did she care for Terrance so very much, then? That thought caused a fresh pang to well up inside my chest.

Lina's—Pauline's—eyes softened. "I had to. I had to marry him. I left England trying to outrun me mistakes. But then . . ." She cast her eyes furtively to Dawson Davies. "Then . . ."

"Spit it out." Dawson Davies ground the words between his clenched teeth.

Pauline's eyes filled with tears. "I found out things I shouldn't have. I was wrong. I tried to use those things to me own advantage." A tear spilled over. "But then you paid, and Lord Saverton, he . . . he didn't. He tried to have me killed!" She sobbed, and Terrance sloppily put an arm around her shoulders. "I knew I had to get somewhere he could never find me. That's why I blackmailed you for such a sum. I had to leave. But I'd met Terrance doing some odd work at the theater. He was kind. But he's a lord; what could I do? When I got the money, I ran. Ran all the way to America. I tried to find work. There was nothin'. No one would hire me. I was nearing the last of my money." She glanced again at Dawson Davies, who still stood impassively with his arms crossed over his chest. "Your money," she amended in a whisper. "When I found the airship was lookin' for workers. I managed a part in the acting troupe on account that I worked some in the London theater." She leaned heavily into Terrance. "And I saw my hero again."

Terrance beamed, his face a wreath of smiles and drunken wrinkles. "In marrying him, I have secured me own future—which I mightn't have otherwise had. In marrying a duke's son, I'm safe. Lord Saverton can't touch me, even if I go back to England." Her chin rose. "Would you have me dead instead?" Her voice cracked. "Can you blame me for taking his protection?" Tears streamed down the woman's face. "Also, did you know that there is a murderer aboard this ship? Someone left Collette—my roommate—dead as a doornail in the middle of our room." Pauline fidgeted with the edge of the blanket. "All this way, and still death chases me. Terrance, don't let them take me!" she wailed into his shoulder.

"There, there, Lina. We took care of the body now. No one will know. They won't find it." Terry patted her hand. "I won't let anyone hurt you." He hiccupped.

Cora's hand flew to her mouth even as my shoulders sagged in relief and my belly threatened to empty its contents.

"I never wished you ill, my lady, but he offered me protection and safety. And . . . and I do care for him. Wouldn't you have done the same?"

"In securing your own well-being, you've stripped me of mine." Cora turned and dashed from the room. The ship toddled, and I slipped as I tried to follow after her, but she rounded the corner and disappeared down a hallway before I could catch her.

Likely she needed time to lick her wounds. I'd find her later and make things right. I had no idea how I could accomplish such a thing, but I knew I had to. In the meantime, I had the legal ramifications of my brother's body moving to contend with.

CHAPTER 61
Cora

I hid in the glassed-in crow's nest. The storm had wrung itself out, and I felt wrung out too. My entire life had gone up in smoke. Utter shambles. There was nothing left for me.

I was as good as ruined.

My fiancé had married another while engaged to me, while aboard my ship—my ship that no longer belonged to me. I choked back the sob that threatened to escape. I was certain the captain had married Terrance and Pauline as much to spite me as anything else. Without my engagement and my marriage, the ship would revert back to the estate and my dowry. My brother couldn't touch it, but neither could anyone else. It was still written in my father's will that the *Lady Air* was to be my dowry, and that I'd keep all proceeds from it. Terrance's spurning of me was a stain I'd carry within society the rest of my days. I'd be at the mercy of whatever scrap of humanity would take a tainted woman.

Because there must be something deadly wrong with a woman for her fiancé—the son of the great Duke of Exford and Debensley—to have so little regard for her.

It would not matter that the fault lay entirely with Terrance and not with me. All the blame would fall at my feet and would be a black smudge upon my character and my family forever.

Bitter tears stung the backs of my eyes, and a lump formed in my throat. My arm ached, and so did my heart. Around me, the sun began to poke through the spent clouds, their wisps flying this way and that with the wind caused by the great turbines. We'd be in Southampton by the afternoon, and my life as I knew it would be over.

Angrily, I swiped at an errant tear that dared to fall over and wet my lashes, dripping slowly across my cheek. I didn't want to feel so weak, so despondent. I didn't want to shatter into a thousand pieces, but my heart was cracking just the same.

A light tap at the door to the private crow's nest had me spinning, hand to my heart.

"Cora? Are you in here?"

Nicholas.

Fissures rent my heart, breaking off a great piece of it that I now knew belonged to the man on the other side of the door.

Incapable of speaking around the ball lodged in my throat, I said nothing as he cracked the door and poked his head in. His green eyes, deep and vibrant, drank me in as he entered the small room and shut the door behind him.

We were alone. Alone where no one but the clouds could see us.

"Cora," he said softly, his eyes crinkling at the edges.

I turned back to the window. I could not—would not—bear his pity. I took a ragged breath, hating how loud it sounded in the small space.

Nicholas cleared his throat. "I have sent word to my father. About Terrance. And other things."

"I am sure he is deeply upset by this unexpected turn of events," I offered lamely.

"I would not repeat his response message to a lady."

I glanced back, noting the slight curve of his lips.

"Cora, I messaged my father regarding other things . . . that concern you."

His long fingers grazed my elbow. My sharp intake of breath was magnified in the room.

"Please look at me," he whispered, the breath of his words ghosting across the side of my face and pitching my heart against my ribs. My eyes closed as I steeled myself.

Slowly, I turned and met his gaze.

He cleared his throat. "It was never made common knowledge that you and *Terrance* were engaged. I've gone back over everything a hundred times in my mind. Even in the press, it only said you were to wed into the house of Exford and Debensley. It never said who you were to marry." I searched his face as his words penetrated the thick fog hazing around my brain.

"Nicholas," I started, unable to finish the thought.

He nodded encouragingly. "We'll go to Grandmama's as planned and settle this. I will speak with father. I *will* make this right."

"How do you plan to make this right?" I whispered. Mary Adelaide Tristan was not known for her kind and gentle ways. I couldn't imagine that she'd welcome me into her innermost circle. And if I could not marry Terrance, then what else?

Nicholas shrugged. "What if I were to . . ." He swallowed nervously. "What if I were to propose you marry someone else of the Tristan line?"

My gaze jerked to his face.

"Nicholas, what . . . what are you saying?"

"If it could be arranged, would you be willing?" he whispered roughly.

Willing to marry *Nicholas* Tristan? My heart pounded against my breastbone, eyes widening.

"I will need to speak to Father and Grandmama, who, admittedly, will be harder to win over to this idea. However, she will have little choice if she wishes to keep the Tristan name intact. It's been announced that you're set to become a Tristan. And there is nothing Grandmama wants more than to have a pristine shine to the family name." He quirked an eyebrow with a partial eye roll, trying to lighten the moment. "She'll likely banish Terrance and his blackmailing wife to the farthest reaches of the realm, never to be seen or heard from again."

"And the stipulations of my father's will? The *Lady Air*? My required marriage?"

"Cora, *I* will see things made right. Will you trust me?" His eyes were intense, full of hope and determination.

My stomach dropped in response, suddenly aquiver with heady anticipation. "I . . ." I searched for the right words. "Nicholas, thank you," I finally said at last. My fingers squeezed around his. It was so inadequate, so small in comparison to the relief I felt—to what I felt for Nicholas as a man—to what he'd done for me and my future.

A soft smile crept over his features, lighting his eyes. "You're welcome." With aching slowness, he reached out and let his finger run down a wisp of auburn hair that had escaped the messy knot still secured in the tortoiseshell comb. Tingles raced over my neck and shoulders as embers glowed hotly in my middle. His gaze tracked to my lips before he cleared his throat and took half a step back in the small enclosure.

Had I imagined it? The bobbing of his Adam's apple told me I hadn't. I bit the inside of my cheek, exuberant that he was thinking about my lips at all, but suddenly anxious and unsure of myself.

"Will I like your grandmother?" I asked, my voice cracking. Heat rushed to my cheeks.

Nicholas tipped a half smile. "Grandmama is a hard woman to please. She likes who she chooses to, and the rest of us be hanged."

I blinked at his blunt words but appreciated his candor. I had not thought to have a husband who would speak to me as his equal. But Nicholas did. And I wanted him. Wanted him as a husband. As a friend. As a constant in my world. I prayed Adelaide Tristan would see the reason of her grandson's words. As I continued gazing up at him, his smile grew larger. His thumb rubbed once over the back of my hand as his eyes darted to my lips once more. My mouth dried.

I smiled. I couldn't help it. It gave me no end of pleasure to know that Nicholas—a man of whom I thought so highly, and the man with whom I was fairly certain I was falling in love—respected me enough to speak so plainly. Including those wild, untamed parts of me I tried to keep hidden. He'd come alongside me, metaphorically taking my hand, but not to bind me. Not to restrict me, but to join me. To encourage me, to keep me safe, and to let me know I was not alone.

For the third or fourth time, Nicholas's gaze flitted to my lips.

"You seem uncommonly preoccupied with my lips," I whispered. Bubbles fizzed like champagne inside me.

His eyes snapped up to mine. "Oh, well, yes. They are"—he cleared his throat—"rather distracting." His eyes twinkled, even as openness scrolled over his expression.

Impossibly delicious heat curled through me as a tingle rushed down my spine.

"Are they?" I asked softly, suddenly feeling shy and girlish.

He nodded, green eyes shining. "You know"—he cleared his throat again—"British society would not approve if a gentleman were to kiss a gentlewoman that was not his fiancée. But I have heard that the rules are slightly more relaxed in America." He paused, gauging my reaction. I stood still, heart hammering, unable to move. I wasn't sure I wanted to.

He continued slowly, "Is . . . is my information correct?" He finished quietly, vulnerable, unsure, his manner so unlike his usual bold confidence as he tentatively met my gaze.

Oh.

Was it possible . . . could Nicholas Tristan be asking if I wanted him to kiss me?

"Should a woman wish to engage in such behavior, a small kiss is acceptable," I whispered past the sudden surge of anxiety, excitement, and trepidation rushing through me with enough potency I thought I might sway on my feet.

A smile charming enough to melt butter slid over Nicholas's features. "Would you know any such woman?"

I couldn't speak, but nodded and swallowed as he stepped closer, fully into my space, though he made no move to touch me beyond where he still held the tips of my fingers in his hand. Even so, my breaths came tight and shallow. Slowly he reached his long fingers out, feathering them along my chin, his hand coming to rest against my cheek and cupping my jaw. My lips parted in surprise, such intimate touching foreign and altogether exciting. Sparks danced in my belly, and I had to lock my knees in place to keep them from quivering.

Flashes of that forbidden night that seemed so long ago when I'd first realized there was a heady attraction to Nicholas danced across my mind's eye as his other hand let go my fingers and slid warm against my waist, just where it had that night.

With the barest hint of pressure, he tilted my face up. With aching slowness, he lowered his lips to mine. The first brush of his lips sent sparks skittering over my skin, burning me with their intensity. Of their own accord, my hands rested against his chest, his hard planes delighting my fingertips even through the silk of his vest and the fine cotton of his shirt. His mouth pressed against mine with more pressure, and a breathy little noise somersaulted up my throat only to be swallowed by Nicholas's lips as they caressed mine ever so gently once more before he pulled back.

My eyelids fluttered open, my entire world rocking on its axis in the most delicious fashion I'd ever experienced.

He blew out a slow, unsteady breath as his eyes roved over my face. My stomach dropped at his awed expression, a silly grin creeping over my mouth.

With a reluctant step back, Nicholas blinked and took a deep breath, then cleared his throat. "Right. I think American society might have a thing or two correct." He sent me a cocky grin, and my cheeks flushed.

"Perhaps." I quirked an eyebrow and flashed him a saucy smile of my own.

The *Lady Air* lurched, jerking as she began her descent.

"Come, Phee and Dawson Davies are having tea and happily reacquainting themselves at last. It seems he may be a decent chap after all. She's begging me to invite him to travel with us to London. What do you think?" His green eyes twinkled.

"Regrettably, I think we could use as many allies as we can get." With reluctance, I tipped my head toward the docks. They were still tiny, but already I could see the black cabs I knew belonged to Scotland Yard. They'd be waiting for us, to collect the bodies of the dead women.

Nicholas eyed the commotion already starting at the docks. "I think you may be right."

───◆───

When we docked with a gentle thump against the Southampton airship harborage, they were waiting. Detective Morris, with whom we'd been in contact via the telegraph, was led directly to the captain's quarters.

Captain Cordello was sour as always, though he had a smug look about him. I secretly wished I could turn the insufferable man over to the police, though he'd done nothing devious enough to warrant police attention.

"Lord Tristan, Miss Beaumont, we'll need to hear the full story. My collogues will take care of the murderess and her victims. Do you wish to come to the station?"

"Forgive the vehemence, Detective Chief Inspector, but the less society knows about this, the better," Nicholas said. I nodded emphatically.

I wanted with all my heart for Nicholas to broach the topic of my retaining my inheritance with his grandmama and his father . . . and retaining a Tristan fiancé, should fate smile upon me. I was utterly certain that such nasty rumors as would start from my association with a police investigation would not endear me to the Tristans.

"Of course." The detective chief inspector's mustache twitched. "Questions here, then?"

I tuned him out momentarily, staring out the window of Captain Cordello's quarters as bobbies swarmed the deck and several of their number escorted Rose across the planks, her hands manacled and a black scowl on her face. I nodded in satisfaction. The murderess was caught. She could do no more harm to my passengers.

We had survived. Against strange odds. I took a breath, letting it out with satisfaction. One battle had been fought and won.

It seemed I had another on the horizon.

I'd face it head on. With courage and fortitude. The maiden voyage of the *Lady Air* had taught me that I had both virtues in abundance. I knew my father would be proud. And I was no longer so alone. I glanced at Nicholas. I had friends who were for me. Friends who cared about me and my well-being.

Friends who had proved themselves worthy throughout the course of my lethal engagement.

ACKNOWLEDGMENTS

I t takes a village, they say, and so it does.

So many hands went into the making of *A Lethal Engagement*, and I'm so grateful for every one of them.

My early readers. You've read so many early versions of my work, but you haven't thrown in the towel yet. I'm so sorry you had to put up with such a mangled version of this story, but thank you for your input, struggling over my clumsy early attempts, and seeing the story I hoped to achieve. Your feedback made it possible! V., Amber, Jess, Meg, you guys rock all the socks.

Brittany Eden, this story simply would not be had you not suggested, "What if Cora were American instead of British?" Your one question changed the entire trajectory of the story and truly made it what it has become. I shall be eternally grateful for all your suggestions, your opining, and all our bookish discussions. They are often a highlight of my week. Also. Thank you for sharing your love of K-dramas and K-pop. You've ruined me for life. But in the best possible way.

Amanda Wright, your endless encouragement and *Attagirl!* attitude have been invaluable. Seriously. What did I do before I met you? You are a sweet gift, and I appreciate your friendship so much. Your words shall ever be immortalized. You are my favorite Red Bull–inebriated beaver.

To my newest circle of encouragement, Nova McBee, Chelsea Bobulski, and Lorie Langdon—I so value your thoughts and your encouragement. Thank you for always uplifting me, validating that what I'm doing is important, and being such wonderful examples. I wouldn't trade you all for the world.

Husband, thank you for the gift of time. I could not write if you did not give me those moments to escape. Likewise, to my sweet children, thank you for letting Mommy put in her headphones now and then and get some work done. You are very patient with me, and I hope someday when you're older, you'll get to enjoy these imaginary worlds as much as I do. I'll take you there, my loves, and we can have grand adventures together. It's so fun getting to see you experiment with your own writing and your own stories. I have no doubt that someday, each one of you will be a master storyteller in your own right. I'm already so proud of each of you.

Mom and Dad, Grandma Dot, Grandma Ann, Landon, Barry and Sally—thank you for your support, for your prayers, for your cheering, for all the questions. Even though you don't always understand what bookish tangent I'm railing about, you always ask and are interested in my life. Mom especially, thank you for reading to me when I was little and instilling a deep, abiding love for stories.

Uncle Gary: "Let them come to us."

Aunt Bonnie, you're *always* first in line to buy the next book!

Crystal, Brianna, and Portia, you guys have been around from the beginning, and you keep coming back. Y'all are the best!

To the entire team at Crooked Lane Books—I have been so thrilled to work with such a talented team of folks. This experience has been amazing, and I could not have asked for better.

Melissa, thank you for your gentle editing approach, for your encouraging corrections and suggestions, and for still letting my voice tell this story, even though we changed quite a bit. The changes have truly made this story shine.

Lastly, dear reader, thank *you* for picking up this book. Books aren't much good without readers to read them. If you're still reading and your eyes haven't glazed over yet, I'd love to hear what you thought of the book. Drop me a line on social media or via email. I respond to every message and email I receive (though it might take a few days sometimes), and I love connecting with readers! Maybe you could make a suggestion for my next mystery or help me name a character.

Until the next book,
-April

Voluntas mea obediens sit et verba mea Deo glorientur.